2nd CHANCE

JAMES PATTERSON

AND ANDREW GROSS

headline

First published in Great Britain in 2002
by HEADLINE BOOK PUBLISHING

This edition published in 2009
by HEADLINE PUBLISHING GROUP

8

Cataloguing in Publication Data is available from the British Library

ISBN 978 0 7553 4927 2

Typeset in Palatino Light by Palimpsest Book Production Limited,
Grangemouth, Stirlingshire

Printed and bound in Great Britain by
Clays Ltd, St Ives plc

Headline's policy is to use papers that are natural, renewable
and recyclable products and made from wood grown in
sustainable forests. The logging and manufacturing processes
are expected to conform to the environmental regulations of
the country of origin.

HEADLINE PUBLISHING GROUP
An Hachette UK Company
338 Euston Road
London NW1 3BH

www.headline.co.uk
www.hachette.co.uk

James Patterson is one of the best-known and biggest-selling writers of all time. He is the author of some of the most popular series of the past decade: the Women's Murder Club, the Alex Cross novels and Maximum Ride, and he has written many other number one bestsellers including romance novels and stand-alone thrillers. He has won an Edgar Award, the mystery world's highest honour. He lives in Florida with his wife and son.

Praise for James Patterson's novels:

'The man is a master of this genre. We fans will have one wish for him: write even faster'   *USA Today*

'Unputdownable. It will sell millions'   *The Times*

'Pacy, sexy, high-octane stuff'   *Guardian*

'Patterson does everything but stick our finger in a light socked to give us a buzz'   *New York Times*

'A novel which makes for sleepless nights'   *Daily Express*

'Breakneck pacing and loop-the-loop plotting'
                  Publishers Weekly

'Reads like a dream'   *Kirkus Reviews*

'A fast-paced, electric story that is utterly believable'
                  Booklist

'Absolutely terrific'   *Bookseller*

'Patterson's action-packed story keeps the pages flicking by'   *The Sunday Times*

'A fine writer with a good ear for dialogue and pacing. His books are always page-turners'   *Washington Times*

'Patterson is a phenomenon'   *Observer*

'Brilliantly terrifying . . . so exciting I had to stay up all night to finish it'   *Daily Mail*

Special thanks to Inspector/Sergeant Holly Pera of the SFPD's Homicide Detail. To her partner, Inspector/Sergeant Joe Toomey. And Pete Ogten, Captain, Ret., SFPD. And again, to Doctor Greg Zorman of Ft. Lauderdale.

But most of all, this is for Lynn and Sue.

Prologue

The Choir Kids

Chapter 1

A aron Winslow would never forget the next few minutes. He recognized the terrifying sounds the instant they cracked through the night. His body went cold all over. He couldn't believe that someone was shooting a high-powered rifle in this neighborhood.

K-pow, k-pow, k-pow . . . k-pow, k-pow, k-pow.

His choir was just leaving the Harrow Street church. Forty-eight young kids streamed past him onto the sidewalk. They had just finished their final rehearsal before the San Francisco Sing-Off, and they had been excellent.

Then came the gunfire. Lots of it. Not just a single shot. A strafing. *An attack.*

K-pow, k-pow, k-pow . . . k-pow, k-pow, k-pow.

'Get down . . .' he screamed at the top of his voice. 'Everybody down on the ground! Cover your heads! Cover up!' He almost couldn't believe the words as they left his mouth.

At first, no one seemed to hear him. To the kids, in their white blouses and shirts, the shots must have seemed like firecrackers. Then a volley of shots rained through the church's beautiful stained-glass window. The depiction of Christ's blessing over a child at Capernaum shattered, glass splintering everywhere, some of it falling on the heads of the children.

'Someone's shooting!' Winslow screamed. Maybe more than one person. *How could that be*? He ran wildly through the kids, screaming, waving his arms, pushing as many as he could down to the grass.

As the kids finally crouched low or dove for the ground, Winslow spotted two of his choir girls, Chantal and Tamara, frozen on the lawn as bullets streaked past them. 'Chantal, Tamara, get down!' he screamed, but they remained there, hugging one another, emitting frantic wails. They were best friends. He had known them since they were little kids, playing four-square on blacktop.

There was never any doubt in his mind. He sprinted towards the two girls, grasping their arms firmly, tumbling them to the ground. Then he lay on top of them, pressing their bodies tightly.

Bullets whined over his head, just inches away. His eardrums hurt. His body was trembling and so were the girls shielded beneath him. He was almost sure he was about to die. 'It's all right, babies,' he whispered.

Then, as suddenly as it had begun, the firing stopped. A hush of silence hung in the air. So strange and eerie, as if the whole world had stopped to listen.

As he raised himself, his eyes fell on an incredible sight. Slowly, everywhere, the children struggled to their feet.

There was some crying, but he didn't see any blood; no one seemed to be hurt.

'Everyone okay?' Winslow called out. He made his way through the crowd. 'Is anyone hurt?'

'I'm okay . . . I'm okay,' came back to him. He looked around in disbelief. This was a miracle.

Then he heard the sound of a single child whimpering.

He turned and spotted Maria Parker, only twelve years old. Maria was standing on the whitewashed wooden steps of the church entrance. She seemed lost. Choking sobs poured from her open mouth.

Then his eyes came to rest on what had made the girl hysterical. He felt his heart sink. Even in war, even growing up on the streets of Oakland, he had never felt anything so horrible, so sad and senseless.

'Oh, God. Oh, no. How could You let this happen?'

Tasha Catchings, just eleven years old, lay in a heap in a flowerbed near the base of the church. Her white school blouse was soaked with blood.

Finally, Reverend Aaron Winslow began to cry himself.

Book One

The Women's Murder Club – Again

Chapter One

On a Tuesday night I found myself playing a game of crazy-eights with three residents of the Hope Street Teen House. I was loving it.

On the beat-up couch across from me sat Hector, a barrio kid two days out of Juvenile; Alysha, quiet and pretty, but with a family history you wouldn't want to know; and Michelle, who at fourteen had already spent a year selling herself on the streets of San Francisco.

'Hearts,' I declared, flipping down an eight and changing the suit, just as Hector was about to lay out.

'Damn, badge lady,' he whined. 'How come each time I'm 'bout to go down, you stick your knife in me?'

'Teach *you* never to trust a cop, fool,' laughed Michelle, tossing a conspiratorial smile my way.

For the past four months I'd been spending a night or two a week at the Hope Street House. For so long, after the terrible bride and groom case earlier that summer, I'd felt completely lost. I took a month off from Homicide; ran down by the Marina; gazed out at the Bay from the safety of my Potrero Hill flat.

Nothing helped. Not counseling, not the total support of my girls – Claire, Cindy, Jill. Not even going back to the job. I had watched, unable to help, as the life leaked out of the person I loved. I still felt responsible for my partner's death in the line of duty. Nothing seemed to fill the void.

So I came here . . . to Hope Street.

And the good news was, it was working a little.

I peered up from my cards at Angela, a new arrival who sat in a metal chair across the room, cuddling her three-month-old baby. The poor kid, maybe sixteen, hadn't said much all night. I would try to talk to Angela before I left for the night.

The door opened and Dee Collins, one of the House's head counselors, came in. She was followed by a stiff-looking black woman in a conservative gray suit. She had Department of Children and Families written all over her.

'Angela, your social worker's here.' Dee kneeled down beside her.

'I ain't blind,' the teenager said.

'We're going to have to take the baby now,' the social worker interrupted, as if completing this assignment was all that kept her from catching the next CalTran.

'No!' Angela pulled the infant even closer. 'You can keep me in this hole, you can send me back to Claymore, but you're not taking my baby.'

'Please, honey, only for a few days,' Dee Collins tried to reassure her.

The teenage girl drew her arms protectively around her

baby, who, sensing some harm, began to cry.

'Don't you make a scene, Angela,' the social worker warned. 'You know how this is done.'

As she came towards the girl, I watched Angela jump out of the chair. She was clutching the baby in one arm and a glass of juice she'd been drinking in the other hand.

In one swift motion she cracked the glass against a table. It created a jagged shard.

'Angela,' I leapt up from the card table, 'put that down. No one's going to take your baby anywhere unless you let her go.'

'This *bitch* is trying to ruin my life,' she glared. 'First, she lets me sit in Claymore three days past my date, then she won't let me go home to my mom. Now she's trying to take my baby girl.'

I nodded, peering into the teenager's eyes. 'First, you gotta lay down the glass,' I said. 'You *know* that, Angela.'

The DCF worker took a step, but I held her back. I moved slowly towards Angela. I took hold of the glass, then I gently eased the child out of her arms.

'She's all I have,' the girl whispered and then started to sob.

'I know,' I nodded. 'That's why you'll change some things in your life and get her back.'

Dee Collins had her arms around Angela, a cloth wrapped around the girl's bleeding hand. The DCF worker was trying unsuccessfully to hush the crying infant.

I went up and said to her, 'That baby gets placed somewhere nearby with daily visitation rights. And by the way, I didn't see anything going on here that was worth putting on file . . . *You?*' The caseworker gave me a disgruntled look and turned away.

Suddenly, my beeper sounded, three dissonant beeps punctuating the tense air. I pulled it out and read the number. *Jacobi, my ex-partner in Homicide. What did he want?*

I excused myself and moved into the staff office. I was able to reach him in his car.

'Something bad's happened, Lindsay,' he said, glumly. 'I thought you'd want to know.'

He clued me in about a horrible drive-by shooting at the LaSalle Heights Church. An eleven-year-old girl had been killed.

'Jesus . . .' I sighed, as my heart sank.

'I thought you might want in on it,' Jacobi said.

I took in a breath. It had been over three months since I'd been on the scene at a homicide. Not since the day the bride and groom case ended.

'So, I didn't hear,' Jacobi pressed. 'You want in, *Lieutenant?*' It was the first time he had called me with my new rank.

I realized my honeymoon had come to an end. 'Yeah,' I muttered back. 'I want in.'

Chapter Two

A cold rain started to fall as I pulled my Explorer up to the LaSalle Heights Church on Harrow Street in the predominantly black section of Bay View. An angry, anxious crowd had formed – a combination of saddened neighborhood mothers, and the usual sullen homeboys huddled in their bright 'Tommy's' – all pushing against a handful of uniformed cops.

'This ain't goddamn Mississippi,' someone shouted as I forced my way through the throng.

'How many more?' an older woman wailed. '*How many more?*'

I badged my way past a couple of nervous patrolmen to the front. What I saw next absolutely took my breath away.

The façade of the white clapboard church was slashed with a grotesque pattern of bullet holes and lead-colored chinks. A huge hole gaped in a wall where a large, stained-glass window had been shot out. Jagged edges of colored glass teetered, like hanging ice. Kids were still scattered all over the lawn, obviously in shock, some being attended to by EMS teams.

'Oh, Jesus,' I whispered under my breath.

I spotted medical techs in black windbreakers huddled over the body of a young girl by the front steps. A couple of plainclothesmen were nearby. One of them was my ex-partner, Warren Jacobi.

I found myself hesitating. I had done this a hundred times. Only months ago I had solved the biggest murder case in the city since Harvey Milk, but so much had happened since then. I felt weird, like I was new at this. Balling my fists together, I took a deep breath and went over to Jacobi.

'Welcome back to the world, Lieutenant,' Jacobi said, with a roll of the tongue on my new rank.

The sound of that word still sent a surge of electricity through me. Heading Homicide had been the goal I had pursued throughout my career: the first female homicide detective in San Francisco; now its first lieutenant. After my old LT Sam Roth opted for a cushy stint up in Bodega Bay, Chief Mercer had called me in. *I can do one of two things, he'd said to me. I can keep you on long-term administrative leave and you can see if you find the heart to do this job again. Or I can give you these, Lindsay.* He pushed a gold shield with two bars on it across the table. Until that moment, I don't think I had ever seen Mercer smile.

'The lieutenant's shield doesn't make it any easier, does it, Lindsay,' Jacobi said, emphasizing that our three-year relationship as partners had now changed.

'What do we have?' I asked him.

'Looks like a single gunman, from out in those bushes.' He pointed to a dense thicket beside the church, maybe fifty yards away. 'Asshole caught the kids just as they came out. Opened fire with everything he had.'

I took a breath, staring at the weeping, shell-shocked kids scattered all over the lawn. 'Anybody see the guy? Somebody did, right?'

He shook his head. 'Everyone hit the deck.'

Near the fallen child a distraught black woman sobbed into the shoulder of a comforting friend. Jacobi saw my eyes fix on the dead girl.

'Name's Tasha Catchings,' he muttered. 'In the fifth grade, over at St Anne's. Good girl. Youngest kid in the choir.'

I moved in closer and knelt over the body. No matter how many times you do this, it's a wrenching sight. Tasha's school blouse was soaked with blood, mixed with falling rain. Just a few feet away a rainbow-colored knapsack still lay on the grass.

'She's it?' I asked incredulously. I surveyed the scene. 'She's the only one who got hit?'

Bullet holes were everywhere, splintered glass and wood. Dozens of kids had been streaming out to the street . . . *All those shots, and only one victim.*

'Our lucky day, huh?' Jacobi snorted.

Chapter Three

Paul Chi, one of my Homicide crew, was interviewing a tall, handsome black man dressed in a black turtleneck and jeans, on the steps of the church. I'd seen him before, on the news. I even knew his name: Aaron Winslow.

Even in shock and dismay, Winslow carried himself with a graceful bearing – a smooth face, jet-black hair cut flat on top, and a football running back's build. Everyone in San Francisco knew what he was doing for this neighborhood. He was supposed to be a real-life hero, and I must say, he looked the part.

I walked over.

'This is Reverend Aaron Winslow,' Chi said, introducing us.

'Lindsay Boxer,' I said, extending my hand.

'*Lieutenant* Boxer,' said Chi. 'She'll be overseeing the case.'

'I'm familiar with your work,' I said. 'You've given a lot to this neighborhood. I'm so sorry for this. I don't have any words for it.'

His eyes shifted towards the murdered girl. He spoke in the softest voice imaginable. 'I've known her since she was a baby. These are good, responsible people. Her mother . . . she brought up Tasha and her brother on her own. These were all young kids. Choir practice, Lieutenant.'

I didn't want to intrude, but I had to. 'Can I ask a few questions? Please.'

He nodded blankly. 'Of course.'

'You see anyone? Someone fleeing? A shape, a glimpse?'

'I saw where the shots came from,' Winslow said, and he pointed to the same thicket of bushes where Jacobi had gone. 'I saw the trailer fire. I was too busy trying to get everyone down. It was madness.'

'Has anyone made any threats recently against you or your church?' I asked.

'Threats . . .?' Winslow screwed his face. 'Maybe years ago, when we first got funding to rebuild some of these houses.'

A short distance away, a haunting wail came from Tasha Catchings' mother as the girl's body was lifted onto a gurney. This was so sad.

The crowd was growing edgy. Taunts and accusations began to ring out. 'Why are you all standing around? Go find her killer!'

'I'd better get over there,' Winslow said, 'before this thing goes the wrong way.' He started to move, then turned with tight-lipped resignation on his face. 'I could have saved that poor baby. I heard the shots.'

'You couldn't save them all,' I said. 'You did what you could.'

He finally nodded. Then he said something that totally shocked me. 'It was an M-16, Lieutenant. Thirty-six-round clip. The bastard reloaded twice.'

'How would you know that?' I asked, surprised.

'Desert Storm,' he answered. 'I was a field chaplain. No way I would ever forget that awful sound. No one ever does.'

Chapter Four

I heard my name called over the din of the crowd. It was Jacobi. He was in the woods behind the church. 'Hey, Lieutenant, come check this out.'

Heading over, I didn't know what kind of person could do such a terrible thing. I had worked on a hundred homicides; usually, drugs, money or sex were at the heart of them. *But this . . . this was meant to shock.*

'Check it out,' Jacobi said, bending down over a spot. He'd found a bullet casing.

'M-16, I bet,' I replied.

Jacobi nodded. 'Little Lady been brushing up in her time off? Shell's a Remington 223.'

'*Lieutenant* Little Lady to you,' I smirked. Then I told him how I knew.

Dozens of empty shells were scattered all around. We were deep in the brush and trees, hidden from the church. The casings were strewn in two distinct clusters about five yards apart.

'You can see where he started firing,' Jacobi said. 'I figure here. He must've moved around.'

From the first cluster of shells there was a clear line of sight to the side of the church. That stained-glass window in full view . . . All those kids, streaming onto the street . . . I could see why no one spotted him. His hiding place was totally protected.

'When he reloaded, he must've moved over there,' Jacobi pointed.

I made my way over and crouched near the second cluster of shells. Something wasn't making sense. The façade of the church was in view, the front steps where Tasha Catchings lay. But only barely.

I squinted through an imaginary sight, leveling my gaze at where Tasha must've been when she was hit. You could barely even fix it into sight. There was no way he could've been aiming for her intentionally. She was struck from a totally improbable angle.

'Lucky shot,' Jacobi muttered. 'What do you think, a ricochet?'

'What's back here?' I asked. I looked around, pushing my way through the thick bushes leading away from the church. No one had seen the shooter escape, so he obviously hadn't made his way along Harrow Street. The brush was about twenty feet deep.

At the end was a five-foot-high chain-link fence, dividing the church grounds from the surrounding neighborhood. The fence wasn't high. I planted my flats and hoisted myself over.

I found myself facing penned-in backyards and tiny row

houses. A few people had gathered, watching the show. To the right, the playgrounds of the Whitney Young projects.

Jacobi finally caught up with me. 'Take it easy,' he huffed. 'There's an audience. You're making me look bad.'

'This is how he must've made his way out, Warren.' We looked in both directions. One led towards an alley; the other towards a row of homes.

I shouted to a group of onlookers who had gathered on a back porch, 'Anyone see anything?'

No one responded.

'Someone was shooting at the church,' I shouted. 'A little girl's been killed. Help us out. We need your help.'

Everyone stood around with the unconfiding silence of people who don't talk to the police.

Then, slowly, a woman of about thirty came forward. She was nudging a young boy ahead of her. 'Bernard saw something,' she said in a muffled voice.

Bernard appeared to be about eight, with cautious round eyes, wearing a gold and purple Kobe Bryant sweatshirt. He was nuzzling into his mother's legs.

'It was a van,' Bernard blurted. 'Like Uncle Reggie's.' He pointed to the dirt road leading to the alley. 'It was parked down *there*.'

I kneeled down, gently smiling into the scared boy's eyes. 'What color van, Bernard?'

The kid nodded, 'White.'

'My brother's got a white Dodge minivan,' Bernard's mother said.

'Was it like your uncle's, Bernard?' I asked.

'Sorta. Not really, though.'

'Did you see the man who was driving it?'

He shook his head. 'I was bringing out the garbage. I only saw it drive away.'

'Do you think you would recognize it again, if you saw it?' I asked.

Bernard nodded.

'Because it looked like your uncle's?'

He hesitated. 'No, because it had a picture on the back.'

'A picture? You mean like an insignia? Or some kind of advertising?'

'Uh-uh,' he shook his head, his moon-like eyes searching around. Then they lit up. 'I mean like that.' He pointed towards a pick-up truck in a neighbor's driveway. There was a sticker of a Cal Golden Bear on the rear bumper.

'You mean a decal?' I confirmed.

'On the door.'

I held the boy gently by the shoulders. 'What did this decal look like, Bernard?'

'Like Mufasa,' the boy said, 'from *The Lion King*.'

'A lion?' My mind raced through anything that seemed familiar. Sports teams, college logos, corporations . . .

'Yeah, like Mufasa,' Bernard repeated. 'Except it had two heads.'

Chapter Five

L ess than an hour later I was pushing through the surging crowd that had built up on the steps of the Hall of Justice. I felt hollowed-out and terribly sad, but knew I couldn't show it here.

The lobby of the granite, tomblike building where I worked was packed with reporters and news crews, shoving their microphones at anyone wearing a badge. Most of the crime reporters knew me, but I waved them off until I could get upstairs.

Then a set of hands grasped onto my shoulders and a familiar voice chimed, 'Linds, we need to talk . . .'

I spun into the face of Cindy Thomas, one of my closest friends, though it also happened she was the lead crime reporter at the *Chronicle.* 'I won't bother you now,' she said above the din. 'But it's important. How about the bar at Susie's, at ten?'

It had been Cindy who, as a stringer buried on the paper's Metro desk, had sneaked into the heart of the bride and groom case and helped blow it wide open. Cindy who, as much as any of us, was responsible for the gold on my shield today.

I managed a smile. 'I'll see you there.'

Upstairs, on four, I strode into the cramped, fluorescent-lit room that the twelve inspectors who managed Homicide for the city called home. Lorraine Stafford was waiting for me, my first appointment, after six successful years in Sex Crimes. And Cappy McNeil, he had come in, too.

Lorraine asked, 'What can I do?'

'You can check for any stolen white vans with Sacramento. Any model. In-state plates. And put out an APB along with it for a sticker of some sort of lion on the rear door.' She nodded and turned away.

'Lorraine,' I stopped her. 'Make that a *two*-headed lion.'

Cappy walked with me while I got myself a cup of tea. He'd been in Homicide for fifteen years and I knew he had supported me when Chief Mercer consulted him about offering me the job. He looked sad, thoroughly depressed. 'I know Aaron Winslow. I played ball with him in Oakland. He's devoted his life to those kids. He really is one of the good guys, Lieutenant.'

All of a sudden Frank Barns from Auto Theft stuck his head in our office. 'Heads up, Lieutenant. Weight's on the floor.'

Weight, in the lexicon of the SFPD, meant Chief of Police Earl Mercer.

Chapter Six

M ercer strode in, all two hundred fifty pounds of him, trailed by Gabe Carr, a mean little weasel who was the department's press liaison, and Fred Dix, who managed community relations.

The Chief was dressed in his trademark dark gray suit, blue shirt and shiny gold cufflinks. I'd watched Mercer manage a number of tense scenes – transit bombings, Internal Affairs stings, serial killers – but I'd never seen his face so tight. He motioned me into my office and, with barely a word, pulled the door shut. Fred Dix and Gabe Carr were already inside.

'I just got off the phone with Winston Gray and Vernon Jones' – two of the city's most outspoken leaders – 'They've assured me they'll plead for restraint, give us some time to find out just what the fuck is going on. Just so I'm clear, by *restraint*, what they mean is, deliver the person or group who's responsible for this, or they'll have two thousand outraged citizens at City Hall Plaza.'

He barely relaxed his face when he stared at me. 'So I'm

hoping, Lieutenant, you got something you want to share . . .?'

I took him through what I had found at the church, along with Bernard Smith's sighting of the white getaway van.

'Van or not,' the mayor's man, Fred Dix, cut in, 'you know where you have to start on this. Mayor Fernandez is going to come down hard on anyone operating in the area espousing a racist or anti-diversity message. We need some heat to fall their way.'

'You seem pretty sure that's what we're looking at,' I said with a non-committal glance. 'Your garden-variety hate crime?'

'Shooting up a church, murdering an eleven-year-old child? Where would *you* start, Lieutenant?'

'That girl's face is going to be on every news report in the country,' Carr, the press liaison, pitched in. 'The effort in the Bay View neighborhood is one of the mayor's proudest accomplishments.'

I nodded. 'Does the mayor mind if I finish my eyewitness interviews first?'

'Don't worry yourself with the mayor,' Mercer cut in. 'Right now, all you have to be concerned with is me. I grew up on these streets. My folks still live in Portal Heights. I don't need a TV soundbite to see that kid's face in my mind. You run the investigation wherever it leads. Just run it fast. And Lindsay . . . nothing gets in the way, you understand?'

He was about to get up. 'And most importantly, I want

total containment on this. I don't want to see this investigation being run on the front page.'

Everyone nodded, and Mercer, followed by Dix and Carr, stood up. He let out a deep blast of air. 'Right now we have one hell of a press conference to muck our way through.'

The others filed out of the room, but Mercer stayed behind. He leaned his thick hands on the edge of my desk, his hulking shape towering over me.

'Lindsay, I know you left a lot on the table after that last case. But all that's done. It's history now. I need everything you have on this case. One of the things you left behind when you took that shield was the freedom to let personal pain interfere with the job.'

'You don't have to worry about me.' I gave him a solid stare. I'd had my differences with the man over the years, but now I was ready to give him everything I had. I had seen the dead little girl. I had seen the church torn up. My blood was on fire. I hadn't felt this way since I left the job.

Chief Mercer flashed me a smile of understanding. 'It's good to have you back, Lieutenant.'

Chapter Seven

A fter a highly charged news conference conducted on the steps of the Hall, I met Cindy at Susie's as we had arranged. The relaxed, laid-back atmosphere at our favorite meeting place was a relief after the frenzied scene at the Hall. Cindy was already sipping a Corona as I arrived.

A lot had happened here – at this very table. Cindy, Jill Bernhardt, the Assistant District Attorney, and Claire Washburn, the Chief Medical Examiner and my closest friend, had started to meet last summer, when it seemed that fate had pulled us all together with links to the bride and groom case. In the process, we had evolved into the closest of friends.

I signaled our waitress, Loretta, for a beer, then planted myself across from Cindy with a worn-out smile. 'Hey . . .'

'Hey, yourself,' she smiled back. 'Good to see you.'

'Good to be seen.'

A TV blared above the bar, a broadcast of Chief Mercer's news conference. 'We believe it was a single gunman,' Mercer announced to a flash of photographer's bulbs.

'You stay for that?' I asked Cindy, taking a welcome swig of my ice-cold beer.

'I was there,' she replied. 'Burns and Hatcher were there, too. They filed the report.'

I gave her a startled look. Ed Burns and Dede Hatcher were her competition on the Crime Desk. 'You losing your touch? Six months ago, I would've found you coming out of the church as soon as we arrived.'

'I'm going at it from another angle,' she said, shrugging.

A handful of people crowded around the bar, trying to catch the breaking news. I took another chug of beer. 'You should've seen this poor little girl, Cindy. All of eleven years old. She sang in the choir. There was this rainbow-colored knapsack with all her books on the ground nearby.'

'You know this stuff, Lindsay.' She gave me a bolstering smile. 'You know how it is. It sucks.'

'Yeah,' I nodded. 'But just once it'd be nice to pick one of them up . . . You know, brush them off, send them home. Just once, I'd like to hand one back their book bag.'

Cindy tapped her fist affectionately on the back of my hand. Then she brightened. 'I saw Jill today. She's got some news for us. She's excited. Maybe Bennett's retiring and she's getting the Big Chair. We should get together and see what's up with her.'

'For sure,' I nodded. 'That what you wanted to tell me tonight, Cindy?'

She shook her head. In the background, all hell was breaking loose in the news conference on the screen –

Mercer promising a swift and effective response. 'You've got a problem, Linds . . .'

I shook my head. 'I can't give you anything, Cindy. Mercer's handling everything. I've never seen him so worked up. I'm sorry.'

'I didn't ask you here to get something, Lindsay.'

'Cindy, if you know something, tell me.'

'I know that boss of yours better be careful what he's committing to.'

I glanced at the screen. '*Mercer* . . .?'

In the background, I heard his voice asserting that the shooting was an isolated incident, how we already had tangible leads, how every available cop would be on the case until we tracked the killer down.

'He's telling the world you're gonna nail this guy *before* it happens again?'

'So . . .?'

Our eyes met solidly. 'I think it already has.'

Chapter Eight

The killer was playing Desert Command and he was a master.

Phffft, phffft, phffft . . . phffft, phffft.

Impassively, he squinted through the illuminated, infrared sight as hooded figures darted into view. As if an extension of his finger, the darkened, maze-like chambers of the terrorist bunker exploded in bursts of orange flame. Shadowy figures burst into narrow halls, *phffft, phffft, phffft.*

He was a champion at this. Great hand-eye coordination. No one could touch him.

His finger twitched on the trigger. *Ghouls, sand mites, towel-heads.* Come at me, baby . . . *Phffft, phffft . . .* Up through the dark corridors . . . He smashed through an iron door, came upon a whole nest of them, sucking on tebouleh, playing cards. His weapon spat a steady, orange death. *Blessed are the peacemakers*, he smirked.

He squinted one more time through the sight, replaying the scene at the church again in his mind, imagining her little face. That little Jemima, with her braided hair, the rainbow-colored knapsack on her back.

Phffft, phffft. A figure's chest exploded. This next kill was for the record. *Got it*! His eye flashed towards the on-screen score. *Two hundred seventy-six enemy dead.*

He took a tug on his Corona and grinned. A new personal record. This score was worth keeping. He punched in his initials: *F.C.*

He stood at the machine in the Playtime arcade in West Oakland, flicking the trigger long after the game had ended. He was the only white guy in the room. The only one. In fact, that was why he chose to be here.

Suddenly, the four large overhead television sets were blaring the same face. It sent a chill down his back, and made him furious.

It was Mercer, the pompous ass who ran the San Francisco cops. He was acting like he had everything figured out.

'We believe this was the act of a single gunman,' he was saying. 'An isolated crime . . .'

If you only knew, he laughed.

Wait until tomorrow . . . you'll see. Just you wait, Chief Asshole.

'What I want to stress,' the Chief of Police declared, 'is that under no circumstance will we permit this city to be terrorized by racial attack . . .'

This city, he spat. *What do you know about this city? You don't belong here.*

He clutched at a C-1 grenade in his jacket pocket. If he

wanted to he could blow everything open right here. *Right now.*

But there was work to do.

Tomorrow.

He was going for another personal record.

Chapter Nine

The next morning Jacobi and I were back canvassing the grounds of the LaSalle Heights Church.

All night long I had fretted over what Cindy had told me about a case that had come across her desk. It involved an elderly black woman in West Oakland, who lived alone in the Gustave White projects. Two days ago, the Oakland Police had found her hanging from a pipe in the basement laundry room, an electrical cord wound tightly around her neck.

At first, the police presumed it was a suicide. No abrasions or defensive wounds were found on her body. But yesterday, during the autopsy, a flaky residue was found packed under her nails. It turned out to be human skin with microscopic specks of dried blood. *The poor woman had been desperately digging her nails into someone.*

She hadn't hung herself after all, Cindy said.

It looked like the woman had been lynched.

As I went back over the crime scene at the church, I felt

uneasy. Cindy could be right. This might be *the second* in an onset of racially driven murders.

Jacobi walked up. He was holding a curled-up *Chronicle*. 'You see this, boss?'

The front page rocked with the blaring headline: *Police Stumped as Girl, 11, is Killed in Church Assault*.

The article was written by Ed Burns and Dede Hatcher, whose careers had been nudged aside by Cindy's work on the bride and groom case. With the newspapers stoking the fire, and the activists Gray and Jones railing on the air, they'd soon be accusing us of sitting on our hands while the terror suspect was running free.

'Your buddies . . .' Jacobi huffed. 'They always make it about us.'

'Uh-uh, Warren,' I shook my head. 'My buddies don't take cheap shots.'

Behind us in the woods, Charlie Clapper's CSU team was going over the ground around the sniper's position. They'd turned up a couple of foot imprints, but nothing identifiable. They would fingerprint the shell casings, grid-search the ground, pick up every piece of lint or dust where the supposed getaway vehicle had been parked.

'Any more sightings on that white van?' I asked Jacobi. In a strange way it was good to be working with him again.

He grumbled and shook his head. 'Got a lead on a couple of winos who hold a coffee klatch on that corner at night. So far, all we have is this.' He unfolded the artist's rendering of Bernard Smith's sketch – a two-headed lion, the sticker on the rear door of the van.

Jacobi scrunched in his cheeks. 'Who are we after, Lieutenant, the Pokémon killer?'

Across the field I spotted Aaron Winslow coming out of the church. A knot of protestors followed him from a police barrier some fifty yards away. As he saw me, his face tensed.

'People want to help any way they can. Paint over the bullet holes, build a new façade,' he said. 'They don't like to look at this.'

'I'm sorry,' I said. 'I'm afraid there's still an active investigation going on.'

He took in a breath. 'I keep playing it over in my mind. Whoever did this had a clear shot. I was standing right *there*, Lieutenant. More in the line of fire than Tasha. If someone was trying to hurt someone, *why didn't they hurt me?*'

Winslow kneeled down and picked up a pink butterfly hair clip from the ground. 'I read somewhere, Lieutenant, that "Courage abounds where guilt and rage run free." '

Winslow was taking this hard. I felt sorry for him; I liked him.

He managed a tight smile. 'It'll take more than this bastard to ruin our work. We won't fold. We'll have Tasha's service here, in this church.'

'We were headed to pay our respects,' I said.

'They live over there. Building A.' He pointed towards the projects. 'I guess you'll find a warm reception, given that there's some of your own.'

I looked at him askance. 'I'm sorry? What was that?'

'Didn't you know, Lieutenant? Tasha Catchings' uncle is a city cop.'

Chapter Ten

I visited the Catchings' apartment, paid my respects, then headed back to the Hall. This whole thing was incredibly depressing.

'Mercer's looking for you,' hollered Brenda, our longtime civilian secretary, as I got into the office. 'He sounds mad. Of course, he always sounds mad.'

I could imagine the folds under the Chief's jaw tightening even deeper with the afternoon headline. In fact, the entire Hall was buzzing with the news that the LaSalle Heights murder victim had been related to one of their own.

There were several other messages waiting for me on my desk. At the bottom of the pile I came across Claire's name. Tasha Catchings' autopsy should be finished by now. I decided to hold off on Mercer until I had something concrete to report, so I called Claire.

Claire Washburn was the sharpest, brightest, most thorough ME the city ever had. Everyone associated with law enforcement knew it, and how she ran the department without a hitch while the Chief Coroner Rhigetti, the mayor's stiff-suited appointee, traveled around the country to forensic conferences working on his political résumé. You wanted something done in the ME's office, you called Claire.

And when I needed someone to set me straight, make me laugh, or just be there to listen, that's where I went, too.

'Where you been hiding, baby?' Claire greeted me with her always upbeat voice that had the ring of polished brass.

'Normal routine,' I shrugged. 'Staff appraisals, case write-ups . . . city-dividing, racially motivated homicides.'

'Just my region of expertise,' she chuckled. 'I knew I'd be hearing from you. My spies tell me you've got yourself a bitch of a case out there.'

'Any of those spies maybe work for the *Chronicle* and drive a beat-up purple Beetle?'

'Or the DA's office, and a BMW 535. How the hell do you think information ever gets down here, anyway?'

'Well, here's one, Claire. Turns out the dead little girl's uncle is in uniform. He's at Northern. And the poor kid ends up being a poster child for the LaSalle Heights project in action. Top-of-the-line student, never once in trouble. Some justice, huh? This bastard leaves a hundred slugs in the church and the one that hits finds its way into her.'

'Unh-uh, honey,' Claire cut me off, 'there were *two* of them in there.'

'*Two*? She was hit twice?' EMS had been all over the body. How could we have failed to catch that?

'If I'm hearing you right, my guess is you think this shot was some kind of accident,' Claire said.

'What are you saying . . .?'

'Honey,' she said, soberly, 'I think you better come on down for a visit.'

Chapter Eleven

The morgue was on the ground floor of the Hall, out a back entrance and accessible from an asphalt path that led from the lobby. It took me no more than three minutes to rush down three flights of stairs.

Claire, in a long, white doctor's coat, met me in the reception area outside her office. Her bright and usually cheery face bore a look of professional concern, but as soon as she saw me, she eased into a smile and gave me a hug.

'How you been, stranger?' she asked, as if the case were a million miles away.

Claire could diffuse the tension in even the most critical of situations. I'd always admired the way she could relax my single-minded focus with just a smile.

'I've been good, Claire. Just swamped since I got the job.'

'I don't get to see you much now that you're Mercer's pet butt-boy.'

'Very funny.'

She smiled that coy, wide-eyed smirk of hers that was

partly, *Hey, I know what you mean*, but maybe a lot more, *You gotta make the time, girl, for those who love you*. But without as much as a reproving word, she led me down an antiseptic, linoleum-tiled hallway towards the morgue's operating room, called the Vault.

She glanced behind her. 'You made it sound like you were sure Tasha Catchings was killed by a stray bullet.'

'That's what I thought. The gunman fired two clips at the church and she was the only one hit. I even went and cased the area where the shots came from. There was no way he had anything even close to a clean shot. But you said *two* . . .'

'Uh-huh,' she nodded. We burst through a closed compression door into the dry, cold air of the Vault. The icy chill and chemical smell always made my skin crawl.

And it was no different now. A single inhabited gurney was visible from its refrigerated vault. A small mound lay on it, covered by a white sheet. It barely filled half the length of the gurney.

'Hold on,' Claire warned. The shock of naked post-op victims, rigid and bloodless, was never an easy sight.

She pulled down the sheet, revealing the child's face. *God, she was young* . . .

I looked at her soft, ebony skin, so innocent, so out of place against the cold, clinical surroundings. Part of me wanted to just reach out and lay a hand against her cheek. She had such a loveable face.

A large puncture wound, freshly cleaned of blood, tore up the flesh around the right side of the child's chest. '*Two* bullets,' Claire explained, 'basically right on top of each other, in rapid succession. I could see why EMS might've missed it. They almost tore through the same hole.'

I could barely contain my astonishment at this. A fit of nausea gripped at my gut.

'The first one exited right through her scapula,' Claire went on, easing the tiny body over on its side. 'The second bounced off the fourth vertebrae and lodged in her spine.'

Claire reached over and picked up a glass Petrie dish resting on a nearby counter. With a tweezer, she held up a flattened lead disk about the size of a quarter. 'Two shots, Linds. The first tore through the right ventricle, doing the trick. She was probably dead before this one even struck.'

Two shots . . . two one-in-a-million ricochets? I replayed the likely position of Tasha as she exited the church, and the killer's line of fire in the woods. One seemed plausible, but *two*.

'Did Charlie Clapper's crew find any bullet nicks in the church above where the girl was found?' Claire inquired.

'I don't know.' It was standard procedure in all homicides to painstakingly match up all bullets with their marks. 'I'll check.'

'What was the church constructed of where she was hit? Wood or stone?'

'Wood,' I said, realizing where she was heading. No way wood on its own would deflect an M-16.

Claire pushed her pair of operating glasses high on her forehead. She had a cheery, amiable face, but when she was certain, as she was now, it had a glow of conviction that admitted no doubt. 'Lindsay, the angle of entry is frontal and clean for both shots. A ricocheting shell would likely have come in from a different trajectory.'

'I went over every inch of the shooter's position, Claire. The way he was firing, he'd have to be a goddamn sharpshooter to set up that shot.'

'You say the fire was sprayed irregularly across the side of the church.'

'In a steady pattern, right to left. And Claire, no one else was struck. A hundred shots, *she was the only person hit*.'

'So, you assumed this was a tragic accident, right?' She peeled off her plastic medical gloves and tossed them deftly into a waste receptacle. 'Well, these two were no accident. They didn't ricochet off of anything. They were straight and perfectly placed. Killed her instantly. You willing to consider the possibility that maybe your gunman hit exactly what he was aiming at?'

I replayed the scene in my mind. 'He would have only had an instant to line up such a shot, Claire. And only a foot or two of clearance from the wall to squeeze it in.'

'Then either God didn't shine on that poor girl last night,' Claire said, with a sympathetic sigh, 'or you better start looking for one hell of a shooter.'

Chapter Twelve

The shocking possibility that Tasha Catchings might not have been a random victim after all dogged me all the way back to the office. Upstairs, I ran into a wall of detectives anxiously awaiting me. Lorraine Stafford informed me there was a positive from the auto search, a '94 Dodge Caravan reported stolen three days ago down the peninsula in Mountain View. I told her to see if any of the characteristics matched.

I grabbed Jacobi and told him to wrap up his bagel and come with me.

'Where we headed?' he groaned.

'Across the Bay. Oakland.'

'Mercer's still looking for you,' Brenda shouted as we hit the hall. 'Whad'ya want me to say?'

'Tell him I'm investigating a murder.'

Twenty minutes later, we had crossed the Bay Bridge, woven through the drab, antiquated skyline that was downtown Oakland, and pulled up in front of the Police

Administration Building on Broadway. Oakland's police headquarters was a short, gray, panel and glass building in the impersonal style of the early Sixties. On the second floor was Homicide, a cramped, dreary office no larger than our own. I'd been here a few times over the years.

Lieutenant Ron Vandervellen stood up to greet us as we were led into his office. 'Hey, I hear congratulations are in order, Boxer. Welcome to the world of sedentary life.'

'I wish, Ron,' I replied.

'What brings you here? You looking to check out how the real world works?'

For years, the San Francisco and Oakland Homicide Departments had maintained a kind of friendly rivalry, they believing that all we dealt with across the Bay was the occasional computer parts salesman found naked and dead in his hotel room.

'I saw you on the news last night,' Vandervellen cackled. 'Very photogenic. I mean *her*,' he grinned at Jacobi. 'So why *are* you here?'

'A little bird named Chipman,' I replied. Estelle Chipman was the elderly black woman Cindy told me had been found hung in her basement.

He shrugged. 'I got a hundred unsolved murders if you guys don't have enough to keep you busy.'

I was used to the Vandervellen barbs, but this time he sounded particularly edgy. 'No agenda, Ron. I just want to look at the crime scene if that's okay.'

'Sure, but I think it's gonna be tough to tie it into your church shooting.'

'Why's that?' I asked.

The Oakland Lieutenant got up, went into the outer office, and came back with a case file. 'I guess I'm having a hard time putting together how a homicide as obviously racially motivated as yours could be committed by one of their own.'

'What are you saying?' I asked. 'Estelle Chipman's killer was *black*?'

He donned a pair of reading glasses, leafed through the file until he came to an official document marked *Alameda County Coroner's Report*.

'Read it and weep,' he muttered. 'If you called, I could've saved you the toll. "Dermal specimens found under the victim's fingernails suggest a hyper-pigmented dermus consistent with a non-Caucasian." Slides are out being tested as we speak.

'You still want to check out the site?' he asked, seemingly enjoying the moment.

'You mind? We're already here.'

'Sure, yeah, be my guest. It's Krimpman's case, but he's out. I can take you though. I don't get out to the Gus White projects much anymore. Who knows, riding with you two supercops, I might pick something up along the way.'

Chapter Thirteen

The Gustave White projects were six identical redbrick high rises on Redmond Street in West Oakland. As we pulled up, Vandervellen said, 'Didn't make much sense. The poor woman wasn't ill, seemed to have okay finances, even went to church twice a week. But sometimes, people just give up. Until the autopsy, it looked legit.'

I reviewed the case file: there were no witnesses, no one had heard any screams, no one saw anybody running away. Only an elderly woman who kept to herself, found hanging from a steam pipe in the basement, her neck at a right angle and her tongue exposed.

At the projects, we walked right into Building C. 'Elevator's on the fritz,' Vandervellen said. We took the stairs down. In the graffiti-marked basement, we came upon a hand-painted sign that read: LAUNDRY ROOM-BOILER ROOM.

'Found her in here.'

The basement room was still criss-crossed with yellow Crime Scene tape. A pungent, rancid odor filled the air. Graffiti was everywhere. Anything that had been here –

the body, the electric wires she was hung with – had already been taken either to the morgue or entered into evidence.

'I don't know what you're looking to find,' Vandervellen said with a shrug.

'I don't know either,' I swallowed. 'It happened late last Friday night?'

'Coroner figures around ten. We thought maybe the old lady came down to do her laundry, that someone surprised her. Janitor found her the next morning.'

'What about security cameras?' Jacobi asked. 'They were all over the lobby and the halls.'

'Same as the elevator – broken,' Vandervellen shrugged.

It was clear Vandervellen and Jacobi wanted to head out as quickly as possible, but something pulled at me to stay. *For what*? I had no idea. But my senses were buzzing *Find me . . . over here*!

'The race thing aside,' Vandervellen called out, 'if you're looking for a connection, I'm sure you know how unusual it is for a killer to switch methods in the midst of a spree.'

'Thanks,' I sniffed back. I had scanned the room, nothing jumped at me. Just the feeling. 'Guess we'll have to solve *this* one on our own. Who knows, by now maybe something's popped up on our side of the pond.'

As he was about to flick off the light, something caught my eye. 'Hold it,' I said.

As if pulled by gravity, I was drawn to the far side of the room, to the wall behind the spot where Chipman had been found hanging. I knelt, examining the concrete wall closely. If I hadn't seen it before it would've passed right by my sight.

A primitive drawing, like a child's, in bright orange chalk. It was a lion. Like Bernard Smith's drawing, but more fierce. The lion's body led into a coiled tail, but it was the tail of something else . . . a reptile? *A serpent*?

And that wasn't all.

The lion had two heads: one a lion, the other possibly a goat.

I felt a knot in my chest, a tremor of revulsion, and recognition, too.

Jacobi came up behind me. 'Find something, Lieutenant?'

I drew a long breath. '*Pokémon*.'

Chapter Fourteen

So now I knew . . .

The cases were probably related. Bernard Smith's sighting of the fleeing van had been on the mark. We had our getaway car. We might have a double killer.

It didn't surprise me that when I finally got back to the Hall, an angry Chief Mercer insisted he be buzzed the minute I walked in.

I closed the door to my office, dialed his extension and waited for the barrage.

'You know what's going on here,' he said, the sting of authority rippling through his voice. 'You think you can stay out in the field all day and ignore my calls? You're *Lieutenant* Boxer now. Your job is to manage your squad. And keep me informed.'

'I'm sorry, Chief, it's just that—'

'A child has been killed. A neighborhood terrorized. We've got some psycho a brick short out there who's trying to turn this place into an inferno. By tomorrow, every African-American leader in this town will be demanding to know what we're going to do.'

'It's gotten deeper than that, Chief.'

Mercer stopped short. 'Deeper than what?'

I told him what I had found in the basement in Oakland. The lion-like symbol that had been at both crimes.

I heard him suck in a deep breath. 'You're saying these two killings are related?'

'I'm saying that before we jump to any fast conclusions, that possibility exists.'

The air seemed to seep right out of Mercer's lungs. 'You get a photo of what you found on that wall over to the lab. And the sketch of what that kid in Bay View saw. I want to know what those drawings mean.'

'It's already in the works,' I replied.

'And the getaway van? Anything back on it yet?'

'Negative.'

A troubling possibility seemed to be forming in Mercer's mind. 'If there's some kind of conspiracy taking place here, we're not going to sit back while this city is held hostage to a terror campaign.'

'We're running the van. Let me have some time on that symbol.' I didn't want to tell him my worst fear. If Vandervellen was right, that Estelle Chipman's killer was black, and if Claire was right, that Tasha Catchings was an intended target, this might not be a racial terror campaign at all.

Even on the phone, I could feel the creases underneath his jaw tighten. I was asking him to take a risk, a big one.

Finally I heard him exhale, 'Don't let me down, Lieutenant. Solve your case.'

As I hung up, I could feel the pressure rising. The world was going to expect me to bust down the door of every hate group operating west of Montana, and already I had real doubts.

On my desk I spotted a message from Jill. 'How about a drink? Six o'clock,' it read. '*All of us.*'

Two days into the case . . . If there was anything that would calm my fears it was Jill, Claire and Cindy, and a pitcher of margaritas at Susie's.

I left a message on Jill's voicemail that I'd be there.

I glanced at a faded blue baseball cap hanging on a wooden coat rack in the corner of my office, with the words, 'It's *Heavenly* . . .' embroidered on the brim. The cap had belonged to Raleigh. He'd given it to me during a beautiful weekend up at Heavenly Valley, where the outside world had seemed to disappear for a while, and both of us opened up to what was starting to take place between us.

'Don't let me mess up,' I whispered. I felt my eyes begin to sting with tears. *God, I wished he was here.* 'You sonovabitch . . .' I shook my head at the hat. 'I miss you.'

Chapter Fifteen

I t took no more than a minute of settling back in our old booth at Susie's to feel the magic begin to spark, and to realize it was happening all over again.

A troublesome case that was getting worse. A pitcher full of high-octane margaritas. My three best friends, all at the top of law enforcement. I was afraid that our murder club was back in business.

'Just like old times?' smiled Claire, scooting her large frame over to make room for me.

'In more ways than you know,' I sighed. Then, pouring myself a frothy drink, 'Jesus, do I need one of these.'

'Tough day?' Jill inquired.

'No,' I shook my head. 'Routine. Piece of cake.'

'That paperwork, it'll drive anyone to drink,' shrugged Claire, taking a sip of her margarita. 'Cheers. Great to see you wenches.'

There was an obvious level of anticipation buzzing through the group. As I took a sip myself, I scanned around. All eyes were centered on me.

'Uh-uh,' I almost spat into my drink. 'I can't get into it. Don't even start.'

'I told you,' Jill croaked, with a confirming smile. 'Things have changed. Lindsay's management now.'

'That's not it, Jill. There's a gag order. Mercer's got this thing shut down. Besides, I thought we were here for you?'

Jill's sharp blue eyes twinkled. 'The representative from the District Attorney's office is willing to cede the floor to her esteemed colleague from the fourth floor.'

'Jesus, guys, I've been back *four days.*'

'What the hell else is anybody in the city talking about?' said Claire. 'You want to hear about my day? I did a full frontal at ten, then a talk at SFU on the pathology of—'

'We could talk about global warming,' Cindy said, 'or this book I'm reading, *The Death of Vishnu.*'

'It's not that I don't want to talk about it,' I protested, 'it's just that it's sealed, confidential.'

'*Confidential*, like what I turned you onto in Oakland?' Cindy asked.

'We have to talk about that,' I said. '*After.*'

'I'll make you a deal,' Jill said. 'You share it with us. Like always. Then I'll share something. You judge which is juicier. Winner pays the check.'

I knew it was only a matter of time before I gave in. How could I keep secrets from my girls? It was all over the news – at least part of it. And there weren't three sharper minds anywhere in the Hall.

I let out an expectant sigh. 'This all stays here.'

'Of course,' Jill and Claire said. 'Duh.'

I turned to Cindy. 'And that means you don't go to press. With any of it. Until I say so.'

'Why do I get the sense I'm always being blackmailed by you?' She shook her head, then acquiesced. 'Fine. Deal.'

Jill filled up my glass. 'I knew we'd break you down eventually.'

I took a sip. 'Nah. I decided to tell you when you said, "tough day?" '

Piece by piece, I took them through the case so far. The decal Bernard Smith had seen on the getaway van. The identical drawing I had found in Oakland. The possibility that Estelle Chipman might have been murdered, and by a black person. Claire's thought that Tasha Catchings may not have been an accidental target after all.

'I knew it,' Cindy shouted with a triumphant beam.

'You got to find out what that lion image represents,' insisted Claire.

I nodded. 'I'm on it. Big time.'

Jill, the DA, inquired, 'Anything out there that actually ties the victims themselves together?'

'Nothing so far.'

'What about motive?' she pressed.

'Everyone's reading them as hate crimes, Jill.'

She nodded cautiously. 'And you?'

'I'm starting to read them differently. I think we have to consider the possibility that someone's using the hate crime scenario as a smokescreen.'

There was a long silence at the table.

'A racial serial killer,' Claire said.

Chapter Sixteen

I had shared my news, all of it bad. Everyone ran it over glumly.

I nodded to Jill. 'Now you.'

Cindy jumped the gun. 'Bennett's not going to run again, is he?' In her eight years in the Prosecutor's office, Jill had shot up to be his Number Two in command. If the old man decided to step down, she was the logical choice to be appointed San Francisco's next DA.

Jill laughed and shook her head. 'He'll be propped up at that oak desk the day he dies. That's the truth.'

'Well, you're holding *something* back,' pressed Claire.

'You're right,' she admitted. 'I am . . .'

One by one, Jill met each of our gazes as if to ratchet up the suspense. Those normally piercing cobalt eyes had never looked so serene. At last, a crooked little smile crept across her face. She let out a sigh, then said, 'I'm pregnant . . .'

We sat there, waiting for her to crack that she was just putting us on. But she didn't. She just kept those sharp eyes blinking right in our faces, until thirty seconds must have gone by.

'You're joking,' I stammered back. Jill was the most driven woman I knew. You could catch her at her desk most any night until after eight. Her husband Rich was a high-rising partner in a venture firm in town. They were fast-track achievers: they mountain-biked in Moab, wind-surfed on the Columbia River in Oregon. *A baby* . . .

'People do do it,' she exclaimed at our amazement.

'I knew it,' Claire slapped the table and exclaimed. 'I just knew it. I saw the look in your eyes. I saw that sheen on your face. I said, something's toasting in that oven. You're talking to an expert, you know. How long?'

'Twelve weeks. I'm due the end of April.' Jill's eyes beamed with the sparkle of a young girl's. 'Other than our families, you're the first people I've told. *Of course.*'

'Bennett's gonna shit Graham crackers,' Cindy cackled.

'He's got three of his own. And it's not like I'm trading it in to go off and grow grapes in Petaluma. I'm just having a baby.'

I found myself smiling. Part of me was so pleased for her I almost wanted to cry. Part of me was even a little jealous. Most of me still couldn't believe it. 'This kid better know what he's in for,' I grinned. 'He'll be rocked to sleep by tapes of California case law.'

'No way,' Jill laughed, defiantly. 'I won't do it. I promise, I won't do it. I'm gonna be a really good mom.'

I stood up and leaned across the table to her. 'This is so great, Jill.' For a moment, we just stared at each other, our eyes glistening. I was so damned happy for her. I remembered when I was scared shitless because of a blood disease I had, and Jill had bared her arms to us and showed us her terrible scars. She explained how she had cut herself in high school and college; how the challenge to always get to the top – Stanford, law school, DA's office – so deeply ruled her life that she could only take it out on herself.

We threw our arms around each other and I squeezed her.

'Was this something you've been thinking about?' Claire asked.

'We've been trying for a couple of months now,' Jill answered, sitting back down. 'I'm not sure it was any conscious decision, other than the timing seemed right.' She looked at Claire. 'The first time I met you, when Lindsay asked me into your group and you talked about *your* kids . . . it just sort of set off a spark in me. I remember thinking, "She runs the ME's office. She's one of the most capable women I know, at the top of her profession, yet this is what she talks about." '

'When you start out working,' Claire explained, 'you have all this drive and focus. As a woman, you feel you have to prove everything. But when you have kids, it's different, natural. You realize it's no longer about you at all. You realize . . . you no longer have to prove anything. You already have.'

'So, hey,' Jill said with glistening eyes, 'I want a little of that, too.

'I never told this to you guys,' she went on, 'but I was pregnant once before. Five years ago.' She took a sip of water and shook the dark hair off the back of her neck. 'My career was in overdrive – you remember, there was that Lafrade hearing, and Rich was a new partner in the firm.'

'It just wasn't the right time for you then, honey,' Claire said.

'That wasn't it,' she answered quickly. 'I wanted it. It was just that everything was so intense. I was pulling stints at the office until ten. It seemed like Rich was always away . . .' She took a breath, a remote cloudiness in her eyes. 'I had some bleeding. The doctor warned me to cut back. I tried, but everyone was pushing on this case, and I was always alone. One day, I just felt my insides explode. I lost it . . . in the fourth month.'

'Oh, Jesus,' Claire gasped. 'Oh, Jill.'

Jill sucked in a breath, and a hushed silence fell over the table.

'So how *are* you feeling?' I asked, concern on my face.

'Ecstatic,' she replied. 'Physically, strong as ever . . .' Then she blinked remotely for a moment and faced us again, taking a breath. 'Truth is, I'm a total wreck.'

I reached for her hand. 'What does your doctor say?'

'He says we'll keep a close watch, and keep the sensationalist cases down to a minimum. Run it in low gear.'

'Do you have that gear?' I asked.

'I do now,' she sniffed.

In her eyes I saw a glorious transformation taking shape, something I had never seen before. She was always successful. She had that beautiful face, that hard-charging drive. Now I could see, at last, that she was happy.

Beautiful tears welled up in her eyes. I had seen this woman stand up in court against some of the toughest bastards in the city; I had seen her go after murderers with an undeterred conviction. I had even seen the scars of self-doubt on the inside of her arms.

But until that moment I had never seen Jill cry.

'*Dammit* . . .' I smiled. I reached for the check. 'I guess I pay.'

Chapter Seventeen

After a few more giddy hugs with Jill, I made my way home to my apartment on Potrero Hill.

It was the second floor of a renovated blue Victorian. Cozy and bright, with an alcove of wide portico windows overlooking the Bay. Sweet Martha, my affectionate Border collie, met me at the door.

'Hey, sweetie,' I said. She wagged up to greet me and threw her paws against my leg.

'So, how was *your* day?' I nuzzled close, smooching her happy face.

I went into the bedroom and peeled off my work clothes, pulling up my hair and putting on the oversized Giants sweatshirt and flannel pajama pants that I lived in when the weather turned cool. I fed Martha, made myself a cup of Orange Zinger, and sat in the cushioned alcove.

I took a sip of tea, Martha perched on my lap. Out in the distance, a grid of blinking airplane lights descending into SFI came into view. I found myself thinking about the unbelievable image of Jill as a mom ... her thin, fit figure, with a bulging belly . . . a shower with just us girls. It made me chuckle. I smiled at Martha. 'Jilly-bean's gonna be a mommy.'

I had never seen her look so complete. It was only a few months ago when my own thoughts ran to how much I would have loved to have had a baby. As Jill said, *I wanted some of that, too.* It just wasn't meant to be . . .

Parenting just didn't seem like the natural occupation in my family.

My own mother died fourteen years ago, when I was twenty-one and just entering the Academy. She had been diagnosed with breast cancer, and my last two years of college I helped take care of her, rushing back from class to pick her up at the Emporium where she worked, preparing her meals, watching over my younger sister, Cat.

My father, a San Francisco cop, walked out on us when I was thirteen. To this day, I didn't know why. I had grown up hearing all the stories – that he handed his paycheck over to the bookies; that he had a secret life away from Mom; that the bastard could charm the pants off of anyone; that one day he lost his heart, and just couldn't put the uniform back on.

Old timers down in the Southern district still asked me how Marty Boxer was. Last I heard from Cat, he was down in Redondo Beach, doing his own thing, private security. They still tell stories about him, and maybe it's good someone can think about him with a laugh. Marty, who once nabbed three perps with the same set of hand-cuffs . . . Marty Boxer, who stopped off to lay a bet with the suspect still in the car. All I could think about was that the bastard let me tend and nurse my mother while she was dying, and never came back.

I hadn't seen my father for eleven years. Since the day I became a cop. I didn't even miss him anymore.

God, it had been ages since I had examined these old scars. Mom had been gone for twelve years. I'd been married, divorced. I'd made it into Homicide. Now I was running it. Somewhere along the way, I met the man of my dreams . . .

I was right when I told Mercer the old fire was back in my stomach.

But I was lying when I told myself I had put Chris Raleigh in the past.

Chapter Eighteen

It was always the eyes that got him. Naked on his bed in the stark, cell-like room, he sat staring at the old black-and-white photographs he had looked at a thousand times.

It was always the eyes . . . that deadened, hopeless resignation.

How they *posed*, even knowing that their life was about to end. Even with the noose wrapped around their neck.

In the loosely bound album he had forty-seven photos and postcards arranged in chronological order. He had collected them over the years. The first, an old daguerreotype dated 9 June 1901, his father had given him. *Dez Jones, lynched in Fayetteville, Indiana.* On the border, someone had written in faded script: 'This was that dance I went to the other night. We sure *played* afterwards. Your son, Sam.' In the foreground, a crowd in suit coats and bowler hats, and behind them, the limply hanging corpse.

He flipped the page. *Frank Taylor, Mason Georgia, 1911.* It had cost him $500 to get the photo but it was worth every penny. From the back of a buggy perched under an oak, the condemned man stared, seconds before his death. On his face, neither resistance nor fear. A small crowd of properly dressed men and women grinned towards the camera as if they were witnessing Lindbergh arriving in Paris. Dressed up as if it was a family portrait.

Their eyes conveyed that the hanging was something proper and natural. Taylor's simply that there wasn't a damn thing he could do about it anyway.

He got off the bed and dragged his slick, muscular frame to the mirror. He had always been strong. He had lifted weights for ten years now. He flinched as he drew blood and mass into his swollen pecs. He massaged a scratch. That old bitch had dug her nails into his shoulder as he wrapped the coil around the ceiling pipes. She had barely drawn blood, but he looked at the scratch with contempt. He didn't like anything that disturbed the complexion of his skin.

He posed in front of the mirror at the seething lion-goat tattooed across his chest.

Soon, all the stupid assholes would see that it wasn't just about hate. They would read his pattern. The guilty had to be punished. Reputations needed to be restored. He had no particular antipathy for any of them. It wasn't the hate.

He climbed back on the bed and masturbated to the photo of Missy Preston, whose tiny neck was snapped by a rope in Childers County, Tennessee, in August of 1931.

Without even a groan, he ejaculated. The forceful rush made his knees quake. That old lady, she had deserved to die. The choir girl, too. He was pumped up!

He massaged the tattoo on his chest. *Pretty soon, I will let you free, my pet . . .*

He opened his photo scrapbook and flipped to the last blank page, just after Morris Tulo and Sweet Brown, in Hutchinson, Kansas, 1956.

He had been saving this spot for the right picture. And now he had it.

He took a tube of roll-on glue and dabbed all over the back of the photo. Then he pressed it on the blank page.

Here's where it belonged.

He remembered her staring up at him, that sad inevitability etched all over her face. *The eyes . . .*

He admired the new addition: Estelle Chipman, those eyes stretched wide, looking at the camera, just before he kicked out the chair from under her feet.

They always posed.

Chapter Nineteen

F irst thing the following morning, I called Stu Kirkwood, who ran a Hate Crimes desk assigned to the police department. I asked him, *personally*, for any leads on the types of groups that might be operating in the Bay Area. My people had talked to Stu earlier, but I needed action fast.

So far, Clapper's CSU team had scoured the area around the church for two days with nothing to show for it, and the only thing we came back with on Aaron Winslow was that no one had a negative thing to say about him.

Kirkwood informed me over the phone that a few organized supremacist groups operated out of northern California, offshoots of the Klan or some crazy Neo-Nazi skinheads. He said that maybe the best thing was to contact the local chapter of the FBI, who kept a much more active eye on them. Gay-bashing was more his thing.

Bringing in the FBI at this stage didn't fill me with enthusiasm. I asked Kirkwood to give me what he had, and an hour later he came up, carrying a plastic bin crammed with blue and red folders. 'Background reading,' he winked, dropping the bin heavily on my desk.

At the sight of the mass of files, my hopes sank. 'You got any ideas about this, Stu?'

He shrugged, sympathetically. 'San Francisco's not exactly a hotbed for these groups. Most of what I gave you here seems pretty benign. They seem to spend more of their time hoisting back a few beers and shooting off ammo.'

I ordered up a salad, figuring I'd spend the next couple of hours at my desk with a bunch of nutcases railing against blacks and Jews. I pulled out a handful of files and opened one at random.

Some sort of militia group, operating up in Greenview, near the Oregon border. *The California Patriots*. Some summary information supplied by the FBI: Activity Type: Militia, sixteen to twenty members. Weapon Assessment: Minor, small to semi-automatic arms, over the counter. Threat: Low/Moderate.

I skimmed through the file. Some printed materials with logos of crossed guns, detailing everything from population shifts from 'the white, European majority,' to media cover-ups on government programs to promote test-tube fertilization of minorities.

I couldn't imagine my killer buying into this claptrap. I didn't see him on the same wavelength at all. Our guy was organized and bold, not some pumped-up backwoods bozo. He had gone to elaborate lengths to hide the murder in the MO of a hate crime. And he had signed them.

Like most serials, *he wanted us to know*.

And to know there would be more.

I leafed through a few more files. Nothing jumped out at me. I was starting to get the feeling this was a waste of time.

Suddenly Lorraine burst into my office. 'We caught a break, Lieutenant. We found the white van.'

Chapter Twenty

I strapped on my Glock and grabbed Cappy and Jacobi on the way out before Lorraine even finished filling me in. 'I want a SWAT team out there,' I yelled.

Ten minutes later, we all screeched up to a makeshift roadblock on San Jacinto, a quiet residential street.

A radio car on routine patrol had spotted a Dodge Caravan parked outside a house in Forest Hills. What made him sure this was the car we were looking for was the decal of a two-headed lion on the rear door.

Vasquez, the young patrolman who had called in the van, pointed towards a tree-shaded Tudor halfway down the block, the white minivan parked at the end of the driveway. It seemed crazy. This was an affluent neighborhood, not a likely haven for criminals or murderers.

But there it was.

Our white van.

And Bernard Smith's Mufasa.

Moments later, an unmarked SWAT vehicle, rigged to look like a cable TV repair truck, pulled onto the street. The team was headed by Lieutenant Skip Arbichaut. I didn't know what the situation entailed, whether we would have a siege, or possibly have to break our way in.

'Cappy, Jacobi and I will go in first,' I said.

This was a homicide operation and I wasn't letting anyone else take the risk. I had Arbichaut deploy his men, two around back, three manning the front, and one with a sledge with us in case we had to bust in.

We strapped on protective vests and black nylon jackets identifying us as police. I clicked my 9mm off safety. There wasn't much time to get nervous.

The SWAT truck started down the street, three black-vested snipers hugging its opposite side.

Cappy, Jacobi and I followed the truck as cover until it pulled to a stop in front of a mailbox marked 610. Vasquez was right. *The van was a match*.

My heart was racing now. I had been in many forced entries before, but none with any more at stake. We wove our way cautiously to the front of the house.

There were lights on inside, some noise from a TV.

At my nod, Cappy pounded the door with his gun. '*San Francisco Police*.' Jacobi and I crouched with our guns ready.

No one answered.

After a few tense seconds, I signaled Arbichaut for a ram.

Suddenly the front door cracked open.

'*Freeze!*' Cappy boomed, swinging his gun into a shooting position. '*San Francisco Police*.'

A wide-eyed woman in powder-blue exercise clothes

stood frozen in the doorway. 'Oh my God,' she screeched, eyes fastened on our weapons.

Cappy yanked her out the front door as Arbichaut's SWAT team rushed the house. He barked, 'Is anyone else at home?'

'Just my daughter,' the frightened woman shrieked. 'She's two.'

The black-vested SWAT team barged past her into the house like they were searching for Elian Gonzalez.

'Is that your van?' Jacobi barked.

The woman's eyes darted towards the street. 'What is this about?'

'Is that your van?' Jacobi's voice boomed again.

'No,' she said, trembling. 'No . . .'

'Do you know who it belongs to?'

She looked again, terrified, and shook her head. 'I've never seen it before in my life.'

It was all wrong, I could see that. The neighborhood, the plastic kids' ladder on the lawn, the spooked mom in the workout clothes. A disappointed sigh expelled from my chest. The van had been dumped here.

All of a sudden, a green Audi knifed its way up to the curb, followed by two police cars. The Audi must have gone right through our roadblock. A well-dressed man in a suit and tortoiseshell glasses jumped out and ran towards the house. 'Kathy, what the hell's going on?'

'*Steve* . . .' the woman hugged him with a sigh of relief. 'This is my husband. I called him when I saw all the police outside our house.'

The man looked around at the eight cop cars, SWAT back-up and the SFPD inspectors standing around with weapons drawn. 'What are you doing at my house? This is insane! This is nuts!'

'We believe that van was the vehicle used in the commission of a homicide,' I said. 'We have every right to be here.'

'A homicide?'

Two of Arbichaut's men emerged, indicating that there wasn't anyone else in the house. Across the street, people were starting to file outside. 'That van's been our Number One priority for two days. I'm sorry to have upset you. There was no way to be sure.'

The husband's indignation rose. His face and neck were beet red. 'You're thinking *we* had something to do with this. With a homicide?'

I figured I had upset their lives enough. 'The LaSalle Heights shooting.'

'Have you people lost your minds? You suspected us in the strafing of a church?' His jaw dropped and he fixed on me incredulously. 'Do you idiots have any idea what I do?'

My eyes fell on his pinstriped gray suit, his blue button-down collar shirt. I had the humiliating feeling I had just been made a fool of.

'I'm chief counsel for the northern California chapter of the Anti-Defamation League.'

Chapter Twenty-One

We *had* been made fools of by the killer. No one on the block knew anything about, or had any connection to the stolen van. It had been dumped there, purposely, to show us up. Even as Clapper's CSU went over it inch by inch, I knew it wouldn't yield shit. I studied the decal and I was sure it was the same one I had seen in Oakland. One head was a lion's; one seemed to be a goat's; the tail suggested a reptile. But what the hell did it mean?

'One thing we learned,' Jacobi smirked. 'The SOB's got a sense of humor.'

'I'm glad you're a fan,' I said.

Back at the Hall, I said to Lorraine, 'I want to know where that van came from, I want to know who it belonged to, who had access to it, every contact the owner had a month prior to its theft.'

I was fuming. We had a vicious killer out there, but not a single clue as to what made him tick. Was it a hate crime or a killing spree? An organized group or a lone wolf? We knew the guy was fairly intelligent. His strikes had been well planned, and if irony was part of his MO, dumping the getaway car where he had was a real *beaut*.

Brenda buzzed in, informing me Ron Vandervellen was on the line. The Oakland cop came on, chuckling. 'Word is, you managed to subdue a dangerous threat to our society masquerading as a legal watchdog in the Anti-Defamation League.'

'I guess that makes our investigations about equal, Ron,' I chuffed back.

'Relax, Lindsay, I didn't call to rub it in,' he said, shifting his tone. 'Actually, I thought I would make your day.'

'I won't argue, Ron.' I could use anything about now. 'What do you have for us?'

'You knew Estelle Chipman was a widow, right?'

'I think you mentioned that.'

'Well, we were doing some standard background on her. We found a son, in Chicago. He's coming to claim the body. Given what's been going on, I thought what he told us was too coincidental to ignore.'

'What, Ron?'

'Her husband died three years ago. Heart attack. Want to guess what the dude did for a living?'

I had the rising feeling Vandervellen was about to blow this thing wide open.

'Estelle Chipman's husband was a San Francisco cop.'

Chapter Twenty-Two

Cindy Thomas pulled up her VW across from the LaSalle Heights Church and let out a long sigh. The church's white clapperboard front had been defaced by a pattern of ugly chinks and bullet holes. A gaping hole where the beautiful stained-glass window had been was sealed with a black canvas tarp.

She remembered seeing it the day the window was first unveiled, on her old beat at the paper. The mayor, some local dignitaries, Aaron Winslow, all made speeches about how the beautiful scene had been paid for through community work. A symbol. She remembered interviewing Winslow, and being impressed with his passion, and also his unexpected humbleness.

Cindy ducked under the yellow police tape and stepped closer to the bullet-ridden wall. On her job at the *Chronicle*, she'd been assigned to stories where people had died. But this was the first one where she felt the human race had died a little, too.

She was startled by a voice. 'You can stare for as long as

you want, but it doesn't get any prettier.'

Cindy spun, and found herself facing a man with a smooth and very handsome face. Kind eyes. She knew him. She nodded. 'I was here when the window was unveiled. It carried a lot of hope.'

'Still does,' Winslow said. 'We didn't lose our hope. Don't worry about that.'

She smiled, staring into his deep brown eyes.

'I'm Aaron Winslow,' he said, shifting a handful of children's textbooks to extend his hand.

'Cindy Thomas,' she replied. His grip was warm and gentle.

'Don't tell me they've put our church as one of the scenic sights on the Thirty Mile Drive.' Winslow started to walk towards the rear of the church, and she followed along.

'I'm not a tourist,' Cindy said. 'I just wanted to see this. Listen,' she swallowed, 'I'd like to pretend I just came by to pay my respects . . . which I did. But I'm also with the *Chronicle*. On the Crime Desk.'

'A reporter,' Winslow exhaled. 'It makes sense now. For years, everything that *really* goes on here – tutoring, literacy training, a national recognized choir – doesn't crank up a story. But one madman acts and now *Nightline* wants to do a town meeting. What do you want to know, Ms Thomas? What does the *Chronicle* want?'

His words stung her a little, but she kind of liked that. He was right.

'Actually, I want to talk to you. I've never forgotten my

first sight of the new window. It was a special day.'

He stopped. He focused his eyes on her, then smiled. 'It was a special day. And actually, Ms Thomas, I knew who you were when I walked up. I remember you. You interviewed me back then.'

Someone called Winslow's name from inside the church, and a woman came out. She reminded him he had an eleven o'clock meeting.

'So, have you seen all you came to see, Ms Thomas? Should we expect you back in another couple of years?'

'No. I want to know how you deal with this. This violence in the face of all you've done, how the neighborhood feels about it.'

Winslow let himself smile, 'Let me clue you in on something. I don't deal in innocence. I've spent too much time in the real world.'

She remembered that Aaron Winslow wasn't someone whose faith was formed through a life of detachment. He'd come up from the streets. He'd been an Army chaplain. Only days before, he'd put himself in the line of fire, and possibly saved lives.

'You came here to see how this neighborhood is responding to the attack? Come see for yourself. Tasha Catchings is being buried tomorrow.'

Chapter Twenty-Three

Vandervellen's stunning disclosure drummed in my head for the rest of the day. *Both murder victims had been related to San Francisco cops.*

It could add up to nothing. They could be two random and unrelated victims. People in different cities, separated by sixty years.

Or it could mean everything.

I picked up the phone and called Claire. 'I need a big favor,' I asked.

'Just how big?' I could feel her grin.

'I need you to take a look at the autopsy of that woman who was hung in Oakland.'

'I can do that. Send it over. I'll take a look.'

'This is where it gets huge, Claire. It's still at the Oakland ME's office. It hasn't been released.'

I waited expectantly as she sighed, 'You must be kidding, Lindsay. You want me to stick my nose into an investigation that's still in progress?'

'Listen, Claire, I know this isn't exactly procedure, but

they've made some pretty important assumptions that could determine this case.'

'Want to tell me what type of assumptions I'd be stepping all over a respected ME's toes to review?'

'Claire, these cases are related. There's a pattern here. Estelle Chipman was married to a cop. Tasha Catchings' uncle was a cop, too. My whole investigation hinges on whether we're dealing with one killer. Oakland believes there's a black man involved, Claire.'

'A black man?' She gasped. 'Why would a black want to do these things?'

'I don't know. But there's starting to be a lot of circumstantial evidence linking both crimes. I have to know.'

She hesitated, sighed. 'Precisely what the hell would I be looking for?'

I told her about the skin specimens they had found under the victim's nails and their ME's conclusion.

'Teitleman's a good man,' Claire responded. 'I'd trust his findings like I would my own.'

'I know, Claire, but he's not you. Please. This is important.'

'I want you to know,' she shot back, 'that if Art Teitleman asked to poke his nose into one of my preliminary investigations, I'd have his parking ticket stamped and politely tell him to go back to his side of the Bay. I wouldn't do this for anyone else, Lindsay.'

'I know that, Claire,' I said with a grateful tone. 'Why do you think I've been working this friendship all these years?'

Chapter Twenty-Four

L ater that afternoon, I sat at my desk as, one by one, my staff called it quits for the day. I couldn't leave with them.

My mind tried over and over to put together the parts. Almost everything I had was based on assumptions. Was the killer black or white? Was Claire right, that Tasha Catchings was intentionally killed? But the lion symbol had definitely been there. *Link the victims*, my instincts said. *There's a connection. But what the hell is it*?

I glanced at my watch and placed a call to Simone Clark in Personnel, catching her just as she was preparing to leave. 'Simone, I need you to pull a file for me tomorrow.'

'Sure, whose do you need?'

'A cop who retired, maybe six, seven years ago. His name was Edward Chipman.'

'That's a while back. It would be out on the docks.' The department out-sourced its old records to a document storage company. 'Early afternoon, okay?'

'Sure, Simone. Best you can do.'

I was still bristling with nervous energy. I took out another stack of Kirkwood's hate files and plopped them on my desk.

I opened one at random. Americans for Constitutional Action . . . Ploughs and Fifes, another hayseed militia group. All these assholes, they seemed like such a bunch of right-wing jerk-offs. Was I wasting my time? Nothing jumped out. Nothing gave me any hope that this was the right track.

Go home, Lindsay, a voice impelled. *Tomorrow, new leads might develop. There was the van, Chipman's file . . . Call it a night. Take Martha for a run.*

Go home . . .

I stacked the files, about to give in, when the top one caught my eye. *The Templars*. A Hell's Angels offshoot out of Vallejo. The original Templars were Christian knights from the Crusades. Immediately, I noticed the FBI's assessment of threat. Their rating was *High*.

I took the file off the pile and leafed further in. There was an FBI report outlining a series of unsolved felonies that the Templars had been suspected of involvement in: bank robberies, hits for hire against Latino and black gangs.

I leafed on, case files, prison records, surveillance photos of the group. Suddenly, the breath emptied out of my lungs.

My eyes fixed on a surveillance shot: a bunch of heavy, muscled, tattoo-lined bikers huddled outside a Vallejo bar they used as a headquarters. One of them hunched over his bike, back to the camera. He had a shaved head, a bandana, and sleeveless denim jacket over massive arms.

On the back of the denim jacket it was the embroidery that caught my eye.

I was staring at a two-headed lion with the tail of a snake.

Chapter Twenty-Five

South of Market, in a rundown warehouse section of the city, a man in a green windbreaker ducked along a shadowy curb. The killer.

This late at night, in this decrepit neighborhood, no one was around, only a couple of scum-bums huddled over a blazing trash can. Abandoned warehouses, day-time businesses with shorted-out electrical signs: CHECKS CASHED TODAY ... METAL WORKS ... EARL KING, CITY'S MOST TRUSTED BAIL BONDSMAN.

His eyes drifted across the street towards Seventh, to the dilapidated shell of an abandoned residential hotel. 303. He had carefully staked the place out over the past three weeks. Half the apartments were vacant, the other half the nightly resting place for homeless bums with nowhere else to go.

Spitting onto the trash-littered street, he threw a black Adidas sports bag over his shoulder and headed around the block onto Sixth and Townsend. He crossed the dingy street towards a boarded-up warehouse marked only by a scratched-out sign: *AGUELLO'S . . . COMIDAS ESPANOL.*

Making sure he was alone, the killer pushed in the paint-chipped metal door, then he ducked inside. His heart was starting to pump pretty good now. He was addicted to the feeling, actually.

A foul odor met him in the lobby, a firetrap that was littered with old newspapers and oily corrugated boxes. He hit the stairs, hoping not to run into any of the homeless scum camped out in the halls.

He climbed all the way to five, where he quickly made his way to the end of the hall. He pushed through a grating and stepped out onto the fire escape. From there it was only a quick flight up to the roof.

The desolate streets gave way to the luminous aura of the city's skyline. His position was in the shadow of the Bay Bridge, which loomed over him like a hulking ship. He rested the black sports bag on an air conditioning vent, unzipped it and carefully removed the parts of a customized PSG-1 sniper's rifle.

At the church I needed maximum saturation. Here I only get one shot.

As traffic rumbled over him on the Bay Bridge freeway, he screwed the long barrel of the rifle to the shaft and locked it in place. Handling guns was like handling a knife and fork to him. He could do this in his sleep.

He fastened on the infrared sight. He squinted through it, amber-colored shapes coming into focus.

He was so much smarter than them. While they were looking for white vans and silly-ass symbols, he was here, about to blow the lid wide open. Tomorrow they would finally begin to understand.

His heart slowed as he aimed across the street towards the rear of the abandoned transient hotel marked 303. On the fourth floor a dimly lit apartment shone through the window.

This was it. The moment of truth.

He calmed his breath to a whisper and licked his dry lips. He aimed at a picture in his mind he had held for so long. He feathered the sight.

Then, when it was just right, he squeezed.

Click . . .

This time he wouldn't even have to sign it. They'd know from the shot. From the target.

Tomorrow every person in San Francisco would know his name.

Chimera.

Book Two

Justice Will Be Served

Chapter Twenty-Six

I knocked on Stu Kirkwood's glass office door, inter-rupting his morning coffee and bagel. I tossed the surveillance shot of the biker wearing the lion with the tail of a snake in front of him. 'I need to know what this is. I need it ASAP, Stu.'

I followed the shot up with two other versions of the same image: the decal on the rear of the white van, and a Polaroid of the basement wall where Estelle Chipman had been killed. *Lion-goat-tail of a snake or lizard.*

Kirkwood stiffened. 'I don't have any idea,' he said as he looked up.

'This is our killer, Stu. So how do we find him? I thought this was your specialty.'

'I told you, gay bashing's more my bag. We could e-mail the pictures down to Quantico.'

'Okay,' I nodded. 'How long will it take?'

Kirkwood straightened up. 'I know a chief researcher down there who I took a seminar with. Let me put in the call.'

'Do it quick, Stu, *then* finish your bagel. And let me know as soon as you get something back. The minute you hear something.'

Upstairs, I nudged Jacobi and Cappy into my office. I slid Kirkwood's Templar file and a copy of the biker photo across my desk. 'You recognize the artist, guys?'

Cappy glanced up. 'You're thinking these dust mites have something to do with the case?'

'I want to know where these guys are,' I said. 'And I want you to be careful. This crew's been implicated in stuff that makes LaSalle Heights seem like a paintball outing. Weapons traffic, aggravated violence, murder for hire. According to the file, they operate out of a bar over in Vallejo called the Blue Parrot. I don't want you busting in there like you're razzing a pimp down on Geary. And remember, *it's not our jurisdiction.*'

'We hear you,' Cappy said. 'No thumping. Just a little R&R. It'll be nice to spend the day out of town.' He picked up the file and tapped Jacobi on the shoulder. 'Your clubs in the trunk?'

'Guys. *Careful,*' I reminded them. 'Our killer's a shooter.'

After they left, I leafed through a handful of messages and opened the morning *Chronicle* on my desk. There was a headline with Cindy's attribution, reading, *Police Widen Church Shooting Probe, Oakland Woman's Death Thought To Be Brought In.*

Quoting 'sources close to the investigation' and 'unnamed police contacts,' she outlined the possibility that we had widened our investigation, citing the lynching in

Oakland. I had given her the green light to go that far.

I speed-dialed Cindy. 'This is "Source Close to the Investigation," calling,' I said.

'No way. You're "Unnamed Contact". "Source Close to the Investigation" is Jacobi.'

'Oh, shit.' I chuckled.

'I'm glad you have your sense of humor. Listen, I have something important I need to show you. Are you going to Tasha Catchings' funeral?'

I looked at my watch. It was scheduled in less than an hour. 'Yeah. I'll be there.'

'Look for me,' Cindy said.

Chapter Twenty-Seven

A biting drizzle was coming down as I arrived at LaSalle Heights.

Hundreds of black-clad mourners were jammed into the bullet-scarred church. A canvas was draped over the gaping hole where the stained-glass window once stood. It flapped like a somber flag whipped by the breeze.

Mayor Fernandez was there, along with other important faces I recognized from city government. Vernon Jones, the activist, was stationed an arm's length from the family. Chief Mercer was there, too. This little girl was getting the biggest funeral the city had seen in years. It made the murder seem even sadder.

Standing in the rear of the chapel, in a short black suit, I spotted Cindy. We both nodded as we caught each other's eye.

I took a seat near Mercer among a delegation from the department. Soon, the famous LaSalle Heights Choir began a haunting rendition of 'Fly Away.' There is nothing more stirring than uplifting hymns resonating through a filled church. I have my own private credo, and it starts not far from what I've seen on the streets, that nothing in life ever breaks down so simply into good and bad, judgment or redemption. But when the swell of voices lifted up the church, it didn't seem wrong to privately ask for mercy to shine down on this innocent soul.

After the choir finished, Aaron Winslow stepped up to a microphone. He was tall and looked very elegant in a black suit. He spoke about Tasha Catchings as only someone who had known her most of her life could: her little-girl's giggle; the poise she showed in being the youngest in the choir; how she wanted to be a diva, or an architect who would rebuild this neighborhood; how only the angels would now get to hear her beautiful voice.

He didn't speak like some gentle minister exhorting people to turn the other cheek. He kept it hopeful, very emotional, but real. I couldn't watch him without thinking that this handsome man had been on the battlefields of Desert Storm, and only the other day had put his life at risk to protect his children.

He said, his voice soft but powerful, that he could not forgive, and he could not help but judge. 'Only saints don't judge,' he said, 'and believe me, I'm no saint. I'm like all of you, just someone who has grown tired of having to make peace with resignation.' He looked towards Chief Mercer. 'Find the killer. Let judgment be in the courts. This isn't about politics, or faith, or even race. It's about the right to be free from hate. I am convinced the world doesn't break in the face of its worst possible deed. The world mends itself.'

People rose up and they clapped, and they cried. I stood with them. My eyes were wet. Aaron Winslow brought such dignity to these proceedings. It was over within an hour. No blazing sermons, only a smattering of 'Amen's'. But a sadness none of us would ever forget.

Tasha's mother looked so strong as she followed the casket out, her young daughter being carried to her final rest.

I filed out to a chorus of 'Will the Circle Be Unbroken,' feeling numb, and broken.

Chapter Twenty-Eight

Outside, I waited for Cindy, and I watched Aaron Winslow mingle among mourners and weeping schoolmates. There was something about him I liked. He seemed genuine and he definitely had a passion for his work, and these people.

'Now there's a man I could share a foxhole with,' said Cindy, coming up to me.

'And just what do you mean by *that*?' I asked.

'I'm not sure. All I can say is I came out here the other day to talk with him, and I left with the hairs on my arms standing up at attention. I felt like I was interviewing Denzel Washington, or maybe that new guy on *NYPD Blue*.'

'You know, ministers aren't the same as priests,' I said.

'Meaning what . . .?'

'Meaning, it's okay to go in foxholes with them. Just to get out of the line of fire, of course.'

'Of course,' she nodded. Then she mimicked an exploding mortar shot, '*Pow . . .!*'

'He is impressive. His speech made me cry. Is that what you meant to show me?'

'No,' she said with a sigh, coming back to the matter at hand. She dug in her black shoulder bag and pulled out a folded piece of paper. 'I know you told me to butt out . . . I guess I've just gotten used to covering your ass.'

'Right,' I said. 'So what do you have for me? We're a team, right?'

As I unfolded the paper, to my shock I found myself staring at the same lion, goat and snake rendering I had just asked Kirkwood to identify. Professional restraint couldn't keep my eyes from opening wide. 'Where did you get this?'

'You *know* what you're looking at, Lindsay.'

'My guess is that it's not Tyco's new toy craze.'

She didn't laugh. 'What it is is a hate group symbol. A white supremacist thing. A colleague at the paper did research on these groups. I couldn't help looking into it after our meeting the other night. This is used by a small, elite group. That's why it was hard to find out about.'

I stared at the image that I had seen over and over again since Tasha Catchings had been killed. 'This thing has a name, doesn't it?'

'It's called a chimera, Lindsay. Pronounced *kim-air-ah*. It's from Greek mythology. According to my source, the lion represents courage, the body of the goat stubbornness and will, and the serpent's tail, stealth and cunning. It means that whatever you do to crush it, it will always prevail.'

I stared at the symbol, the chimera, the bile grinding in my gut. 'Not this time.'

'I haven't run with it,' Cindy pressed. 'But it's out there. Everybody thinks these murders are connected. This symbol is the key, right? Let me give you a second definition I found: "*a grotesque product of the imagination.*" That fits, right?'

I found myself nodding. *Back to square one. Hate groups.* Maybe even the Templars. Once Mercer found out, we'd be busting the doors down on every group we could find. But how the hell could the killer be black? It didn't make sense to me.

'You're not mad at me, are you?' Cindy asked.

I shook my head. 'Of course I'm not mad. So that source of yours, did he tell you just how they killed this *kim-air-ah* back then?'

'He said they called in some big hero who rode a winged horse and cut off its head. Nice to have dudes, or dudesses, like that around in a pinch, huh?' She looked at me seriously. 'You have a winged horse, Lindsay?'

'No,' I shook my head again. 'I've got a Border collie.'

Chapter Twenty-Nine

Claire met me in the lobby of the Hall, just as I returned with a salad. 'Where you heading?' I asked.

She kept my eye, coyly, dressed in an attractive purple coat dress, a Tumi leather briefcase slung over her shoulder. 'Actually, I was coming to see you.'

Claire had a look on her face that I had learned to recognize. You wouldn't call it smugness or self-importance, Claire didn't run that way. It was more of a twinkle that read, *I found something*. Or more like, *sometimes I even amaze myself.*

'You had lunch?' I asked.

She snickered, 'Lunch? Who has time for lunch? Since ten-thirty I've been under a microscope across the Bay covering for you.' She peeked into my bag and caught a glimpse of my curried chicken salad. 'That looks tempting.'

I pulled it back. 'That depends. On what you came up with.'

She pushed me into the elevator.

'I had to promise Teitleman box seats to the Philharmonic

to calm him down,' Claire said as we got to my office. 'You can consider it Edmund's treat.' Edmund was her husband, who for the past six years had played kettle drums for the San Francisco Philharmonic.

'I'll send him a note,' I said as we sat around my desk. 'Maybe I can get Giants tickets.' I set out my lunch.

'You mind?' she asked, dangling a plastic fork over the salad. 'Saving your ass is tiring work.'

I pulled the container away. 'Like I said. Depends on what you have.'

Without hesitating, Claire speared a piece of chicken. 'Didn't make sense, did it, why a black man would be acting out hate crimes against his own race?'

'All right,' I said, pushing the container her way. 'What did you find out?'

She nodded. 'Mostly, it was pretty much like you told me. None of the normal abrasions or lacerations you would connect with forced submission. But then there were those unusual dermal specimens from under the subject's nails. So we scoped it. True to form, they did reveal a hyper-pigmented skin type. As the report said, "normally consistent with a non-Caucasian male." Samples are out being histopathologied as we speak.'

'So what are you saying?' I pressed. 'The person who killed that woman was black?'

Claire leaned over, lifting the last piece of chicken out from under my reach. 'At first blush, I could see how someone might feel that way. If not African-American, then a dark Latino or Asian. Teitleman was inclined to agree, until I asked him to perform one last test.

'I ever tell you,' she mooned her wide, brown eyes, 'I did my residency at Moffitt in dermopathology?'

'No, Claire.' I found myself shaking my head and smiling. She was so good at what she did.

She shrugged. 'No, huh. I don't know how we overlooked that. Anyway, basically, what a lab is going to be looking for is whether that hyper-pigmentation is *intra*-cellular, as in mellanocytes, which are the dark pigmented cells which are much more concentrated in non-Caucasians, or *inter*-cellular, *in* the tissue, more on the surface of the skin.'

'English, Claire. Is the subject white or black?'

'Mellanocytes,' she continued as if I hadn't asked, 'are the dark skin cells concentrated in people of color.' She pushed up her sleeve. 'You're looking at Mellanocyte Central here. Trouble is, the sampling found under the Chipman lady's nails didn't have a one. All that pigment was *inter*-cellular – surface coloration. On top of that, it was a bluish hue, atypical for naturally occurring mellonin. Any self-respecting dermapathologist would've caught that.'

'Caught *what*, Claire?' I asked, fixing on her smug grin.

'Caught that it wasn't a black man who did that terrible thing,' she said, emphatically, 'but a white man with some topical pigmentation. *Ink*, Lindsay. What that poor woman dug her nails into was the killer's tattoo.'

Chapter Thirty

A fter Claire left, I was buoyed by her discovery. This was good stuff. Brenda knocked and handed me a manila folder. 'From Simone Clark.' It was the file I had requested from Personnel. *Edward R. Chipman.*

I lifted it out of the envelope and began to read.

Chipman had been a career street patrolman out of Central, who retired in 1994, with the rank of sergeant. He had twice received a Captain's Commendation for bravery on the job.

I stopped at his photo. A narrow, chiseled face with one of those bushy Afros popular in the Sixties. It was probably taken the day he joined the force. I pieced through the rest of the contents. What would make someone want to kill this man's widow? There wasn't a single censure on his record. For excessive force or anything else. In his twenty-year career, the officer never fired his gun. He was part of the Police Outreach Unit in the Potrero Hill projects and a member of a minority action group called the Officers for Justice, which lobbied for and promoted the interests of black officers. Chipman, like most cops, had one of those proud, uneventful careers, never in trouble, never under review, never in the public eye. Nothing in there drew the slightest connection to Tasha Catchings, or to her uncle, Kevin Brevin.

Had I read more into the whole thing than was there? Was this even a serial thing? My antennae were crackling. *I know there's something. C'mon, Lindsay.*

Suddenly, I was hammered back to reality by Lorraine Stafford knocking at my door. 'You got a minute, Lieutenant?'

I asked her in. The stolen vehicle, she informed me, belonged to a Ronald Stasic. He taught Anthropology at a local community college down in Mountain View. 'Apparently the van was stolen from the parking lot outside where he works. The reason it was late being reported missing was that he went to Seattle for a night. Job interview.'

'Who knew he was going to be away?'

She flipped through her notes. 'His wife. The college administrator. He teaches two classes at the college and tutors freshmen at other schools in the area.'

'Any of these students show an interest in his van or in where he parked?'

She snickered. 'He said half these kids come to class in BMWs and Saabs. Why would they be interested in a six-year-old van?'

'What about that sticker on the back?' I had no idea if Stasic had anything to do with these killings, but his van did have the same symbol on it that had turned up in the Oakland basement.

Lorraine shrugged. 'Said he never saw it before. I said I'd check his story and asked if he'd take a lie detector on that. He told me to go right ahead.'

'You better check if any of his friends, or his students, have any weird political leanings.'

Lorraine nodded. 'I will, but this guy's totally legit, Lindsay. He acted like he was jerked out of his skin.'

As the afternoon wound down, I had the shaky feeling we were nowhere on this case. I was sure it was a serial, but maybe our best chance was this guy with the chimera embroidered on his jacket.

My phone rang, startling me. It was Jacobi. 'Bad information, LT. We've been outside this damned Blue Parrot place all day. *Nothing*. So we managed to find out from the bartender the dudes you're looking for are history. They split, five, six months ago. Toughest guy we've seen was some weightlifter wearing a Rock Rules T-shirt.'

'What do you mean by *split*, Warren?'

'Split, moved on. Somewhere south. According to the dude, one or two guys who used to hang around with them still come in from time to time. Some big red-headed dude. But basically they hit the road. *Permanent-mente* . . .'

'Keep on it. Find me the red-headed dude.' Now that the van led nowhere, and I had no connection between the victims, that lion and snake symbol was all we had.

'Keep on it?' Jacobi whined. 'How long? We could be out here for days!'

'I'll send out a change of underwear,' I said, and hung up.

For a while I just sat there, rocking back in my chair with a mounting dread. It had been three days since Tasha Catchings was killed, and three days before that, Estelle Chipman.

I had nothing. No significant clues. Only what the killer had left us. This damned chimera.

And the knowledge . . . *serials kill. Serials don't stop until you catch them.*

Chapter Thirty-One

Patrolman Sergeant Art Davidson responded to the 1-6-0 the minute he heard the call. '*Disturbance, domestic violence. 303 Seventh Street upstairs. Available units respond.*'

He and his partner, Gil Herrera, were only four blocks away on Bryant. It was almost eight, their shift was over in ten minutes.

'You want to take it, Gil?' said Davidson, glancing at his watch.

His partner shrugged. 'Your call, Artie. You're the one with the wild party to go to.'

Some wild party. It was his seven-year-old's birthday. Audra. He had called in on his break, and Carol said if he got home by nine-thirty she'd keep her up for him so that he could give her the Britney Spears makeup mirror he had picked out. Davidson had five kids and they were his life.

'What the hell,' Davidson shrugged. 'It's what we get paid the big bucks for, right?'

They hit the siren, and in less than a minute Mobil 2-4 pulled up in front of the dismal and dilapidated entrance to 303 Seventh, the tilted sign of the defunct *Driscoll Hotel* hanging over the front door.

'People still camping out in this dump?' Herrera sighed. 'Who the hell would live here?'

The two cops grabbed their nightsticks and a large flashlight and stepped up to the front door. Davidson pulled it open. Inside, the place smelled of feces, urine, probably rats. 'Hey, anybody here?' Davidson called out. 'Police.'

Suddenly, from above, they heard the sound of shouting. Some kind of argument.

'On it,' Herrera said, bounding up the first flight.

Davidson followed.

On the second floor, Gil Herrera went down the hall, banging his flashlight on doors. '*Police, police* . . .'

In the stairwell, Davidson suddenly heard the sounds again – loud, frantic voices. A crash, as if something was broken. The noise came from just above him. He headed up the last flight of stairs on his own.

The noises grew even louder. He stopped in front of a shut door. Apartment 52. '*Bitch!* . . .' someone yelled. The sound of a plate shattering. A woman seemed to beg. 'Stop him, he's going to kill me. Stop him, please . . . Somebody help me. Please.'

'Police,' Art Davidson responded, and drew his gun. He yelled, 'Herrera, up here. *Now!*'

He jammed all his weight on the door. It opened. The

inside was dimly lit, but from an interior room, more light and the arguing voices . . . closer . . . screaming.

Art Davidson clicked his gun off safety. Then he barged through the open door into the room. To his amazement, no one was in there.

There was a dim yellow light angling from an exposed bulb. A metal chair with a large boom-box on it. Loud voices coming from the speakers.

The words were the same ones he'd heard earlier, 'Stop him, he's going to kill me!'

'What the hell?' Davidson squinted in disbelief.

He walked over to the stereo, kneeled down and turned off the power. The loud blaring argument came to a halt.

'*What the fuck* . . .?' Davidson muttered. 'Somebody playing games.'

He looked around. The pitiful room looked like it hadn't been occupied in a while. His eyes were drawn to the window, then beyond it, across the street, an adjoining building. He thought he saw something. What was it?

Ping . . .

His eye caught the tiniest pinprick of a yellow spark, so quick it was like the snap of a finger, the blink of a firefly on a dark night.

Then the window splintered and a blunt force slammed into Art Davidson's right eye. He was dead before he hit the floor.

Chapter Thirty-Two

I had just about gotten home when the distress call crackled in: 'Available units, proceed to 303 Seventh near Townsend.'

1-0-6 . . . Officer in trouble.

I pulled my Explorer to the curb. Listened to the call. *EMS's to the scene,* the district captain called in. The quick, urgent exchanges convinced me the situation was critical.

The hairs on my arms were standing on edge. It was an ambush, a long-distance shot. Like LaSalle Heights. I threw my car in gear and executed a quick U-turn down Potrero, slamming onto Third Street and headed for downtown.

When I pulled up four blocks from Townsend and Seventh, bedlam was in reign. Barricades of black-and-whites, flashing lights, uniforms everywhere, radios crackling in the night.

I drove ahead, holding my police ID out the window, until I couldn't go any further. Then I left my car and ran towards the center of the commotion. I grabbed the first patrolman I could find. 'Who is it? Do you know?'

'Patrol cop,' he said. 'Out of Central. Davidson.'

'*Oh shit* . . .' My heart sank. I felt nauseous. I knew Art Davidson. We had gone through the Academy at the same time. He was a good cop, a good guy. Did it mean anything that I knew him?

Then a second wave of fear and nausea. *Art Davidson was black.*

I pushed my way through the crowd towards a rundown tenement where a ring of EMS trucks were parked. I ran into Chief of Detectives, Sam Ryan, coming out of the building, holding a radio to his ear.

I pulled him aside. 'Sam, I heard it was Art Davidson. Any chance . . .?'

Ryan shook his head. '*Chance*? He was lured there, Lindsay. Rifle shot to the head. Single shot, we think. He's already been pronounced.'

I stood to the side, a whirring wail growing louder and louder inside my skull, as if some private, unknowable fear had revealed itself only to me. I was sure it was *him*. Chimera. Murder Number Three. He only needed one shot this time.

I brandished my badge to the uniformed cops at the entrance and hurried into the rundown building. Some EMS techs were coming down the stairs. I kept going past them. My legs felt heavy and I could hardly breathe.

On the third floor landing a uniformed cop barreled past me, shouting, 'Coming down! Everybody get out of the way.'

A couple of medical techs appeared – and two more cops carrying a gurney. I couldn't turn my head away. 'Hold it here,' I said.

It was Davidson. His eyes still and open. A crimson, dime-sized peephole above his right eye. Every nerve in my body seemed to go slack. I remembered that he had children. *Did these murders have something to do with kids?*

'Oh, Jesus, Art,' I whispered. I forced myself to study his body, the bullet wound. I finally touched the side of his forehead. 'You can take him down now,' I said. *Fuck.*

I made my way to the next floor somehow. A crowd of angry plainclothesmen were gathered outside an open apartment. I saw Pete Starcher, an ex-homicide detective who worked with IAB, coming out.

I went up to him. 'Pete, what the hell happened?'

Starcher had always had an edge for me. He was one of those cynical old-timers. 'You got business here, Lieutenant?'

'I knew Art Davidson. We went through school together.' I didn't want to give him any inkling of why I was here.

Starcher sniffed, but he filled me in. The two patrolmen were responding to a 911 in the building. There was only a tape recorder there. It was all set up, orchestrated. 'He was suckered. Some sonovabitch wanted to kill a cop.'

My body grew numb. I was sure it was him. 'I'm going to look around.'

Inside, it was just like Starcher had said. Spooky, weird, unreal. The living room was empty. Walls stripped of paint and cracks in the plaster. As I wandered into the adjoining room, I froze. There was a pool of blood soaked into the floor; blood splattered on the wall where the bullet had probably lodged. *Poor Davidson.* A portable tape deck sat on a folding chair in the center of the room.

I looked to the window, a hanging pane of splintered glass.

Suddenly, everything was clear to me. There was a cold spot at the center of my chest.

I went to the open window. I leaned out, looked across the street. There was no sign of Chimera, or anybody. But I knew . . . I knew because he had told me – with the accuracy of the shot, the choice of the victim. *He wanted us to know it was him.*

Chapter Thirty-Three

'It was him, Lindsay, wasn't it?'

Cindy was on the phone. It was after eleven. I was trying to pull my wits together at the end of an insane, horrible night. I had just come in from taking Martha on a late walk. All I wanted was to take a hot shower and wash the image of Art Davidson's body out of my mind.

'You *have* to tell me. It was the same guy, Chimera. Wasn't it?'

I threw myself on my bed. 'We don't know. There was nothing at the scene.'

'You *know*, Lindsay. I know you know. We both know it was him.'

I just wanted her to let me be and curl up into bed. 'I don't know,' I said, wearily. 'It could be.'

'What caliber was the gun? Did it match Catchings'?'

'Please, Cindy, don't try to play detective on me. I knew the guy. His partner said it was his kid's seventh birthday. He had five children.'

'I'm sorry, Lindsay,' Cindy finally came back in a softer,

gentler voice. 'It's just that it's like the first murder. The shot that no one else could make.'

We sat a while on the phone without talking. She was right. I knew she was right. Then she said, 'You've got another one, don't you, Lindsay?'

I didn't answer, but I knew what she meant.

'Another pattern killer. A cold-blooded marksman. And he's targeting blacks.'

'Not just blacks,' I sighed.

'Not just blacks . . .?' Cindy hesitated, then she came back in a rush. 'The Oakland crime reporter got a rumor out of Homicide there. About the Chipman widow. Her husband was a cop. First Tasha's uncle. Then her. Now Davidson makes three. Oh Jesus, Lindsay.'

'This stays with us,' I insisted. 'Please, Cindy. I need to sleep now. You don't realize how hard this is for us.'

'Let us help, Lindsay. All of us. We want to help you.'

'I will, Cindy. I need your help. I need all of your help.'

Chapter Thirty-Four

I thought of something during the night. The building had been empty. No one else could have heard the shouting. *It could only have been the killer who called 911.*

I got right on it in the morning. Lila McKendree ran Dispatch. She had been on the board when the Davidson call came in.

Lila was plump, rosy-cheeked, and quick to smile, but no one was more professional or could coolly juggle serious situations like an air traffic controller.

She set up the tape of the actual 911 call in the squad room. The entire detail huddled around. Cappy and Jacobi had come in before heading back out to Vallejo.

'It's on a three-loop reel,' Lila explained. She pressed the PLAYBACK key.

In a few seconds we were going to hear the killer's voice for the first time.

'San Francisco Police, 911 Hotline,' a dispatcher's voice came on.

There wasn't another sound in the squad room.

An agitated male voice shot back, 'I need to call in a disturbance . . . Some guy's beating up on his wife.'

'Okay,' the operator replied. 'I'll need to start with your location. Where is this disturbance taking place?'

There was an interfering background noise like a TV or traffic, making it difficult to hear. '303 Seventh. Fifth floor. You better send someone out. It's starting to sound real bad.'

'You said the address was 303 Seventh?'

'That's right,' the killer said.

'And who am I speaking with?' the operator asked.

'My name's Billy. Billy Rephon. I live down the hall. You better hurry.'

We all looked around, surprised. *The killer gave a name? Why?*

'Listen, sir,' the dispatcher asked, 'are you able to hear what's going on as I'm talking to you?'

'What I can hear,' he said, 'is some spook getting the living shit beat out of her.'

The dispatcher hesitated. 'Yes, sir. Can you determine if there's been any physical injury so far?'

'I'm no doctor, lady, I'm just trying to do the right thing. Just send someone!'

'Okay, Mr Rephon, I'm calling a patrol car now. What I want you to do is exit the building and wait for the officers. They're on the way.'

'You better move quick,' the killer said. *'Sounds like someone's about to get hurt.'*

After the transmission ended, there was the follow-up

recording of the outgoing dispatch call.

'The call came from a mobile phone,' Lila said, shrugging her broad shoulders. 'No doubt cloned. Here, it's starting up again on a three-cycle loop.' In a moment the tape came on a second time. This time, I listened closely for what the voice could tell me.

I need to call in a disturbance . . . It was a worried voice, panicked but cool.

'The guy's a good fucking actor,' Jacobi huffed.

My name's Billy. Billy Rephon . . .

I clenched a wooden chair as I listened to the dispatcher's well-intended instructions. 'Exit the building and wait for the officers. They're on the way.' All the while, he was sitting behind a rifle scope, waiting for his prey to show up.

You better move quick, he sneered. *Someone's about to get hurt.*

This time I heard the mocking indifference in his voice. Not even the slightest tone of compassion for what he was about to do. In the last warning, I even detected a hint of a cold chuckle: *Quick* . . . *Someone's about to get hurt.*

'That's all I have,' Lila McKendree said. 'The killer's voice.'

Chapter Thirty-Five

The Davidson murder changed everything.

A bold headline in the *Chronicle* shouted, *Murdered Cop Thought To Be Third In Terror Spree*. The front-page article, with Cindy's by-line, cited the accurate, long-range rifle shots, and also the symbol used by active hate groups that had been found at the scenes.

I headed down to the CSU lab and found Charlie Clapper curled up behind a metal desk in the lab, wearing a lab coat, munching on a breakfast of Doritos chips. His salt and pepper hair was oily and tousled, and his eyes sagged like heavy bags. 'I've slept at this desk twice this week,' he scowled. 'Doesn't anyone get killed during the day anymore?'

'In case you didn't notice, I haven't been getting my normal beauty rest the last week,' I shrugged back. 'C'mon, Charlie, I need something on this Davidson thing. He's killing our own guys.'

'I know he is.' The rotund CSU man sighed. He hoisted himself up and shuffled over to a counter. He picked up a small Ziploc sandwich bag with a dark, flattened bullet in it.

'Here's your slug, Lindsay. Took it out of the wall behind where Art Davidson got dropped. One shot. Lights out. Check with Claire if you like. The sonovabitch can definitely shoot.'

I lifted up the shell and tried to pull a reading.

'Forty caliber,' Clapper said. 'My first read is that it's from a PSG-1.'

I frowned. 'You're sure about this, Charlie?' Tasha Catchings had been killed with an M-16.

He pointed towards a scope. 'Be my guest, Lieutenant. I figure, ballistics must be a lifelong study of yours.'

'I didn't mean that, Charlie. I was just hoping for a match on the Catchings girl.'

'Reese is still working on it,' he said, grabbing a chip out of the Doritos bag. 'But don't bet on it. This guy was clean, Lindsay. Just like at the church. No prints, nothing left behind. The tape machine's standard, could've been bought anywhere. Set off by a long-distance remote control. We even traced what we thought to be his route up there through the building and dusted everything from the railings to the window locks. We did turn up one thing . . .'

'What's that?' I pressed.

He walked me over to a lab counter. 'Partial sneaker print. Off the tar on the roof where the shot came from. Looks like a standard shoe. But we did take out some traces of a fine white powder. No guarantees it even came from him.'

'Powder?'

'Chalk. Resin,' Charlie said. 'That narrows it down to about fifty million possibilities. If this guy's signing his pictures, Lindsay, he's making it tough to find.'

'He *signed* it, Charlie,' I said with conviction. 'It was the shot.'

'We're sending the 911 tape out for a voice reading. I'll let you know when we get it back.'

I patted him appreciatively. 'Get some sleep, Charlie.'

He lifted the Doritos bag. 'Sure I will. After breakfast.'

Chapter Thirty-Six

I went back to the office and sank disappointedly into my chair. I had to know more about that Chimera. I was about to dial Stu Kirkwood at the Hate Crimes desk when a cadre of three men in dark suits came into the squad room.

One of them was Mercer. No surprise. He had been on the morning talk shows, pushing for calm. I knew facing tough questions without concrete results didn't sit well with him.

But the other, accompanied by his press liaison, was a man I had never seen on the floor in eight years in Homicide.

It was the mayor of San Francisco.

'I don't want the slightest bit of bullshit,' Art Fernandez, San Francisco's two-term mayor said. 'I don't want the standard protecting the ranks, and I don't want any misplaced reflex to control the situation.' He shifted his eyes on a narrow track between Mercer and me. 'What I want is an honest answer. Do we have a read on this situation?'

We were crammed into my tiny, glass-enclosed office. Outside, I could see staffers standing around, watching the circus.

I fumbled under my desk to get my pumps back on. 'We do not,' I admitted.

'So Vernon Jones is right,' the major exhaled, sinking into a chair across from my desk. 'What we have is an out-of-control spree of hate-driven killings on which the police have no handle, but the FBI may.'

'No, that's not it,' I replied.

'That's not it?' He arched his eyes. He furrowed his brow towards Mercer. 'What is it I don't understand? You've got a recognized hate group symbol, this Chimera, found at two of the three crime scenes. Our own ME believes the Catchings girl was the intended target of this madman.'

'What the lieutenant was saying,' Mercer cut in, 'was that this may not be simply a hate crime issue.'

My mouth was a little cottony, and I swallowed. 'I think it's deeper than a hate crime spree.'

'*Deeper*, Lieutenant Boxer . . . Just what is it you believe we have?'

I stared straight at Fernandez. 'What I think we have is someone with a personal vendetta. Possibly a single assailant. He's couching his murder in the MO of a hate crime.'

'A vendetta, you say,' Carr, the mayor's man chimed in. 'A vendetta against blacks, but not a hate crime. Against black children and widows . . . *but not a hate crime*?'

'Against black *cops*,' I said.

The mayor's eyes narrowed. 'Go on.'

I explained that Tasha Catchings and Estelle Chipman had been related to cops. 'There has to be some further relationship, though we don't know what it is yet. The killer is organized, haughty in the way he's leaving his clues. I do *not* believe a hate crime killer would leave their mark on the hits. The getaway van, the little drawing in Chipman's basement, that cocky 911 tape. I don't think this is a hate crime spree. It's a vendetta – calculated, *personal*.'

The mayor looked at Mercer. 'You go along with this, Earl?'

'Protecting the ranks aside . . .' Mercer smiled tightly, 'I do.'

'Well I don't,' Carr said. 'Everything points to a hate crime.'

There was silence in the cramped room; the temperature suddenly felt like 120 degrees.

'So it seems I have two choices,' the mayor said. 'Under the Hate Crimes Legislation, Article Four, I can call in the FBI, who, I believe, keep a close watch on these groups . . .'

'They have no fucking idea how to run a homicide investigation,' Mercer protested.

'Or . . . I can let the lieutenant do her job. Tell the Feds we got it all handled ourselves,' the mayor said.

I met his eyes. 'I went to the Academy with Art Davidson. You think you want to catch his killer any more than me?'

'Then catch him,' the mayor said, and rose.

'Just so we know what's at stake,' said Mercer.

I was nodding back glumly when Lorraine burst through

my door. 'Sorry to interrupt, Lieutenant, but it's urgent. Jacobi called in from Vallejo. He said make the place up nice and neat for an important guest. They found the biker from the Blue Parrot.

'They found Red.'

Chapter Thirty-Seven

About an hour later, Jacobi and Cappy entered the squad room. They were pushing a large, red-headed biker type, his hands cuffed behind his back.

'Look who decided to drop in,' Jacobi smirked.

Red jerked his arms defiantly out of Cappy's grip as the policeman shoved him into Interrogation Room One, where he tripped over a wooden chair and crashed to the floor.

'Sorry, Big Fella,' Cappy shrugged. 'Thought I warned you about that first step.'

'Richard Earl Evans,' Jacobi announced. 'AKA Red, Boomer, Duke. Don't feel insulted if he doesn't stand up and shake hands.'

'This is what you thought I meant by "no contact," ' I said, looking cross, but secretly delighted that they had brought him in.

'The guy's got a CCI sheet so long it begins with "Call me Ishmael," ' Jacobi grinned. 'Theft, aggravated mischief, attempted murder, two weapons charges.'

'Behold,' exclaimed Cappy, producing a dime bag of marijuana, a five-inch hunter's blade and a palm-sized Beretta .22-caliber pistol out of a Nordstrom's shopping bag.

'He know why he's here?' I asked.

'Nah,' Cappy grunted, 'we busted him on the gun charge. Let him cool his jets in the back seat.'

The three of us crowded into the small interrogation room facing Richard Earl Evans. The creep leered up at us with a smug grin, a sleeve of tattoos covering both arms. He wore a black T-shirt with block letters on the back: IF YOU CAN *READ* THIS . . . THE BITCH MUST'VE FALLEN OFF!

I nodded, and Cappy freed him from the cuffs. 'You know why you're here, Mr Evans?'

'I know you guys are in deep shit if you think I'm talking to you,' Evans grunted, sniffing a mixture of mucus and blood. 'You got no teeth in Vallejo.'

I raised the bag of dope. 'Santa seems to have brought you a lot of naughty toys. Two felonies . . . still on parole for a weapons charge. Time at Folsom, Quentin. My sense is that you must like it there, 'cause next time up, you qualify for the thirty-year lease.'

'One thing I do know,' Evans rolled his eyes, 'is you didn't drag me all this way for some two-bit weapons rap. The sign on the door says *Homicide*.'

'No, big fella, you're right,' Cappy injected, 'tossing your sorry ass in jail on a gun charge is only a hobby for us. But depending upon how you answer a few questions, that weapons rap could determine where you spend the next thirty years.'

'Pupshit,' the biker grunted, leveling his cold, hard eyes in his face. 'That's all you assholes got on me.'

Cappy shrugged, then brought the flat end of an unopened soda can down hard on the biker's exposed hand.

Evans yelped in pain.

'Damn, I thought you said you were thirsty,' Cappy said, contritely.

Red leered at Cappy, no doubt imagining running over the cop's face with his Honda Road Rider.

'But you're right, Mr Evans,' I said, 'we didn't ask you down here to go over your current possessions, though it wouldn't take much to hand your sorry ass right over to the Vallejo police. But today could work out lucky for you. Cappy, ask Mr Evans if he'd like another drink.'

Cappy moved, and this time Evans jerked his hand off the table.

Then the big cop opened the can and placed it in front of him, grinning widely. 'This all right, or would you prefer a glass?'

'See,' I assured him, 'we can be nice. Truth is, we don't give a shit about you. All you have to do is answer a few questions and you'll be headed home, compliments of the SFPD. You never have to see us again. Or we can lock your three-time loser ass on the eighth floor for a few days until we remember we got you here and notify the Vallejo police. And, when it comes to a third felony offense, we'll see about just how many "teeth" we really have.'

Evans ran his hand across the bridge of his nose, dabbing at the blood. 'Maybe I will take a swig of that soda, if you're still offering.'

'Congratulations, son,' Jacobi said. 'That's the first thing you done that makes sense since we set eyes on you.'

Chapter Thirty-Eight

I laid out a black-and-white surveillance photo of the Templars in front of Red's startled face. 'First thing we need to know is where can we find your buddies?'

Evans looked up, grinning. 'So that's what this is all about?'

'C'mon, sharp as nails,' pressed Jacobi, 'the lieutenant asked a question.'

One by one, I spread three more photos showing various members on the table.

Evans shook his head. 'Never ran with those guys.'

The last photo I put down was a surveillance shot of *him*.

Cappy reached out, all two hundred fifty pounds of him, and raised the biker by the shirt, lifting him out of his seat. 'Listen, codshit, you're only lucky we're not concerned here with what you sorry bunch of losers got off doing. So act smart, and you'll be outta here, and we can go on to what we do give a shit about.'

Evans shrugged. 'Maybe I did run a bit with them. But

no more. Club's disbanded. Too much heat. I ain't seen these guys around here in months. They split. You wanna find them, start with *5 South*.'

I looked at the two inspectors. As much as I doubted whether Evans would actually turn over on his buddies, I believed him.

'One more question,' I said. 'A big one.' I laid down the photo of the biker with the leather chimera jacket. 'What does this mean to you?'

Evans sniffed. 'The dude's got bogus taste in attire?'

Cappy leaned forward.

Evans recoiled. 'It's a symbol, man. Means he's in the Movement. A patriot.'

'A patriot?' I asked him. 'What the hell is that supposed to mean?'

'An advocate of the white race, the self-determination of a free and orderly society.' He smiled at Cappy. 'Present company excluded, of course. 'Course, none of this shit necessarily reflects my personal views.'

'Did this guy head off to the Sun Belt, too?' Jacobi asked.

'Him? Why, what do you think he's done?'

'There he goes,' Cappy stood over him, 'answering questions with questions again.'

'Look,' Evans swallowed, 'the brother only hung with us a short while. I don't even know his real name. Mac . . . McMillan, McArthur? What'd he do?'

I figured there was no reason not to tell him what we thought. 'What's the word about what happened in LaSalle Heights?'

Red finally flinched. His pupils widened. All of a sudden, it was falling into place. 'You think my old dudes lit up that church? *This guy . . . Mac*?'

'You know how we could talk to him?' I said.

Evans grinned. 'That's a tough order. Even for you.'

'Try us,' I said. 'We're resourceful.'

'I'm sure you are, but this fucker's dead. Back in June. He and a partner blew themselves up, in Oregon. Sonovabitch must've read somewhere you could turn cowshit into a bomb.'

Chapter Thirty-Nine

In the small blacktop parking lot adjacent to the LaSalle Heights Church, Cindy Thomas climbed out of her VW. Her stomach growled, telling her that it didn't quite know what she was doing here.

She took a breath and opened the large oak door into the main chapel. Just yesterday it had been filled with the choir's resonating sound. Now it was eerily quiet, the pews empty. She walked through the chapel and into a connecting building.

A carpeted hallway led to a row of offices. A black woman, glancing up from a copy machine, asked, 'Can I help you? What do you want?'

'I'm here to see Reverend Winslow.'

'He's not seeing visitors now,' the woman said.

Winslow's voice rang out from one of the offices. 'It's all right, Carol.'

Cindy was led to his office. It was small, crowded with books. He was wearing a black T-shirt and khakis, and didn't look like any minister she'd ever known.

'So, we managed to get you back after all,' he said. Then, finally, he smiled.

He had her take a seat on a small couch and he sat in a well-worn red leather chair. A pair of glasses were resting on a book and she instinctively sneaked a peek. *A Heart-breaking Work of Staggering Genius.* Not what she would have expected.

'You mending?' she asked.

'Trying to. I read your story today. It was terrible about that policeman. It's true? Tasha's murder might be tied up with two others?'

'The police think so,' Cindy answered. 'The ME believes she was deliberately shot.'

Winslow grimaced and then shook his head. 'I don't understand. Tasha was just a little girl. What possible connection could there be?'

'It wasn't so much Tasha,' Cindy held eye contact with Aaron Winslow, 'as what she represented. All the victims apparently have a link to San Francisco cops.'

Winslow's eyes narrowed. 'So tell me, what brings you back so soon? Your soul aching? Why are you here?'

Cindy lowered her eyes. 'The service yesterday. It was moving. I felt chills. It's been a long time for me. Actually, I think my soul has been aching. I just haven't bothered to notice.'

Winslow's look softened. She'd told him a small truth, and it had touched him. 'Well, good. I'm glad to hear you were moved.'

Cindy smiled. Incredibly, he made her feel at ease. He

seemed centered, genuine, and she'd heard nothing but good things about him. She wanted to do a story on him, and she knew it would be a good one, maybe a great story.

'I bet I know what you're thinking,' Aaron Winslow said.

'Okay,' she said, 'shoot.'

'You're wondering . . . the man seems together enough, not completely weirded out. He doesn't seem like a minister. So what is he doing making his living working like this?'

Cindy flashed an embarrassed smile. 'I admit, something like that did cross my mind. I'd like to do a story about you and the Bay View neighborhood.'

He seemed to be thinking it over. But then he changed the subject on her.

'What is it you like to do, Cindy?'

'Do . . .?'

'In the big, bad world of San Francisco you cover out there. After you call in your story. What moves you besides your job at the *Chronicle*? What are your passions?'

She found herself smiling. 'Hey, I ask the questions. I want to do a story on *you*. Not the other way around,' she said. 'All right. I like yoga. I take a class twice a week on Chestnut Street. You ever do yoga?'

'No, but I meditate every day.'

Cindy smiled some more. She wasn't even sure why. 'I'm in a women's book club. Two women's clubs, actually. I like jazz.'

Winslow's eyes lit up. 'What kind of jazz? I like jazz myself.'

Cindy laughed. 'Okay, now we're getting somewhere. What kind of jazz do you like?'

'Progressive. Interpretive. Anything from Pinetop Perkins to Coltrane.'

'You know the Blue Room? On Geary?' she asked.

'Of course I know the Blue Room. I go there Saturday nights, whenever Carlos Reyes is in town. Maybe we could go sometime. As part of your story. You don't have to answer right now.'

'Then you agree to let me do a piece on you?' Cindy said.

'I agree . . . to let you do a piece on the neighborhood. I'll help you with it.'

A half hour later, in her car, Cindy sat letting the engine run, almost too astonished to put it in gear. *I don't believe what I just did . . .* Lindsay would rap her in the head. Question whether her gadgets were working properly.

But they were working. They were *humming* a little, actually. The tiny hairs on her arms were standing straight on edge.

She had the beginnings of what she thought might be a good story, maybe a prize winner.

She'd also just accepted a date from Tasha Catchings' pastor, and she couldn't wait to see him again.

Maybe my soul has been aching, Cindy thought, as she finally drove away from the church.

Chapter Forty

It was close to seven on that Friday. The end of a long, insane, incredibly stressful week. Three people had died. My only good leads had come and gone.

I needed to talk to somebody, so I went down to three, where the DA's staff were located. Two doors down from the big man himself was Jill's corner office.

The executive corner was dark, offices empty, staff scattered for the weekend. In a way, though I needed to vent, I was sort of hoping Jill – the *new* Jill – would've already gone home, and was maybe picking through swatch books for her baby's room.

But as I approached, I heard the sound of classical music coming from within. Jill's door was cracked half-open.

I knocked gently, and pushed it. There was Jill, in her favorite easy chair, knees tucked tightly into her chest, a yellow legal pad resting on her lap. Her desk was piled high with briefs.

'Why are you still here?' I asked.

'Snagged,' she sighed, raising her hands in a mock

arrest. 'It's just this goddamn Perrone thing. Closing arguments Monday morning.' Jill was at the end of a high-profile case in which a derelict landlord was being charged with manslaughter when a faulty ceiling caved in on an eight-year-old child.

'You're pregnant, Jill. It's after seven o'clock.'

'So is Connie Sperling, for the defense. They're calling it the Battle of the Bulge.'

'Whatever they're calling it, so much for the shift of gears.'

Jill turned down the CD player and extended her long legs. 'Anyway, Rich's out of town. What else is new. I'd only be doing the same thing if I were at home.' She cocked her head and smiled. 'You're checking up on me.'

'No, but maybe someone should.'

'Good Lord, Lindsay, I'm just preparing notes, not running a 10k. I'm doing fine. Anyway,' she glanced at her watch, 'since when did you turn into the poster girl for keeping everything in perspective?'

'I'm not pregnant, Jill. All right, all right, I'll stop lecturing.'

I stepped inside her office, eyed her Women's Final Four Soccer photo from Stanford, framed diplomas, and pictures of her and Rich rock climbing and running with their black Lab, Snake Eyes.

'I still have a beer in the fridge if you want to sit,' she said, tossing her legal pad on the desk. 'Pull a Buckler's out for me.'

I did just that. Then I shifted the black Max Mara suit

jacket hastily thrown over a cushion and sank back in the leather couch. We tilted our bottles, and both of us blurted in the same breath, 'So, how's your case?'

'You first,' Jill laughed.

I spread my thumb and index finger barely a half-inch apart to indicate, basically zip. I took her through the maze of dead ends: the van, the Chimera sketch, the surveillance photo of the Templars; that CSU had come up with nothing on the Davidson ambush.

Jill came over and sat beside me on the couch. 'You want to talk, Linds? Like you said, you didn't come up here to make sure I was behaving myself.'

I smiled guiltily, then placed my beer on the coffee table. 'I need to shift the investigation, Jill.'

'Okay,' she said, 'I'm listening. This is just between us.'

Piece by piece, I laid out my theory that the killer was not some reckless, hate-mongering maniac, but a bold, plotting, pattern killer, acting out a vendetta.

'Maybe you're over-reaching,' Jill replied. 'What you *do* have is three terror crimes aimed at African-Americans.'

'So why these victims, Jill? An eleven-year-old girl? A decorated cop? Estelle Chipman, whose husband has been dead for three years?'

'I don't know, honey. I just nail 'em to the wall when you turn them over.'

I smiled. Then I leaned forward. 'Jill, I need you to help me. I need to find some connection between these victims. I know it's there. I need to check out past cases in which a white plaintiff was victimized by a black police officer.

That's where my gut leads me. It's where I think those killings might start. It has something to do with revenge.'

'What happens when the next victim never had anything to do with a police officer? What are you gonna do then?'

I looked at her imploringly. 'Are you going to help me?'

'Of course I'm going to help you,' she shook her head at me. 'Duh . . . Anything you can give me that can help me narrow it down?'

I nodded. 'Male, white. Maybe a tattoo or three.'

'That oughta do it.' She rolled her eyes.

I reached out and squeezed her hand. I knew I could count on her. I looked at my watch. Seven-thirty. 'I better let you finish up while you're still in your first trimester.'

'Don't go, Lindsay,' Jill held my arm. 'Stick around.'

I could see something on her face. That clear, professional intensity suddenly weakened into a thousand-yard stare.

'Something wrong, Jill? Did the doctor tell you something?'

In her sleeveless vest, with her dark hair curled around her ears, she looked every bit the power lawyer, Number Two in the city's legal department. But there was a tremor in her breath. 'I'm fine. Really. Physically, I'm fine. I should be happy, right? I'm gonna have a baby. I should be riding the air.'

'You should be feeling whatever you're feeling, Jill.' I took her hand.

She nodded, glassily. Then she curled her knees up to

her chest. 'When I was a kid, I would sometimes wake up in the night. I always had this little terror, this feeling that the whole world was asleep, that around this whole, huge planet, I was the only one left awake in the world. Sometimes, my father would come in and try and rock me to sleep. He'd be downstairs in his study, preparing his own cases, and he'd always check on me before he turned in. He called me his Second Chair. But even with him there, I still felt so alone.'

She shook her head at me, tears glistening in her eyes. 'Look at me. Rich's away for two nights and I turn into a fucking idiot,' she said.

'I don't think you're an idiot,' I said, stroking her pretty face.

'I can't lose this baby, Lindsay. I know it seems stupid. I'm carrying a life. It's *here*, always in me, right next to me. How is it I feel so alone?'

I held her tightly by the shoulders. My father had never been there to rock me to sleep. Even before he left us, he worked the third shift and would always head to McGinty's for a beer. Sometimes I felt like the heartbeat that was closest to me was the pulse of the bastards I had to track down.

'I know what you mean,' I heard myself whisper. I held Jill. 'Sometimes I feel that way, too.'

Chapter Forty-One

On the corner of Ocean and Victoria, a man in a green fatigue windbreaker hunched, chewing a burrito, as the black Lincoln slowly made its way down the block. He had waited here dozens of nights, stalked his next prey for weeks.

The person he had watched for so long lived in a pleasant stucco house inside Ingleside Heights, just a short walk away. He had a family, two girls in Catholic school; his wife was a registered nurse. He had a black Lab; sometimes it bounded out to greet him as his car pulled up. The Lab was named 'Bullitt', like the old movie.

Usually, the car drove by around seven-thirty. A couple of times a week, the man got out to walk. It was always at the same spot, on Victoria. He liked to stop at the Korean market, chat with the owner as he picked out a melon or some cabbages. Playing the big man walking among his people.

Then he might mosey into Tiny's News, stuff his arms with a few magazines: *Car and Driver*, *PC World*, *Sports*

Illustrated. Once, he had even stood behind him in the line as he waited to pay for his reading material.

He could have taken him out. Many times. One dazzling shot from a distance.

But no, this one had to be up close. Eye to eye. This murder would make the entire city of San Francisco take notice. This would take the case international, and not many got that big.

His heart sprung alive as he huddled in the damp drizzle, but this time the black Lincoln merely passed by.

So it won't be tonight, he exhaled. *Go home to your little wife and dog. But soon . . . You've grown forgetful*, he thought, balling his burrito into the wrapper and tossing it in a trash bin. *Forgetful of the past*. But it always finds you.

I live with the past every day.

He watched as the black Lincoln, its windows dark, made its customary left turn onto Cerritos and disappeared into Ingleside Heights.

You stole my life. Now I'm going to take yours.

Chapter Forty-Two

I worked hard through most of the weekend, only taking Sunday morning off to run Martha by the Bay and do my tai chi on the Marina Green. By noon I was in jeans and a sweatshirt, back at my desk. By Monday, the investigation was listing towards 'the dead zone,' no new angles to work. We were putting out releases just to keep the press off our tail. Each stalled line of questioning, each frustrating dead end only narrowed the time to when Chimera would strike again.

I was dropping off some case files back to Jill when the elevator door opened and Chief Mercer ambled in. He looked surprised when he saw me, but not displeased.

'Come, take a ride with me,' he said.

Mercer's car was waiting along the side entrance of Eighth Street. As the police driver leaned back, Mercer told him, 'West Portal, Sam.'

West Portal was a diverse, middle-class neighborhood out of the center of the city. I didn't know why Mercer would be dragging me out there in the middle of the day.

As we rode, Mercer asked a few questions, but stayed mostly silent. A tremor shot through me: *he's gonna take me off the case.*

The driver pulled onto Monroe, a residential street I had never been on before. He parked in front of a small blue Victorian across from a high school playground. A pick-up basketball game was going on.

I blinked first. 'What was it you wanted to talk about, Chief?'

Mercer turned to me. 'You have any personal heroes, Lindsay?'

'You mean like Amelia Earhart or Margaret Thatcher?' I shook my head. I had never grown up with any of those. 'Maybe Claire Washburn,' I grinned.

Mercer nodded. 'Arthur Ashe was always one of mine. Someone asked him if it was hard to cope with AIDS and he answered, "Not nearly as hard as it was to deal with growing up black in the United States." '

His expression deepened. 'Vernon Jones tells the mayor that I've lost sight of what's really at stake in this case.' He pointed towards the blue Victorian across the street. 'You see that house? My parents' house. I was raised there.

'My father was a mechanic in the transit yards and my mother did the books for an electrical contractor. They worked their whole lives to send me and my sister to school. She's a trial litigator now, in Atlanta. But this is where we're from.'

'My father worked for the city, too,' I nodded.

'I know I never told you, Lindsay, but I knew your father.'

'You knew him?'

'Yeah, we started out together. Radio cops, out of Southern. Even shifted together a few times. *Marty Boxer* . . . Your father was a bit of a legend, Lindsay, and not necessarily for exemplary duty.'

'Tell me something I don't know.'

'All right . . .' he paused. 'He was a good cop then. A damned good cop. A lot of us looked up to him.'

'Before he bagged out.'

Mercer looked at me. 'You must know by now, things happen in a cop's life that don't always break down so easily into choices the rest of us can understand.'

I shook my head. 'I haven't spoken to him in eleven years.'

Mercer nodded. 'I can't speak for him as a father, or as a husband, but is there a chance that as a man, or at least a cop, you've judged him without knowing all the facts?'

'He never stuck around long enough to present the facts,' I said.

'I'm sorry,' Mercer said. 'I'll tell you some things about Marty Boxer, but another time.'

'Tell me what? When?'

He drew down the privacy barrier and instructed his driver that it was time to head back to the Hall. 'When you find Chimera.'

Chapter Forty-Three

L ater that night, as his town car slowed in the evening traffic near his home, Chief Mercer spoke up from the back seat. 'Why don't I get out here, Sam.'

His driver, Sam Mendez, glanced back. The mandate from the Hall was: no unnecessary risks.

Mercer was firm on the matter. 'Sam, there's more cops on patrol in a five-block radius here than there are back at the Hall.' There was usually a patrol car or two cruising on Ocean and one stationed across from his home.

The car eased to a stop. Mercer opened the door and thrust his heavy shape onto the street. 'Pick me up tomorrow, Sam. Have a good night.'

As his car pulled away, Mercer lugged his thick briefcase in one hand and threw his tan raincoat over his shoulder with the other. He experienced a surge of freedom and relief. These little after-work excursions were the only times he felt free.

He stopped at Kim's Market and picked out the sweetest-looking basket of strawberries, and some choice plums, too. Then he wandered across the street to the Ingleside Wine Shop. He decided on a Beaujolais that would go with the lamb stew Eunice was making.

On the street, he glanced at his watch and headed towards home. On Cerritos, two stone pillars separated Ocean from the secure enclave of Ingleside Heights. The traffic disappeared behind him.

He passed the low stone house belonging to the Taylors. A noise rustled from a hedge. 'Well, well . . . Chief?'

Mercer stopped. His heart was already pounding.

'Don't be shy. I haven't seen you in years,' the voice said again. 'You probably don't remember.'

What the hell was going on?

A tall, muscular man stepped out from behind the hedge. He was wearing a cocky smirk, a green wind-breaker wrapped around him.

A vague recognition came over Mercer, a familiarity in the face he couldn't quite place. Then all at once it came back to him. Suddenly, everything made sense and it took his breath away.

'This is such an honor,' the man said. 'For *you*.'

He had a gun, heavy and silver. It was extended towards Mercer's chest. He knew he had to do something. Ram him. Get to his own gun somehow. He needed to act like a cop on the street again.

'I wanted you to see my face. I wanted you to know why you were dying.'

'Don't do this. There are cops everywhere around here.'

'Good. That makes it even better for me. Don't be

scared, Chief. Where you're going, you'll be running into a lot of your old friends.'

The first shot struck him in the chest, a burning, clothes-searing thud that buckled his knees. Mercer's first thought was to shout. Was it Parks or Vasquez stationed in front of his house? Only precious yards away. But his voice died inaudibly in his chest. *Jesus, God, please save me.*

The second shot tore through his throat. He didn't know if he was up or down. He wanted to charge the killer. He wanted to take this bastard down. But his legs felt paralyzed, inert.

The man with the gun was standing over him now. The bastard was still talking to him, but he couldn't hear a word. His face kept melting in and out of focus. A name flashed in his mind. It seemed impossible. He said it twice just to be sure, his breath pounding in his brain.

'That's right,' the killer said, leveling the silvery gun. 'You've solved the case. You figured out Chimera. Congratulations.'

Mercer thought he should close his eyes, when the next bright orange flash exploded in his face.

Chapter Forty-Four

I will always remember what I was doing when I heard the news. I was home, tending a pot of farfalle on the stove. 'Aida' by Sarah McLachlan was playing on the stereo.

Claire was coming over. I'd lured her for dinner with my famous pasta with asparagus and lemon sauce. Not lured her, actually, *begged*. I wanted to talk about something other than the case. Her kids, yoga, the California Senate race, why the Warriors sucked. *Anything . . .*

I will never forget . . . Martha sat toying with a headless San Francisco Giants mascot bear that she had appropriated to her side of the property list. I was chopping basil; I checked on the pasta. Tasha Catchings and Art Davidson had drifted out of my mind. Thank God.

The phone rang. A selfish thought knifed through me, hoping that it wasn't Claire; that at the last minute she was bagging out of our date.

I cradled the phone in the nape of my neck and answered, 'Yo.'

The voice was Sam Ryan's, the department's Chief of

Detectives. Ryan was my administrative superior in the chain of command. At the sound of his voice, I knew something had to be seriously wrong.

'Lindsay, something terrible has happened.'

My body went numb. It was like someone had reached inside my chest and squeezed my heart in their indifferent fist. I listened to Ryan speak. *Three shots from point blank range . . . Only a few yards from his house. Oh my God . . . Mercer . . .*

'Where is he, Sam?'

'Moffitt. Emergency surgery. He's fighting.'

'I'll be right down. I'm on my way.'

'Lindsay, there's nothing you can do here. Get out to the scene.'

'Chi and Lorraine will cover it. I'll be right down.'

The doorbell buzzed. As if in a trance, I rushed over, opened it.

'Hey,' said Claire.

I didn't say a word. In an instant, she recognized the pallor on my face. 'What's happened?'

My eyes were wet. 'Claire . . . he's shot Chief Mercer.'

Chapter Forty-Five

We raced down the steps, climbed into Claire's Pathfinder and made the dash from Potrero to the California Medical Center all the way over in Parnassus Heights. The entire ride, my heart pumped madly and hopefully. The streets blurred by – Twenty-fourth, Guerrero, then across the Castro on Seventeenth to the hospital atop Mt Sutro.

Barely ten minutes after I got the call, Claire spun the Pathfinder into a restricted parking space across from the hospital entrance.

Claire ID'd herself to a nurse at the front desk, asking for an up-to-date report. She looked worried as she charged inside the swinging doors.

I ran up to Sam Ryan. 'What's the word?'

He shook his head. 'He's on the table now. If anyone can take three bullets and make it through, it's him.'

I flipped open my cell phone and patched into Lorraine Stafford at the scene. 'Things are crazy here,' she said. 'There's people from Internal Affairs, and some goddamn city *crisis* agency. And the fucking press. I haven't been able to get close to the radio cop who was first on the scene.'

'Don't let *anyone* other than you or Chi get close to that scene,' I told her. 'I'll be out there as soon as I can.'

Claire came back out of the ER. Her face was drawn. 'They've got him open now, Lindsay. It doesn't look good. His cerebral cortex was penetrated. He's lost a ton of blood. It's a miracle he's hung on as long as he has.'

'Claire, I've got to get in there to see him.'

She shook her head. 'He's barely alive, Lindsay. Besides, he's under anesthesia.'

I had this mounting sense that I owed it to Mercer, each unresolved death. That he knew, and if he died, the truth would die with him, too. 'I'm going in there.'

I pushed through the doors leading to the OR, but Claire held onto me. As I looked into her eyes, the last glimmer of hopefulness drained out of my body. I had always fought with Mercer, battled him. He was someone to whom I felt I always had something to prove, and prove again and again. But in the end, he had believed in me. In the strangest of ways I felt like I was losing a father all over again.

Barely a minute later, a doctor in a green smock came out, peeling off latex gloves. He said a few words to one of the mayor's men, then to the Assistant Chief.

'The Chief's dead,' Tracchio uttered.

Everyone stood staring blankly ahead. Claire put an arm around me and hugged.

'I don't know if I can do this,' I said, holding firmly onto her shoulder.

'Yes, you can,' she said.

I smiled tightly and caught Mercer's doctor as he was headed back to the ER. I introduced myself. 'Did he say anything when he was brought in?'

The doctor shrugged. 'He held on for a while, but whatever he said was incoherent. Just reflexive. He was on life support from the moment he came in.'

'His brain was still working, wasn't it, doctor?' He had faced his killer head on. Taken three shots. I could see Mercer holding on, just long enough to say something. '*Anything* you remember?'

His tired eyes searched for something. 'I'm sorry, Lieutenant. We were trying to save his life. You might try the EMS techs who brought him in.'

He went back inside. Through the window in the ER doors, I caught a glimpse of Eunice Mercer and one of their teenage daughters, tearfully hugging in the corridor.

My insides felt like they were ripping apart, a knot of nausea building up in my chest.

I ran into the ladies room. I bent over the sink and splashed cold water all over my face. 'Goddamn it! God-damn it!'

When my body calmed, I looked up in the mirror. My eyes were dark, hollow and blank; voices drummed loudly in my head.

Four murders, they tolled . . . *Four black cops*.

Chapter Forty-Six

Lorraine Stafford walked me down from the stone gate on Cerritos.

'The Chief was on his way home,' she bit her bottom lip. 'He lived a couple of houses down that way. No witnesses, but his driver's over there.'

I went to the spot where Mercer had been found. Charlie Clapper's team was already combing all around it. It was a quiet residential street, the walk path guarded by a high hedge that would've blocked off anyone from seeing the killer.

The spot had already been chalked off. Blotches of blood soaked the pavement inside the outline of his body. The remains of his last evening, some plastic bags containing magazines, fruit and a bottle of wine were scattered around.

'Didn't he have a car stationed in front of his house?' I asked.

Lorraine nodded towards a young uniformed officer leaning against the hood of a black-and-white. 'By the time he got down here, the perp had fled and the Chief was bleeding out.'

It became clear the killer had been lying in wait. He must've hidden in the bushes until Mercer came by. He must've known. Just like he knew with Davidson.

From up on Ocean, I saw Jacobi and Cappy coming towards us. The sight of them made me exhale with relief.

'Thanks for coming down,' I whispered.

Then Jacobi did something totally uncharacteristic. He grasped my shoulder and looked firmly in my eyes. 'This is gonna get big, Lindsay, Feds are gonna come in. Anything we can do, anything you need, anytime you need to talk about it, you know I'm here for you.'

I turned to Lorraine and Chi. 'What do you need to finish up here?'

'I want to check along the escape route,' Chi said. 'If he had a car parked, someone must've seen it. Otherwise, maybe someone saw him come out on Ocean.'

'Fucking Chief,' Jacobi sighed. 'I always thought the guy would hold a news conference at his own funeral.'

'We still classifying this as a hate crime, Lieutenant?' Cappy sniffed.

'I don't know about you,' I said, 'but I hate this bastard pretty bad.'

Chapter Forty-Seven

Jacobi was right about one thing. The next morning, everything *had* changed. Anthony Tracchio was named Acting Chief. He had been the Chief's administrative right hand, but had never come up through the ranks. On the Chimera case, I was now reporting to him.

A joint task force was set up to handle Mercer's homicide. It wasn't until I got upstairs that I found out precisely what 'joint' meant. A feeding frenzy of every news organization in the country was massing on the outside steps, setting up their camera crews, clawing for interviews. 'No leaks,' Tracchio warned brusquely. 'No contact with the press. All interviews go through me.'

When I got back to my office, two tan-suited FBI agents were waiting in the outer room. A polished, preppy black man named Ruddy in an Oxford shirt and yellow tie, who seemed in charge. And the typical hard-nosed field agent named Hull.

The first thing out of Ruddy's mouth was to tell me how nice it was to be working with the officer who had solved the bride and groom case. The second thing was to ask for the Chimera files. All of them. Tasha. Chipman. Davidson. Whatever we had on Mercer.

Ten seconds after they left I was on the phone to my new boss. 'Guess I know what you meant by "joint",' I said.

'Crimes against public officials are a Federal offense, Lieutenant. There's not much I can do,' said Tracchio.

'Mercer said this was a *city* crime, Chief. He said city personnel ought to see it through.'

Tracchio sent my heart into a tailspin. 'I'm sorry. Not anymore.'

Chapter Forty-Eight

L ater that afternoon, I drove out to Ingleside Heights to
talk with Chief Mercer's wife. I felt I needed to do it
myself. A line of cars was already stretched along the street
around the Chief's home. A relative answered the door
and told me Mrs Mercer was upstairs with family.

I stood around, checking out faces I recognized gathered
in the living room. After a few minutes, Eunice Mercer
came down the stairs. She was accompanied by a
pleasant-looking, middle-aged woman who turned out to
be her sister. She recognized me and walked my way.

'I'm so sorry. I can't believe it,' I said, squeezing her hand
first, then hugging her.

'I know,' she whispered. 'I know you've just gone
through this yourself.'

'I promise you, I know how tough this is. But I need to
ask you a few questions,' I finally said to her.

She nodded, and her sister floated back among the
guests. Eunice Mercer took me into a private den.

I asked her many of the same questions I had put forth

to the relatives of other victims. Had anyone recently threatened her husband? Calls to the house? Anyone suspicious watching the house?

She shook her head, no. 'Earl said this was the only place where he actually felt like he lived in the city, not just ran the police force.'

I changed tack. 'You ever come across the name Art Davidson before this week?'

Eunice Mercer's face went blank. 'You think Earl was killed by the same man who did these other horrible things?'

I took her hand. 'I think these murders were all committed by the same man.'

She massaged her brow. 'Lindsay, *nothing* makes sense to me right now. Earl's murder. That book.'

'Book . . .?' I asked.

'Yes. Earl always read car magazines. He had this dream, when he retired . . . This old GTO he kept in a cousin's garage. He always said he was gonna tear it down and build it up from scratch. But that book he had stuffed in his jacket . . .'

'What book?' I was squinting at her hard.

'A young doctor at the hospital returned it to me, along with his wallet and keys. I never knew he had such an interest in that sort of thing. Those old myths . . .'

Suddenly, my pulse was racing. 'Can you show me what you're talking about?'

'Of course,' Eunice Mercer said. 'It's over here.' She left the den, and in a minute came back. She handed me a paperback copy of a book every schoolkid reads. *Mythology,* by Edith Hamilton.

It was an old dog-eared copy, looked like it had been leafed through a thousand times. I riffled through the pages and spotted nothing.

I ran down the table of contents. Then I saw it. Halfway down, page 141. It was underlined. *Bellerophon Kills the Chimera.*

Bellerophon . . . Billy Rephon.

My heart clenched. It was the name he'd used on the 911 call about Art Davidson. He had called himself Billy Rephon.

I flipped to page 141. It was there. With an illustration. The lion rearing. The goat's body. The serpent's tail.

Chimera.

The bastard was telling us he had killed Chief Mercer.

A surge rippled through me. There was something else on the page. A sharp, edgy script, a few words, scrawled above the chapter heading in bold-faced ink:

More to come . . . justice will be served.

Chapter Forty-Nine

L eaving Mercer's home, I drove around in a sweat, terror-filled at what I knew to be the truth.

All my instincts had been right. This was no random racist murder spree. This was a cold, calculating killer. He was taunting us, the same way he had with the white van. With that cocky tape. Billy Rephon.

Finally I said, *fuck it*. I called the girls. I couldn't hold back any longer. They were three of the sharpest law enforcement minds in the city. And this bastard had told me there were going to be more killings. We set up a meeting at Susie's.

'I need your help,' I said, panning their faces in our usual booth at the restaurant.

'That's why we're here,' Claire said. 'You call, we come running.'

'*Finally*,' Cindy chuckled. 'She admits she's nothing without us.'

'This Kiss' by Faith Hill was drowning out a basketball game on the TV, but in the corner booth the four of us were huddled in our own purposeful world. God, it was good to have everybody back together again.

'Everything's screwed up with Mercer gone. The FBI's come in. I don't even know who's in control. All I know is that the longer we wait, the more people are going to be killed.'

'This time there have to be some rules,' Jill said, tugging on a Buckler's non-alcoholic beer. 'This isn't a game. That last case, I think I broke every rule I took an oath to uphold. Withholding evidence, using the DA's office for personal use. If anything had gotten out, I'd be doing my cases from the eighth floor.'

We laughed. The eighth floor of the Hall was where the holding cells were located.

'Okay,' I agreed. It was the same for me. 'Anything we find we take to the task force.'

'Let's not go overboard,' said Cindy with a mischievous laugh. 'We're here to help you, not to make the careers of some uptight, bureaucratic men.'

'The Margarita Posse lives,' laughed Jill. 'Jesus, I'm glad we're back.'

'Don't you *ever* doubt it,' said Claire.

I looked around at the girls. The women's murder club. Part of me bristled with apprehension. Four people were dead, including the highest-ranking police officer in the city. The killer had proved he could strike anywhere he wanted to.

'Each murder has become more high profile, and more daring,' I said, filling them in on the latest, including the book stuffed in Mercer's jacket. 'He no longer needs the subterfuge of the racial MO. It's racial, all right. I just don't know why.'

Claire took us through the Chief's autopsy, which she had finished up that afternoon. He was hit three times at close range with a .38 gun. 'My impression is, the three shots were spaced at measured intervals. I could tell by the pattern that the wounds bled out. The last one was to the head. Mercer was already on the ground. It makes me think they may have confronted each other. That he was trying to kill him slowly. Or that they were even talking. I guess where I'm headed is that it's likely Mercer knew his killer.'

'You checked into the possibility that all these officers were somehow connected?' Jill cut in. 'Of course you have. You're Lindsay Boxer.'

'Of course I have. There's no record any of them had even met. Their careers don't seem to have crossed. They were all different ages. We can't find anything that puts them together.'

'Somebody hates cops. Well, actually, a lot of people do,' Cindy said.

'I just can't find the link. This started out in the guise of a hate crime. The killer wanted us to view the murders in a certain way. He wanted us to find his clues. And he wanted us to find the Chimera. His fucked-up symbol.'

'But if this is a personal vendetta,' Jill thought aloud, 'it doesn't make sense that it would lead back to some organized group.'

'Unless he was setting someone up,' I said.

'Or unless,' Cindy said, chewing her lip, 'the Chimera doesn't lead back to a hate group at all. Maybe this book is his way of telling us it's something else.'

I stared at her. We all did. 'We're waiting, Einstein.'

She blinked remotely, then shook her head. 'I was just thinking out loud.'

Jill said she would dig into any grievance cases against a black officer who had wronged or injured a white. Any act of vengeance that might explain the killer's mindset. Cindy would do the same at the *Chronicle*.

It had been a long day and I was exhausted. I had a task force meeting at seven-thirty the next morning. I looked each of my friends in the eye. 'Thank you, thank you.'

'We're gonna solve this sucker with you,' Jill said. 'We're going to get Chimera.'

'We've got to,' Claire said. 'We need you to keep picking up the bar bill.'

For a few more minutes we chatted about what we all had going on the next day, when we could get together again. We were starting to cook now. Jill and Claire had their cars parked in the lot. I asked Cindy, who lived in the Castro section, near me, if she needed a ride.

'Actually,' she said with a smile, 'I have a date.'

'Good for you. Who is your next victim?' Claire exclaimed. 'When do we get to check him out?'

'If you supposedly mature, talented women want to ogle like a bunch of schoolkids, I guess *now*. He's picking me up.'

'I'm always up for a good ogle,' Claire said.

I snorted out a laugh. 'You could be meeting Mel Gibson *and* Russell Crowe and it wouldn't rock my boat tonight.'

As we pushed through the front door, Cindy tugged my arm. 'Hold onto your oars, honey.'

We all saw him at once. We all ogled, and my boat was rocked.

Waiting outside, looking altogether sexy and handsome, dressed entirely in black, was Aaron Winslow.

Chapter Fifty

I couldn't believe it. I stood there, gawking. I looked at Cindy, then back at Winslow, my surprise slowly giving way to a blushing smile.

'Lieutenant,' Winslow nodded, cutting through the awkward murk. 'When Cindy said she was meeting friends, I wasn't expecting to find you here.'

'Yeah, me too,' I stammered back.

'We're headed to the Blue Door,' Cindy said to the crowd, going through the introductions. 'Pinetop Perkins is in town.'

'Terrific,' nodded Claire.

'*Beatific*,' snipped Jill.

'Anybody care to join?' Aaron Winslow asked. 'If you haven't heard it, there's nothing like Memphis jazz.'

'I'm in the office at six tomorrow,' said Claire. 'You two go along.'

I leaned over to Cindy and whispered, 'You know, when we were talking foxholes the other day, I was only joking.'

'I know you were,' Cindy said, looping her arm around mine. 'But I wasn't.'

Claire, Jill and I stood with our jaws open and watched the two of them disappear around the corner. Actually, they looked kind of cute together, and it was only a date to hear some music.

'Okay,' Jill said, 'tell me I wasn't dreaming.'

'You weren't dreaming, girl,' Claire replied. 'I just hope that Cindy realizes what she's getting herself into.'

'Uh-uh,' I shook my head. 'I hope *he* does.'

During the ride home, I entertained myself with the notion of Cindy and Aaron Winslow. It almost pushed out of my head the reason we had gotten together in the first place.

I turned my Explorer onto Brannan and waved good-bye to Claire, who was heading over to 280. As I made the turn, I caught a glimpse of a white Toyota pulling out down the block behind me.

My mind was wrapped up with what I had just done, getting the girls involved in this horrible case. I had countermanded a direct order from the mayor, *and* my commanding officer. This time there was no one backing me up. No Roth, or Mercer.

A Mazda with two teenage girls in it pulled up behind me. We had stopped at a light on Seventh. The driver was talking a mile a minute on her cell phone, while her companion sung along obliviously to the stereo.

As we started up, I kept my eye on them for a block, until they veered onto Ninth. A blue minivan had taken the Mazda's place.

I made a right onto Potrero under the underpass to 101, heading south. The blue van turned.

To my surprise, I saw that same white Toyota lurking thirty yards behind.

I continued on. A silver BMW had sped up in the left lane and pulled up behind me. Behind it, a city bus. It looked like the mystery car had gone.

Who could blame you for getting a little jumpy, with what was going on? I said to myself. My picture had been in the paper and on the TV news.

I made my usual right on Connecticut, and started the climb up the Potrero Hill. I was hoping Mrs Taylor next door had come by to walk Martha. And I was thinking of stopping in the market on Twentieth for some Edy's Vanilla Twirl.

Two blocks up, I glanced a last time in my rearview mirror. The white Toyota crept into view.

Either the sonovabitch lived on the same block, or the bastard was following me.

It had to be Chimera.

Chapter Fifty-One

My heart was pounding; the hairs on the back of my neck stood erect. I squinted in the rearview mirror and ran the plate numbers over in my head: California . . . PCV 182. I couldn't make out the person driving. *This was insane . . .* But I sure wasn't imagining it.

I pulled into an open parking spot in front of my building. I waited in the car until I saw the hood of the Toyota rise over the lip of Twentieth Street, then pause at the base of the last hill. My blood ran cold.

I had let the bastard trail me right to my house.

I reached in the glove compartment and took out my Glock. I checked the clip. *Stay calm. You're gonna take this asshole down. You're going to nail Chimera right now.*

I hunched in my car, scrolling through my options. I could call it in. A patrol car could be here in a matter of minutes. But I had to find out who it was. The appearance of a police car would scare him away.

My heart beat madly. I palmed my gun and opened the car door. I slipped out into the night. *Now what?*

On the first floor of my apartment building there was a back door which led to an alley underneath my terrace. From there, I could wrap around the block near the park at the top of the hill. If the bastard stayed outside, I could double back and maybe surprise him.

I hesitated in the doorway, just long enough to see the Toyota creeping slowly up the street. My hands fumbled in my bag for the key. I jammed it in the lock.

I was inside. From a small window I watched the Toyota. I strained to catch a glimpse of the driver but his interior lights were off.

I undid the bolt to the back door, crept out into the alley behind my building.

I ran behind the cover of the houses to the cul de sac at the top of the hill. From there, I reversed back, hugging the shadows of the buildings along the opposite side of the street.

Behind him . . .

The Toyota had parked across from my building, its lights dimmed.

The driver in the front seat was smoking a cigarette.

I crouched behind a parked Honda Accord, clasping my gun. *This is what it's all about, Lindsay.*

Could I take Chimera in the car? What if the doors were locked?

Suddenly, I saw the car door open, the interior lights flash on. The bastard's back was turned to me as he climbed out of his car.

He was wearing a dark, weatherproof jacket, a floppy

cap pulled over his eyes. He was glancing up at my building. *My apartment.*

Then he headed across the street. No fears.

Take him down. Now. The bastard had come for me. He'd threatened me in Mercer's book. I moved out from the cover of the line of parked cars.

My heart was racing so fast and loud, I was afraid he would suddenly spin around. *Now! Do it! You've got him!*

I stepped up, the Glock firm in one hand. I wrapped the other around his neck, pulled, kicked his legs out from under him.

He toppled to the ground, landing hard on his back. I pinned him there. I pressed the barrel of my gun to the back of his head.

'Police, asshole! Hands out wide.'

A painful groan came from him. He spread his arms. *Was it Chimera?*

'You wanted me, you bastard, well you got me. Now, turn around.'

I relaxed my knee just enough for him to maneuver around. As he did, my heart almost stopped.

I was staring into the face of my father.

Chapter Fifty-Two

Marty Boxer rolled onto his back and groaned, the air squeezed out of his lungs. He still had a glimmer of the rugged handsomeness I remembered as a kid, but it was different – older, leaner, worn. His hair had thinned and the once-lively blue eyes seemed washed out.

I hadn't seen him in eleven years.

'What are you doing here?' I wanted to know.

'Right now,' he gasped, rolling onto his side, 'having the shit beat out of me by my daughter.'

I felt a hard slab jutting out of his jacket pocket. I pulled out an old department-issued Smith and Wesson .40 caliber. 'What the hell is this? How you say hello?'

'It's a dangerous world out there,' he groaned again.

I rolled off of him. The sight of him was an affront, a sudden illumination of memories I'd shut off years ago. I didn't offer to help him up. 'What were you doing? Following me?'

Slowly, he edged himself into a sitting position. 'I'm

gonna pretend you didn't know it was your old man dropping in, Buttercup.'

'*Please* don't call me that,' I shot back at him.

Buttercup was his pet name for me when I was about seven and he was still at home. My sister, Cat, was Horsefly; I was Buttercup. Hearing that name brought a surge of bitter memories. 'You think you can drop in here after all these years, scare the shit out of me, and get away with it by calling me "Buttercup". I'm not your little girl. I'm a Homicide Lieutenant.'

'I know that. And you deliver a hell of a takedown, baby.'

'Consider yourself lucky,' I said, clicking my Glock onto safety.

'Who the hell were you expecting, anyway?' he said as he massaged his ribs. 'The Rock?'

'That doesn't matter. What does matter is just what you're doing here.'

He sniffed, guiltily. 'I'm definitely starting to pick up, Buttercup, that you might not be entirely thrilled to see me?'

'I don't know that I am. Are you sick?'

His blue eyes sparkled. 'Can't a guy check up on his firstborn without his motives being called into account?'

I studied the lines on his face. 'I haven't seen you in eleven years and you act like it's been a week. You want an update? I was married, now I'm divorced. I got into Homicide. Now I'm Lieutenant. I know that's a bit sketchy, but it brings you up to date, Dad.'

'You think so much time has passed that I can't look at you as a father?'

'I don't know how you look at me,' I said.

My father's blue eyes suddenly warmed and he smiled. 'God, you do look beautiful . . . *Lindsay.*'

His expression was that same twinkling, guiltless mug I had seen a thousand times as a kid. I shook my head in frustration. 'Marty, just answer my question.'

'Look,' he swallowed, 'I know sneaking up on you didn't win me any style points, but do you think I could at least talk my way into a cup of coffee?'

I stared incredulously at the man who had left our family when I was thirteen. Who had stayed away all the time my mother was sick. Who I had thought of as a coward or a cad or even worse for most of my adult life. I hadn't seen my father since he sat in the back row on the day I was sworn in as a cop. I didn't know if I wanted to slug him, or take him in my arms and give him a hug.

'Just *one,*' I said, holding out a hand and hoisting him up. I brushed off some loose gravel from his lapel. 'You talked yourself into one cup of coffee, *Buttercup.*'

Chapter Fifty-Three

I made a pot of coffee for my father and a cup of Red Zinger for me. I gave him a quick tour, introducing him to Martha, who almost against my silent instructions took a liking to dear old dad.

We sat on my white canvas couch, Martha curled up at my father's feet. I gave him a damp cloth and he dabbed at a scratch on his cheek.

'Sorry about the bruise,' I said, cradling the hot mug on my knees. *Kind of sorry.*

'I've earned worse,' he shrugged with a smile.

'Yeah, you have.'

We sat facing each other. Neither of us knew quite where to begin. 'So, I guess this is where you bring me up to date on what you've been up to for the last eleven years?'

He swallowed and put down the mug. 'Sure. I can do that.' He took me through his life, which seemed more like a sputtering spiral of bad luck. He had been an Assistant Chief, which I guess I knew, down in Redondo Beach.

Then he left to go into private security. Celebrities. Kevin Costner. Whoopi Goldberg. 'Even went to the Oscars,' he chuckled. He'd gotten married again, this time for only two years. 'Found out I was under-qualified for the job,' he quipped with a self-effacing wave. Now he was back in security, no celebrities, doing odd-jobs.

'Still gambling?' I asked.

'Only mind bets. In my head,' he replied. 'Had to give it up when I ran out of funds.'

'Still root for the Giants?' I asked. When I was a kid, he used to take me after his shift to this bar called Robbie Crusoe's out in Sunset. He'd prop me up on the counter where he and his buddies would watch the afternoon games from Candlestick. I'd loved being with him back then.

He shook his head. 'Nah, gave them up when they traded away Will Clark. I'm a Dodger fan now. I would like to go to the new park, though.' Then he looked at me for a long time.

It was my turn now. How to relate the past eleven years of my life to my father?

I took him through as much as I could handle, leaving out anything related to Mom. I told him about my ex, Tom, how it didn't work out. ('Chip off the old block,' he snickered. 'Yeah, but at least I stayed,' I replied.) How I pushed for Homicide, and finally got it.

He nodded, glumly. 'I read about that big case you worked on. Even down south it was all over the news.'

'A real resumé launcher.' I told him how, a month after,

I'd been offered the job as Lieutenant.

My father leaned forward and placed a hand on my knee. 'I wanted to see you, Lindsay. A hundred times. I don't know why I didn't. I'm proud of you. Homicide's top of the line. When I look at you, you're so . . . strong, in control. So beautiful. I only wish I could take a little of the credit.'

'You can. You taught me I had no one to rely on but myself.'

I got up, refilled his cup, and sat down again, facing him. 'Look, I'm sorry things haven't worked out for you. I really am. But it's been eleven years. Why are you here?'

'I called Cat, to see if you'd want to hear from me. She told me you'd been sick.'

I didn't need to relive this. It was hard enough just looking at him. 'I was sick,' I nodded. 'I'm better now. Hopefully I'll stay that way.'

My heart was tight against my chest. This was starting to get uncomfortable. 'So, how long have you been following me?'

'Since yesterday. I sat across from the Hall in my car for three hours, trying to find the right way in. I didn't know if you'd want to see me.'

'I don't know if I do, Daddy.' I tried to find the right words, and I felt the edge of tears welling in my eyes. 'You were never there. You ran out on us. I can't just change the way I've felt for all these years.'

'I don't expect you to, Lindsay,' he said. 'I'm becoming an old man. An old man who knows he's made a million mistakes. All I can do now is try and reverse some of them.'

I looked at him, half shaking my head in disbelief, half smiling and dabbing at my eye. 'Things are crazy here now. You heard about Mercer?'

'Of course,' my father exhaled. I waited for him to say something, but he simply shrugged. 'I saw you on the news. You *are* stunning. Do you know that, Lindsay?'

'Dad, please. Don't.' This case needed everything I had right now. It was madness. Here I was facing my father again. 'I don't know if I can handle this now.'

'I don't know either,' he said, tentatively reaching out for my hand. 'What about we try?'

Chapter Fifty-Four

At nine the next morning, Morris Ruddy, the FBI senior agent, scribbled a point on a yellow legal pad. 'Okay, Lieutenant, when did you first determine the Chimera symbol pointed towards the white supremacist movement?'

My head still whirred from the events of the night before. The last place I wanted to be was cooped up in a task force meeting, talking to the Feebies.

'Your office clued us in,' I replied. 'In Quantico.'

It was a bit of a lie, of course. Stu Kirkwood had only confirmed what I had already learned from Cindy.

'Subsequently, since you had that knowledge,' the FBI man bore in, 'how many of these groups have you checked out?'

I gave him a frustrated look that read, *we might actually start making some progress if we could get out of this goddamn room.*

'You read the files I gave you. We looked into two or three.'

'You looked into *one*.' He raised an eye.

'Look,' I explained, 'we don't have a history of these groups operating in this area. The method used in these killings seemed consistent with other cases I had worked. I made a determination we were dealing with a serial killer. I'll admit, it's a gut call.'

'From these four distinct acts,' Ruddy continued, 'you narrowed it down to the fact that this was the act of a single UNSUB, right?'

'Yeah. From *that*, and eight years working Homicide.' I didn't like his tone.

'Look, Agent Ruddy, this isn't a hearing,' Sam Ryan, my Chief of Detectives, finally said.

'I'm merely trying to determine how much of an effort we still have to coordinate in this area,' the FBI man replied.

'Look,' I insisted, 'these Chimera clues weren't exactly popping out at us in press releases. The white van was sighted by a seven-year-old kid. The second was on a wall of graffiti at the crime scene. Our ME suggested that the Catchings' shooting might not have been a random bullet.'

'But even now,' Ruddy said, 'after your own Chief of Police has been murdered, you still believe these killings aren't politically motivated?'

'The killings might be politically motivated. I don't know the killer's total agenda. But it's one guy and he's a nutcase. Where the hell is this going?'

'Where it's *going* is murder number *three*,' the other agent, Hull, cut in. 'The Davidson shooting.' He hoisted his solid frame out of his seat and stepped over to a flipchart, on which each separate murder and the pertinent details were listed in neat columns.

'Murders one, two and four,' he explained, 'all had ties to this Chimera. Davidson's murder doesn't tie in at all. We want to know what makes you so sure we're dealing with the same guy?'

'You didn't see the shot,' I said.

'According to what I have,' Hull leafed through his notes, 'Davidson was killed with a bullet from a totally different weapon.'

'I didn't say "ballistics", Hull, I said *the shot*. It was precision, marksman-caliber. Just like the one that killed Tasha Catchings.'

'I guess my point,' Hull continued, 'is that we have no tangible evidence linking the Davidson murder with the other three. If we stick to the facts, rather than Lieutenant Boxer's hunch, there's nothing to suggest we're not dealing with a *politically* motivated series of events. Nothing.'

At that moment there was a knock at the conference room door, and Charlie Clapper stuck his head in. Sort of like a shy groundhog peeking out of his cave.

Clapper nodded towards the FBI guys, then winked at me. 'I thought you'd be able to use this.'

He put a black-and-white rendering of a large sneaker tread on the table.

'You remember that shoe print we pulled off of the tar at the shooter's position in Art Davidson's killing?'

'Of course,' I said.

He placed a second rendering, side by side. 'This is one we were able to take from a patch of wet soil behind the Mercer scene.'

The imprints were identical.

A hushed silence filled the room. I looked at Agent Ruddy first, then Agent Hull.

"Course, they're just a standard pair of Reebok cross trainers,' Charlie explained.

Out of a pocket in his white lab coat, he removed a slide. On it were traces of tiny grains of powder. 'We picked this up at the Chief's crime scene.'

I leaned over and stared at traces of the same white chalk.

'One killer,' I said. 'One shooter.'

Chapter Fifty-Five

I called the girls together for a quick lunch. I couldn't wait to see them.

We met at Yerba Buena Square, and sat in the courtyard outside the new IMAX, watching the kids play in the fountains, munching on take-out salads and wraps. I went through everything, from the moment I left them at Susie's, to the suspicion that someone was following me, to taking down my father outside my apartment.

'My God,' uttered Claire. 'The prodigal father.'

For a moment, it was as if a bio-dome of silence had shut us off from the rest of the world. Everybody fixed on me with incredulous faces.

'When was the last time you'd seen him?' Jill asked.

'He was at my graduation from the Academy. I didn't invite him, but he knew somehow.'

'He followed you!' Jill gasped. 'From our meeting? Like some kind of creepy perp? *Yick*,' she said, cringing.

'Typical Marty Boxer,' I exhaled. 'That's my dad.'

Claire put her hand on my arm. 'So, what did he want?'

'I'm still not sure. It's like he wanted to make amends. He said my sister Cat told him I was sick. He followed the bride and groom case. He said he wanted to tell me how proud he was of me.'

'That was months ago,' Jill snorted, taking a bite of a chicken and avocado wrap. 'He sure took his time.'

'That's what I said,' I nodded back.

Cindy shook her head. 'He just decided *after eleven years* to show up at your door?'

'I think it's a good thing, Lindsay,' injected Claire. 'You know me – positive.'

'A good thing, that after eleven years he marches back in with a guilty conscience?'

'No, a good thing because he needs you, Lindsay. He's alone, right?'

'He told me he got married again for two years, but he's divorced. Imagine, Claire, finding out years after the fact that your father got married again.'

'That's not the point, Lindsay,' Claire replied. 'He's reaching out. You shouldn't be too proud to accept it.'

'How *do* you feel?' inquired Jill.

I wiped my mouth, took a sip of iced tea, and then a long breath. 'The truth? I don't even know. He's like some ghost from the past who brings back a lot of bad memories. Everything he's touched has only hurt people.'

'He's your father, honey,' Claire said. 'You've carried this hurt around since I've known you. You should let him in, Lindsay. You could have something you never had before.'

'He could also kick her in the shins again,' said Jill.

'Gee,' Cindy looked over at Jill, 'the prospect of mother-hood hasn't exactly made you all soft and gooey, has it?'

'One date with the Reverend,' Jill chuffed back, 'and suddenly you're the conscience of the group? I'm impressed.'

We looked at Cindy, all of us suppressing smiles.

'That's true,' nodded Claire. 'You don't think you're going to get off the hook, do you?'

Cindy began to blush. Never since I'd known her had I seen Cindy Thomas blush.

'You guys do make quite the couple,' I sighed.

'I like him,' Cindy blurted. 'We talked for hours. At a bar. Then he took me home. The end.'

'Sure,' Jill grinned. 'He's cute, he's got a steady job, and if you're ever tragically killed, you don't have to worry about who will preside over your service.'

'I hadn't thought of that one,' Cindy finally smiled. 'Look, it was one date. I'm doing a piece on him and the neighborhood. I'm sure he won't ask me out again.'

'But will you ask him out again?' said Jill.

'We're friends. No, we're friendly. It was a great couple of hours. I guarantee, all of you would have enjoyed your-selves. It's *research*,' Cindy said, and folded her arms.

We all smiled. But Cindy was right – none of us would have turned down a couple of hours with Aaron Winslow.

As we crumpled our meals back into paper bags, I turned to Jill. 'So, how're you feeling? You okay?'

She smiled. 'Pretty good, actually.' Then she linked her hands around her barely swollen belly and puffed out her cheeks, as if to say, *Fat* . . . 'I've just got this last case to finish up on. Then, who knows, I might even take some time off.'

'I'll believe that when I see it,' chortled Cindy. Claire and I mooned our eyes in support.

'Well, you just might be surprised,' Jill said.

'So what're you gonna do?' Claire turned to me as we got up to leave.

'Keep trying to link the victims. They'll connect.'

She kept her eyes on me. 'I meant about your dad.'

'I just don't know. It's already a bad time, Claire. Now Marty comes barging in. If he wants dispensation, he can wait in line.'

Claire stood up, crumpling her paper bag into a ball. She shot me one of her wise smirks.

'You obviously have a suggestion?' I said.

'Naturally. Why not do what you normally do in situations of doubt and stress.'

'And that is . . .?'

'Cook the man a meal.'

Chapter Fifty-Six

The next afternoon, Cindy hunched over her computer at the *Chronicle*, sipping a Stewart's Orange Crème as she scrolled down another futile query.

Somewhere, in the deepest bin of her memory, there was something she had filed away, a nagging recollection she couldn't place. *Chimera* . . . the word used in another context, some other form that would help the case.

She'd gone through CAL, the *Chronicle*'s on-line archives, and come back with zilch. She had browsed through the usual search engines – Yahoo!, Jeeves, Google. Her antennae were buzzing on high mode. She felt, as did Lindsay, that this fantastical monster led somewhere other than hate groups. It led to one very twisted and clever individual.

C'mon, she exhaled, jabbing the ENTER key in frustration, *I know you're in here somewhere*.

The day was nearly gone and she'd come back with nothing. Not even a lead for tomorrow morning's edition. Her editor would be pissed. *We have readers*, he would growl. *Readers want continuity*. She'd have to promise him something. But what? The investigation was stalled.

When she found it, she was in Google, wearily eyeing down the eighth page of responses. It hit her like a slap.

CHIMERA ... See Hellhole, an exposé of prison life in Pelican Bay, by Antoine James. Posthumous publication of prison hardships, cruelties, life of crime.

Pelican Bay ... Pelican Bay was where they threw the worst of the worst troublemakers in the California prison system. Violent offenders who couldn't be controlled anywhere else.

She remembered now that she had read about Pelican Bay in the *Chronicle*, maybe two years before. That was where she'd heard of Chimera. It was how it fit. It was what had been needling her for the past two days.

She spun her chair over to the CAL terminal on a nearby shelf. She pushed her glasses up on her forehead and typed in the query. *Antoine James.*

Five seconds later, a response came up. One article, 10 August 1999. Two years before. Written by Deb Meyer, a Sunday section feature writer. Headlined: *Posthumous Journal Details Nightmare World of Violence Behind Bars.*

She clicked on the display bar, and in another few seconds a facsimile of the article flashed on the screen. It was a Lifestyle article in a Sunday Metro section. Antoine James, while serving a ten-to-fifteen sentence at Pelican Bay for armed robbery, had been stabbed and killed in a prison squabble. He had kept a journal detailing the unsettling story of life on the inside, alleging a routine of forced snitching, racial attacks, beatings by guards, and perpetual gang violence.

She printed off the article, closed out of CAL, and spun her chair back across to her desk. She leaned back in her chair and rested her feet on a stack of books. She scanned the page.

'From the moment they process you through the doors, life in Pelican Bay is a constant war of guard intimidation and gang violence,' James had written in a black composition book. 'The gangs provide your status, your identity, your protection, too. Everyone pledges out, and whatever group you belong to controls who you are and what's expected of you.'

Cindy's eyes raced further down. The prison was a viper's nest of gangs and retaliation. The blacks had the Bloods and the Daggers as well as the Muslims. The Latinos had the Nortenos in their red headbands and the Serranos in their blue, and the Mexican Mafia, Los Eme. Among the whites, there were the Guineas and the Bikers, and some white trash shitbags called the Stinky Toilet People. And the supremacist Aryans.

'Some of the groups were ultra-secret,' James wrote. 'Once you were in, nobody touched you.

'One of these white groups was particularly nasty. All "max" guys, serving violent felony time. They'd cut a brother open just to bet on what he had to eat.'

Adrenaline shot through Cindy as she stopped on the next sentence.

James had a name for the group – *Chimera*.

Chapter Fifty-Seven

I was just finishing up for the day – nothing further on the four victims and the white chalk still a mystery – when I got a call from Cindy.

'The Hall still under Martial Law?' she quipped, referring to the mayor's moratorium on the press.

'Trust me, it's no picnic on the inside either.'

'Why don't you meet me? I've got something.'

'Sure. Where?'

'Look out your window. I'm right outside.'

I peered out and saw Cindy, leaning on a car parked under the freeway overpass on Seventh and Harrison. It was almost seven. I cleared my desk, called a quick good-night to Lorraine and Chi, and ducked out the rear entrance. I ran across the street and went up to Cindy. She was in a short skirt, embroidered jean jacket, with a faded khaki knapsack slung over her shoulder.

'Choir practice?' I winked.

'You should talk. Next time I see you in SWAT gear I'll assume you have a date with your dad.'

'Speaking of Marty, I called him. I asked him over tomorrow night. So, Deep Throat, what's so important that we're meeting out here?'

'Good news, bad news,' Cindy said. She pulled off her knapsack and came out with an 8"×11" manila envelope. 'I think I found it, Lindsay.'

She handed me the envelope, and I opened it: a *Chronicle* article dated two years ago. Plus a prison diary, *Hellhole*, by someone named Antoine James. A few passages were high-lighted in yellow. I began to read.

Aryan . . . worse than Aryan. All max guys. White, bad and hating. We didn't know who they hated worse, us, the 'swarms' they had to share their meals with, or the cops and guards who had put them there.

These bastards had a name for themselves. They called themselves Chimera . . .

My eyes fixed on the word.

'They're animals, Lindsay. The worst troublemakers in the penal system. They're even committed to carrying out each other's hits on the outside.

'That's the good news,' she said. 'Bad news is, it's Pelican Bay.'

Chapter Fifty-Eight

I n the anatomy of the California State Prison system, Pelican Bay was *the place where the sun don't shine.*

The following day, I took Jacobi and req'd a police helicopter for the hour's flight up the coast to Crescent City, near the Oregon border. I had been to Pelican Bay twice before, to meet with a snitch on a murder case, and to attend a parole hearing for someone I had put away. Each time, as I flew over the dense, redwood forest surrounding the facility, it left a hole in the pit of my stomach.

As a law enforcement agent – and as a woman – this was the kind of place you don't want to go. There's a sign, as they process you through the front gate, warning that if you're taken hostage you're on your own. *No negotiations.*

I had arranged to meet with Assistant Warden, Roland Estes, in the main administrative building. He kept us waiting for a few minutes. When he showed up, Estes was tall and serious, with a hard face and tight blue eyes. He had that clenched-fist unconfidingness that comes from years of living under the highest discipline.

'I apologize for being late,' he said, taking a seat behind his large oak desk. 'We had a disturbance down in O block. One of our resident Nortenos stabbed a rival in the neck.'

'How'd he get the knife?' Jacobi asked.

'No knives,' Estes smiled thinly. 'He used the filed-down edge of a gardening hoe.'

I wouldn't have Estes's job for a heartbeat, but I also didn't like the reputation this place had for beatings, intimidation and the motto, Snitch, Parole, or Die.

'So, you said this was related to Chief Mercer's murder, Lieutenant?' The warden leaned forward.

I nodded, removing a case file from my bag. 'To a possible string of murders. I'm interested in what you may know about a prison gang here.'

Estes shrugged. 'Most of these inmates have been in gangs from the time they were ten. You'll find that every territory or gang domain that exists in Oakland or East LA exists here.'

'This particular gang is called Chimera,' I said.

Estes registered no immediate surprise. 'No starting with the small stuff, huh, Lieutenant? So what is it you want to know?'

'I want to know if these murders lead to these men in Chimera. I want to know if they're as bad as they're made out to be. And I want to know the names of any reputed members who are now on the outside.'

'The answer to your first two questions is yes,' Estes nodded, flatly. 'It's a sort of trial by fire. Prisoners who can take the worst we can dish out. The ones who have been in the SHUs, isolation, for a substantial time. It earns them rank – and certain privileges.'

'Privileges?'

'Freedom. In the way we define it here. From being debriefed. From snitching.'

'I'd like a list of any paroled members of this gang.'

The warden smiled. 'Not many get paroled. Some get transferred to other facilities. I suspect there are Chimera offshoots at every max facility in the state. And it's not like we have a file of who's in and who's not. It's more like, who gets to sit next to the Big Motherfucker at mess.'

'But you know, don't you? You know who's in.'

'*We* know,' the warden nodded. He stood up as if our interview had come to an end. 'It'll take some time. Some of this I need to consult on. But I'll see what I can do.'

'While I'm here, I might as well meet with *him*.'

'Who, Lieutenant?'

'The Big Motherfucker. The head of Chimera.'

Estes looked at me. 'Sorry, Lieutenant, no one gets to do that. No one gets into the Pool.'

I looked Estes in the eyes. 'You want me to come back with a state order to get it done? Listen, our Chief of Police is dead. Every politician in this state wants this guy caught. I've got backing all the way. You already know that. Bring the bastard up.'

The warden's taut face relaxed. 'Be my guest, Lieutenant. But he doesn't leave. You go to him.'

Estes picked up his phone and dialed a number. After a pause, he muttered, sharply, 'Get Weiscz ready. He has a visitor. It's a woman.'

Chapter Fifty-Nine

We went through a long underground walkway, accompanied by Estes and a club-toting head guard named O'Koren.

When we came to a stairway marked SHU-C, the warden led us up, waving at a security screen, then through a heavy compression door that opened into the ultra-modern prison ward.

Along the way, he filled me in. 'Like most of our inmates, Weiscz came in from another facility, Folsom. He was the leader of the Aryan Brotherhood there, until he strangled a black guard. He's been "iso-ed" here for eighteen months now. Until we start sending people to the Death House in this state, there's nothing more we can do to him.'

Jacobi leaned over and whispered, 'You sure of what you're doing here, Lindsay?'

I *wasn't* sure. My heart was starting to gallop and my palms had busted out in a nervous sweat. 'That's why I brought you along,' I winked.

'*Yeah,*' Jacobi muttered.

Pelican Bay's isolation unit was unlike anything I had ever seen. Everything was painted a dull, sterile white. Burly, khaki-uniformed guards, of both sexes, but uniformly white, manned glassed-in command posts.

Monitors and security cameras were everywhere. *Everywhere.* The unit was configured like a pod with ten cells, the compression-sealed doors tightly shut.

Warden Estes stopped in front of a metal door with a large window. 'Welcome to ground zero of the human race,' he said.

A muscular, balding senior guard, holding a face-visor and some sort of Uzi-like taser gun, came up. 'Weiscz had to be extracted, Warden. I think he'll need a few moments to loosen up.'

I looked up at Estes. '*Extracted?*'

Estes sniffed. 'You would think after being holed up a couple of months, he'd be happy to get out. Just so you know what's coming next, Weiscz was uncooperative. We had to send a team in to pretty him up for you.'

He nodded towards the window. 'There's your man . . .'

I stepped in front of the solid, pressure-sealed door. Strapped to a metal chair, his feet bound in irons, his hands cuffed from behind, hunched a hulking, muscular shape. His hair was long and oily and straggly, and he wore a thin, unkempt goatee. He was dressed in an orange, short-sleeve jumpsuit, open at the chest, revealing ornate tattoos covering his pumped-up arms and chest.

The warden said, 'There'll be a guard in there with you

and you'll be monitored at all times. *Stay away from him.* Don't get closer than five feet. If he as much as juts his chin in your direction, he'll be immobilized.'

'The guy's bound and chained,' I said.

'This sonovabitch eats chains,' Estes said. 'Believe it.'

'Anything I can promise him?'

'Yeah,' Estes smirked, 'a Happy Meal. You ready?'

I winked at Jacobi, who widened his eyes in caution. My heart nearly stopped, like a skeet shot exploded out of the sky.

'Bon voyage,' Estes muttered. Then he signaled the control booth. I heard a *kashoosh* as the heavy compression door unlocked.

Chapter Sixty

I stepped into the stark, white cell. It was completely empty, except for a metal table and four chairs, all bolted to the floor, and two security cameras high up on the walls. In a corner stood a silent, tight-lipped guard holding a stun-gun.

Weiscz barely acknowledged me. His legs were fastened and his hands tightly cuffed behind the chair. His eyes had a steely, inhuman quality to them.

'I'm Lieutenant Lindsay Boxer,' I said, stopping about five feet from him.

Weiscz said nothing, only tilted his eyes towards me. Narrow, almost phosphorescent slits.

'I need to talk to you about some murders that have taken place. I can't promise you much. I'm hoping you'll hear me out. Maybe help.'

'Blow me,' he spat with a hoarse voice.

The guard took a step towards him and Weiscz stiffened, as if he'd taken a jolt from the *taser*. I put up my hand to hold him back.

'You may know something about them,' I continued, a chill shooting down my spine. 'I just want to know if they make sense to you. These killings . . .'

Weiscz looked at me curiously, probably trying to size up if there was something he could get from this. 'Who's dead?'

'Four people. Two cops. One was my Chief of Police. A widow, and an eleven-year-old girl. All black.'

An amused smile settled over Weiscz's face. 'In case you haven't noticed, lady, my alibi's air tight.'

'I'm hoping you may know something about them.'

'Why me?'

From my jacket pocket, I took out the same two Chimera photos I had shown Estes, and held them in front of his face. 'The killer's been leaving these behind. I believe you know what it means.'

Weiscz grinned broadly. 'I don't know what you came in here for, but you don't fucking know how that warms my heart.'

'The killer's a Chimera, Weiscz. You cooperate, you could gain back some privileges. They can always move you out of this hole.'

'Both of us know I'll never get out of this hole.'

'There's always something, Weiscz. Everybody wants something.'

'There is something,' he finally said. 'Come closer.'

My body stiffened. 'I can't. You know that.'

'You got a mirror, don't you?'

I nodded. I had a makeup mirror in my purse.

'Shine it on me.'

I looked at the guard. His head twitched a firm no.

For the first time, Weiscz looked in my eyes. 'Shine it on me. I haven't seen myself in over a year. Even the shower fixtures are dulled here so you can't see a reflection. These bastards just want you to forget who the fuck you were. I want to see.'

The guard stepped forward. 'You know that's impossible, Weiscz.'

'Fuck you, Labont.' He glared up viciously at the cameras. 'Fuck you too, Estes.' Then he turned back to me. 'They didn't send you in here with much to bargain with, did they?'

'They said I could take you out for a Happy Meal,' I said with a slight smile.

'Just you and me, huh?'

I glanced at the guard. 'And *him*.'

Weiscz's goatee split into a smile. 'These bastards, they know how to ruin everything.'

I stood there, nervously. I didn't laugh. I didn't want to show the slightest empathy for him.

But eventually I sat myself at the table across from Weiscz. I fumbled in my bag, took out a compact. Any minute I expected a loud voice to blare over the intercom, or the stone-faced guard to rush over and knock it away. To my amazement, no one interfered. I cracked the compact open, looked at Weiscz, then I turned it towards him.

I don't know what he looked like before, but he was a horrific sight now. He stared at himself, wide-eyed, the truth of his harsh confinement settling in. He fixed on the mirror as if it were the last thing he would see on earth. Then he looked at me and grinned. 'Not much to go on for that blow-me thing, is there?'

I don't know why, but I gave him a begrudging smile.

Then he twisted his neck around to the cameras. 'Fuck you, Estes!' he roared. 'See? I'm still there. You try to squeeze me out, but I'm still there. The reckoning is going on without me. Chimera, baby . . . Glory to the unstained hand who stills the rabble and swarm.'

'Who would do this?' I pressed. 'Tell me, Weiscz.' He knew. I knew he knew. Someone he had shared a cell with. Someone he had traded histories with in a prison yard.

'Help me, Weiscz. Someone you know is killing these people. You've got nothing to gain anymore.'

His eyes lit up with a sudden fury. 'You think I give a shit about your dead niggers? Your dead cops? Soon the state will be gathering them up anyway. Putting them in pens. An eleven-year-old nigger whore, some monkeys dressed up as cops. I only wish it was my finger on the trigger. We both know, whatever I say to you, I'll never get as much as a second meal out of these bastards. The minute you leave Labont's gonna stun me. There's a better chance you'll suck my dick.'

I shook my head, stood up, and motioned for the door.

'Maybe one of your own assholes has come to his senses,' he yelled with a smirk. 'Maybe that's what it was, an inside job.'

A tremor of rage burned through me. Weiscz was an

animal. There wasn't an ounce of humanity in him. All I wanted to do was slam the door in his face. 'I did give something to you, even if it was for a moment.'

'And don't be so sure you didn't get something in return. You'll never catch him. He's Chimera . . .' Weiscz jerked his head down to his chest, pointing towards a tattoo high on his shoulder. All I could make out was the tail of a snake. 'We can endure as much as you can dish, cop lady. Look at me . . . they stuff me in this hellhole, they make me eat my own shit, but I can still win.' Suddenly he was loud and angry again, twisting at his restraints. 'Victory comes in the end. God's grace is the white race. Long live Chimera . . .'

I moved away from him and Weiscz twisted defiantly. 'So what about that Happy Meal, bitch.'

As I got to the door, I heard a zap, followed by a garbled grunt, and turned as the guard pumped a thousand watts into Weiscz's twitching chest.

Chapter Sixty-One

We came back to town with a few names, courtesy of Estes. Recent parolees thought to be members of Chimera. Back at the Hall, Jacobi parceled out the list to Cappy and Chi.

'I'm gonna start calling a few POs,' he said to me. 'You want to join?'

I shook my head. 'I have to leave early, Warren.'

'Whatsamatter, don't tell me you got a date?'

'*Yeah,*' I nodded back. No doubt my eyes sort of lit into an incredulous smile. 'I've got a date.'

The downstairs buzzer rang about seven.

When I opened the door, my father was peeking out from behind a catcher's mask, his hands outstretched in a defensive pose. 'Friends?' he asked, an apologetic smile sneaking through.

'Dinner,' I smiled, begrudgingly. 'That's the best I can do.'

'That's a start,' he said, stepping in. He had cleaned

himself up. He was wearing a brown sports jacket, pressed pants, an open-collared white shirt. He handed me a bottle of red wine wrapped in paper.

'You didn't have to,' I said, unfurling the wine, then gasping in surprise as I read the label. It was a first growth Bordeaux, Chateau Latour, the year – *1966*.

I looked at him. 1966 was the year I was born.

'I bought it a year after you were born. It was about the only thing I took with me when I left. I always figured we'd drink it on your graduation or something, maybe your wedding.'

'You kept it all these years.' I shook my head.

He shrugged. 'Like I said, I bought it for you. Anyway, Lindsay, there's nothing I'd rather do than drink it here tonight.'

Something warm rose inside me. 'You're making it hard to continue to completely hate you.'

'*Don't* hate me, Lindsay.' He tossed me the catcher's mask. 'This doesn't fit. I don't ever want to have to use it again.'

I took him into the living room, poured him a beer and sat down. I had on a wine-colored Eileen Fisher sweater, my hair pulled up in a ponytail. His eyes seemed to twinkle at me.

'You look gorgeous, Buttercup,' my father said.

When I scowled, he smiled. 'I can't help it, you just do.'

For a while we talked, Martha lying beside him as if he were an old friend. We talked about trivial things, things we knew. Who was left from his old cronies on the force.

Cat, and the new granddaughter he hadn't seen. Whether Jerry Rice would call it quits. We skirted the subject of Mercer and the case.

And as if I was meeting someone for the first time, I found him different than I imagined. Not garrulous and boastful and full of stories as I remembered, but humble and reserved. Almost contrite. And he still had his sense of humor.

'I've got something to show you,' I said. I went into the hall closet and came back with the satin Giants baseball jacket he'd given me when I was ten. It was embroidered with a number '24' and had the name 'Mays' on the front chest.

My father's eyes flashed in surprise. 'I'd forgotten about that. I got it from the equipment manager in 1968.' He held it in front of him and looked at it a long time, like an old relic that had made the past suddenly vivid. 'You have an idea what that thing must be worth today?'

'I always called it my inheritance,' I told him.

Chapter Sixty-Two

I did a salmon on the grill in a ginger-miso sauce, fried rice with peppers, leeks and peas. I remembered that my father liked Chinese. We cracked the '66 Latour. It was a dream wine, silky and gem-like. We sat in the alcove overlooking the Bay. My father said it was the best bottle of wine he'd ever tasted.

The conversation gradually drifted towards more personal things. He asked what kind of man I had been married to, and I admitted, unfortunately, someone like himself. He asked if I resented him, and I had to tell him the truth. 'Yeah. A lot, Dad.'

Gradually, we even talked about the case. I told him how tough it was to solve, how I held it against myself that I couldn't crack it. How I was sure it was a serial, but four murders into the case, I still had nothing.

We talked for three more hours, until after eleven, the wine gone, Martha asleep at his feet. Every once in a while I had to remind myself that I was talking to my own father. That I was sitting across from him for the first time in my adult life. And slowly, I began to see. He was just a man who had made mistakes, and who had been punished for them. He was no longer someone I could blindly resent, or hate. He hadn't murdered anybody. He wasn't Chimera. By the standards I dealt with, his sins were forgivable.

Gradually, I could no longer hold back the question I'd been wanting to ask for so many years. 'I have to know the answer to this. Why did you leave?'

He leaned back against the couch. His blue eyes looked so sad. 'There's nothing I could say that would make sense of it to you. Not now. You're a grown woman. You're on the force. You know how things get. Your mother and I . . . let's just say we were never a good match, even for the old school. I had squandered most of what we had on the games. I had a lot of debts, borrowed money on the street. That's not exactly kosher for a cop. I did a lot of things I wasn't very proud of . . . as a man, and as a cop.'

I noticed his hands were trembling. 'You know how sometimes, someone commits a crime simply because the situation gets so bad that, one by one, the options just close off and they're unable to do anything else? That's how it was for me. The debts, what was going on on the job . . . I didn't see any other choice. I just left. I know it's a little late to say this, but I've regretted it every day of my life.'

'And when Mom got sick?'

'I was sorry when she got sick. But by then I had a new life, and no one made it seem like I was welcome to come back. I thought it would hurt her more than help.'

'I know Mom always told me you were a pathological liar.'

'That's the truth, Lindsay,' my father said. I liked the way he admitted it. I liked my father, actually.

I had to get up, shift gears. I started taking the dishes into the kitchen. My chest was heaving. I felt like I might be going to cry. My father was back and I was starting to realize how much I had missed him. In a crazy way, I still wanted to be his girl.

My father helped with the dishes. I rinsed them off and he loaded them in the dishwasher. We barely said a word. My whole body was vibrating.

When the dishes were done, we just sort of turned and met each other's eyes. 'So where're you staying?' I asked.

'With an ex-cop buddy of mine, Ron Fazio. He used to be a district sergeant out in Sunset. He's got me on his couch.'

I washed out a pasta pot. 'I have a couch,' I said.

Chapter Sixty-Three

A ll the following day we pounded on the list of names
Warden Estes and his people had given us. Two we
crossed off immediately. A computer check indicated they
had become reassociated with the California Penal System,
presently residing in other institutions.

Something Weiscz had said the day before had stuck in
my head.

'I gave you something,' I had said, as the convict raved
about the white race.

'And I gave you something back,' he glared. The words
hung in my mind. They had first hit me at two in the
morning and I rolled back to sleep. They had accompanied
me on my morning drive. And they were still with me now.

I gave you something back . . .

I slipped my feet out of my pumps and stared out the
window at the freeway ramp starting to back up with
traffic. I tried to retrace my encounter with Weiscz.

He was an animal who never had a chance of seeing the
light of day. Still, I felt there had almost been a moment

with him, a bond. All he wanted in that hellhole was to see what he looked like. *I gave you something back.*

So what did he give me?

You think I give a shit about your dead niggers, he had seethed. *Long live Chimera,* he had hollered as they put him under . . .

Then, slowly, my mind settled on it.

Maybe one of your own assholes finally came to his senses. Sounds like an inside job.

I didn't know if I had gone off the deep end or what. Was I reaching for something that wasn't there? Was Weiscz actually telling me something he could never be held accountable for?

An inside job . . .

I dialed Estes at Pelican Bay. 'Any of your inmates up there ever been an ex-cop?' I asked.

'A cop . . .?' The warden paused.

'Yeah.' I explained why I wanted to know.

'Excuse my French,' Estes shot back, 'but Weiscz was fucking with you. He was trying to get inside your head. The bastard hates cops.'

'You didn't answer my question, Warden.'

'A cop?' Estes grunted a derisive snort. 'We had a bad narcotics inspector out of LA, Bellacora. Shot three of his informants. But he was transferred out. To my knowledge, he's still in Frenso.' I remembered reading about the Bellacora case. It was as dirty and low as law enforcement got.

'We had a customs inspector, Benes, who was running a

dope ring on the side at San Diego Airport.'

'Anyone else?'

'No, not in my six years.'

'What about before that, Estes?'

He grunted impatiently, 'How far back do you want me to go, Lieutenant?'

'How long has Weiscz been there?'

'Twelve years.'

'Then that's how far.'

It was clear the warden thought I was crazy. He hung up saying he would have to get back to me.

I put down the phone. This was wild – trusting Weiscz for anything. He hated cops. I was a cop. He probably hated women, too.

Suddenly, Brenda, my secretary, burst in. She looked stunned. 'Jill Bernhardt's assistant just called in. Ms Bernhardt's collapsed.'

'Collapsed . . .?'

Brenda nodded blankly. 'She's bleeding. Downstairs. She needs you down there, *now*.'

Chapter Sixty-Four

I raced down the stairs to the third floor and then to Jill's office.

As I charged in, she was on the couch, reclined.

An EMS team, which had fortunately been at the morgue, was already present. There were towels, *bloody* towels, stuffed under her dark blue skirt. Her face was averted, but she looked as gray and listless and afraid as I had ever seen her. In an instant, it was clear what had happened.

'Oh, Jill,' I said, kneeling beside her. 'Oh, sweetie. I'm here.'

She smiled when she saw me, slightly wary and afraid. Her normally sharp blue eyes reflected the color of dismal skies. 'I lost it, Lindsay,' she said. 'I should've quit work. I should've listened to them. *To you.* I thought I wanted the baby more than anything, but maybe I didn't. I lost it.'

'Oh, Jill,' I grasped her hand. 'It wasn't you. Don't say that. This was medical. There was a chance of this. You knew that going in. There was always this risk.'

'It was *me*, Lindsay.' Her eyes suddenly welled with tears. 'I think I didn't want it badly enough.'

A female EMS tech asked me to step away, and they hooked Jill up to an IV line and a monitor. My heart went out to her. She was usually so strong and independent. But I had seen a transformation in her; she had been looking forward to this baby so much. How did she deserve this?

'Where's Rich, Jill?' I leaned down to her.

She sucked in a breath. 'Denver. April reached him. He's on his way back.'

Suddenly, Claire burst into the room. 'I came as soon as I heard,' she said. She glanced worriedly at me, then asked the med tech, 'What do you have?'

She was told that Jill's vitals were good, but she'd lost a lot of blood. When Claire mentioned the baby, the technician shook her head.

'Oh, honey,' Claire clasped her hand, kneeling down. 'How're you feeling?'

Tears were running down Jill's face. 'Oh, Claire, I lost it. I lost my baby.'

'You're going to be all right. Don't worry. We're going to take good care of you.' Claire stroked a curl of damp hair off Jill's forehead.

'We have to move her now,' the EMS tech said. 'Her doctor's been called. She's waiting for us at Cal Pacific.'

'We're going with you,' I said. 'We're gonna be with you all the way.'

Jill forced a smile, then stiffened. 'They're going to operate, aren't they?'

'I don't know,' Claire replied.

'I know they are.' Jill shook her head. She had more resolve than anyone I knew, but the scary truth forming in her eyes was something I'll remember the rest of my life.

The door opened and another EMS tech wheeled in a gurney. 'It's time to go,' said the woman who'd been working on her.

I bent down close to Jill. 'We're going to be with you,' I said.

'Don't leave me,' she said, and held my hand.

'You can't get rid of us that easily.'

'Homicide chicks, right?' Jill murmured with a tight smile.

They eased her onto the gurney. Claire and I helped. A bloody towel fell limply onto the floor of her spotless office.

'It's going to be a boy,' Jill whispered, letting out a pained breath. 'I wanted a boy. I guess I can admit it now.'

I folded her hands gently on her lap.

'I just didn't want it badly enough,' she said, and then she finally started to sob and couldn't stop.

Chapter Sixty-Five

W e rode in the back of the EMS truck with Jill, ran alongside the gurney as they wheeled her up to Obstetrics, and waited as her doctors tried to stop the bleeding.

As they moved her into the OR, she gripped my hand. 'They always seem to win,' she murmured. 'No matter how many of these bastards you put away, they always find a way to win.'

Cindy rushed down to the hospital, and the three of us hung there, waiting to see Jill. About two hours in, her husband, Rich, hurried in. We exchanged some awkward hugs, and part of me wanted to tell him, *don't you fucking realize this baby was for you*? When the doctor came out, we let them be alone.

Jill was right. She had miscarried the child, partly due to the stress of her job.

Afterwards, Claire, Cindy and I filed out of the hospital onto Fillmore Street. No one wanted to go home. There was this Japanese place nearby that Cindy knew. We went there and sat around drinking beer and sake.

It was hard to accept how Jill, who worked tirelessly at the office, who rock climbed at Moab and biked the rough terrain in Sedona, had twice been denied a child.

'The poor girl's just too damn hard on herself,' sighed Claire, warming her hands with her sake cup. 'We all told her she had to ratchet it down.'

'Jill doesn't have that gear,' said Cindy.

I picked up a California roll and turned it over and over in the sauce. 'She did it to please Rich. You could see it on her face. She keeps that impossible schedule. She doesn't give anything up. And he's running around the country wining investment bankers.'

'She loves him,' protested Cindy. 'They're a team.'

'They're not a team, Cindy. Claire and Edmund are a team. The two of them, they're a race.'

'It's true,' exhaled Claire. 'That girl always has to be Number One. She can't fail.'

'So which one of us is any different?' Cindy asked. She looked around. Waited.

There was a moment of protracted silence. Our gazes met with a contrite smile.

'But it's deeper than that,' I said. 'Jill's different. She's tough as nails, but in her heart she feels alone. Any of us could be where she is now. We're not invincible. Except you, Claire. You have this mechanism that just keeps it together, you and Edmund and your kids, like that fucking battery rabbit, on and on and on.'

Claire smiled. 'Someone has to provide the balance

around here. You saw your dad the other night, didn't you?'

I nodded. 'It went pretty well. I guess. We talked, we got some things out.'

'No fisticuffs?' Cindy asked.

'No fisticuffs,' I smiled. 'When I opened the door, he had on a catcher's mask, I'm serious.'

Claire and Cindy laughed out loud.

'He brought me this bottle of wine. Fancy, French first-grown. 1966. He bought it the year I was born. Kept it all these years. How do you figure that? He never even knew if he'd ever see me again.'

'He knew he'd see you again,' Claire said with a smile. She sipped her sake. 'You're his beautiful daughter. He loves you.'

'So how'd you leave it, Lindsay?' Cindy asked.

'I guess you could say we agreed to a second date. Actually, I told him he could stay with me for a while.'

Cindy and Claire both blinked.

'We told you to loosen up and see him, Lindsay,' Cindy snorted. 'Not ask him to share the rent.'

'What can I tell you? He was camped out on someone's couch. It seemed like the right thing to do.'

'It is, honey,' Claire smiled. 'Here's to you.'

'Uh-uh,' I shook my head. 'Here's to Jill.'

'Yeah, here's to Jill,' Cindy said, lifting her beer.

We all clinked. Then it was quiet for a moment or two.

'I don't mean to change the subject,' Cindy said, 'but you want to share where you are on the case?'

I nodded. 'We're looking into the Chimera names

Warden Estes gave us. But this afternoon I came up with a new theory.'

'New theory?' Cindy wrinkled her brow.

I nodded. 'Look, this guy's a trained shooter. He's left no clues. He's been one step ahead of us on every move. He knows how we work.'

Cindy and Claire were listening. Not a word. I told them what Weiscz had said to me. *An inside job . . .*

'What if Chimera isn't a crazy, racist killer from one of these radical groups?' I leaned forward. 'What if he's a cop?'

Chapter Sixty-Six

In a dark bar, Chimera sipped his Guinness. The best for the best, he thought.

Next to him, a white-haired man with a blotchy red, dry-as-parchment face was downing Tom Collins's, glancing up at the TV. The news was on. An insipid reporter was giving the latest on the Chimera case, getting it all wrong, insulting the public, insulting *him*.

He kept his eyes peeled across the street through the bar's large window. He had followed the next victim here. This one he would relish. All those cops, chasing down the wrong leads. This kill would really set them on their heels.

It's not over, he muttered under his breath. *And don't ever get the idea that I'm predictable. I'm not.*

The drunk old-timer next to him gave him a nudge. 'I think the bastard's one of *them*,' he said.

'One of *them*?' Chimera asked. 'Watch your elbows. And what the hell are you talking about?'

'Black as the ace of spades,' the old man spat. 'They're combing through those hate groups. Ha, what a laugh.

This is some sick jungle-bunny minus one jar on the shelf. Probably plays in the NFL. Hey, Ray,' he called to the bartender, 'probably plays in the NFL . . .'

'What makes you say that?' Chimera asked, his dark eyes flicking across the street. He was curious about what his public was thinking. Maybe he ought to do more man-on-the-street interviews like this one.

'You think any motherfucker with a set of brains would leave clues like that?' the old man whispered conspiratorially.

'I think you're jumping a little fast, old-timer,' Chimera finally grinned. 'I think this killer's pretty smart.'

'How smart can you be to be a fucking murderer?'

'Smart enough not to get caught,' Chimera said.

The man scowled back at the screen. 'Yeah, well, when it comes out, you watch. They're looking under the wrong rug. There's gonna be one big surprise. Maybe it's OJ. Hey, Ray, someone should check if OJ's in town . . .'

He had taken just about as much as he could of the drunk. But he was right about one thing. The San Francisco cops were lost in space. Man, they didn't have a clue. Lieutenant Lindsay Boxer was nowhere on this. Not even close to him.

'I'll bet you something,' Chimera grinned at the old man. He put his face close to the man's, his eyes wide. 'If they catch him, I'll bet you he has green eyes.'

Suddenly, across the street, he spotted his target on the move. *Well, maybe this will help Lieutenant Boxer focus. A hit real close to home. A little sidebar that he just couldn't resist.*

He tossed a few dollars on the bar.

'Hey, what's the rush?' the old man turned to him. 'Let me buy you another brew. Hey, what the hell, *you got green eyes, buddy.*'

Chimera spun out of his seat. 'Gotta go. There's my date.'

Chapter Sixty-Seven

O n the long drive home, Claire Washburn kept coming back to what had happened to poor Jill. The whole ride down 280 to her home in Burlingame, she couldn't put the terrible thought away.

She exited the highway at Burlingame and wound her way up into the hills. Her head pounded with weariness. It had been such a long day. These terrible murders, pulling the city apart. Then Jill losing her baby.

The digital clock on the dashboard said twenty past ten. Edmund was playing tonight. He wouldn't be home until sometime after eleven. She wished he would be there. Tonight of all nights.

Claire swung onto Skytop, and a few yards later into the driveway of her modern Georgian home. The house was dark, that's how it was these days now that Edmund Jr was away at college. Reggie, her high school sophomore, was no doubt in his room playing video games.

All she wanted to do was to peel off her work clothes

and slip quietly into her pajamas. Put an end to this horrible day . . .

Inside, Claire called out for Reggie and, hearing no response, flashed through the mail on the kitchen table and brought it into the study. She leafed absently through a Ballard Design catalog.

The phone rang. Claire tossed down the catalog and picked up the receiver. 'Hello?'

There was a hollow pause, as if someone was waiting.

Maybe one of Reggie's friends.

'*Hello?*' Claire called again. 'Once, twice, last time . . .' Still no answer. 'Good-bye.'

She placed the phone back on the hook.

A shiver of nervousness went through her. Even after all these years, when she was alone in the house, an unexpected noise, the lights on in the basement, sent a tremor through her.

The phone rang again. This time she picked it up quickly. '*Hello* . . .'

Another annoying pause. This was starting to get her pissed. 'Who is this?' she demanded.

'Take a guess,' a male voice said.

Claire's breath came to a stop. She glanced at her Caller ID. 'Listen, 901-4476,' she said, 'I don't know what your game is or how you got our number. If you've got something to say, say it fast.'

'You know about Chimera?' the voice replied. 'You're speaking to him. Aren't you honored?'

Claire froze. She arched upright in her chair. Her mind

shot into gear: *Chimera was a police department name.* Had it ever been in print? Who knew she was involved in the investigation?

She pressed a separate line, about to punch in 911. 'You better tell me who this really is,' she said.

'I told you. The old bitch was Number One,' the voice replied. 'The little black choir girl, the fat, unsuspecting cop, the boss . . . You know what they all had in common, don't you? Think about it, Claire Washburn. Do *you* have anything in common with the first four victims?'

Claire's body had begun to shake. Her mind drew a mental picture of the elaborate shots that had killed the first victims.

Her eyes shifted outside the study window, to the darkness around her house.

The voice came back, *'Lean a little to the left, huh, Doc?'*

Chapter Sixty-Eight

C laire spun just as the first bullet splintered through the glass.

A second shot shattered the study window and Claire felt burning pain sear her neck. She was down on the floor as a third and fourth shot exploded into the room.

She yanked down the phone, frantic for a dial tone. Her fingers stabbed 911. A startled cry came from her throat. There was blood on the floor, blood from her own neck, seeping onto her dress, her hands. Her heart beat madly. *How bad was it? Had it severed the arterial vein?*

Then she looked to the doorway and her blood froze. *Reggie . . .*

'Mom!' he exclaimed. His eyes were bulging, paralyzed with fear. He was only wearing a T-shirt and briefs. *He was a target.*

'Reggie, get down,' she screamed at him. 'Someone's shooting at the house.'

The boy dove to the floor and Claire scrambled over to him. 'It's okay. Just stay down. Let me think,' she whispered. 'Don't you raise your head an inch.'

The pain in her neck was excruciating, like the skin had been sheared off. She could breathe, though. If the bullet had pierced her arterial, she'd be choking. The gash was surface, had to be.

'Mom, what's going on?' Reggie whispered. His body was trembling like a leaf. She'd never seen him this way.

'I don't know . . . *Just stay down, Reggie.*'

Suddenly, four more shots blazed from outside. She held her son tight. Whoever it was was shooting blindly, trying to hit anything. *Did the killer know she was still alive?* A jolt of panic set in. *What if he came in the house? Did the killer know about her son? He knew her name!*

'Reggie,' she gasped, cupping his head between her hands. 'Get down in the basement. *Lock the door.* Call 911. Crawl! Now! On your stomach!'

'I'm not going to leave you,' he cried.

'Go,' her voice replied, sharply. '*Go now. Do as I say. Stay down! I love you, Reggie.*'

Claire pushed Reggie forward. 'Call 911. Tell them who you are and what's happening. Then call Dad in the car. He should be on his way home.'

Reggie shot her a last pleading look, but he understood. He crawled, face and body pressed to the floor. *Good boy. Your mother didn't raise any dumb ones.*

Another blast of gunfire came from outside. Sucking in a breath, Claire pleaded, 'Please God, don't let that bastard come into our house. Don't let that happen, I beg You.'

Chapter Sixty-Nine

C himera squeezed off four more rounds through the shattered window, smoothly swiveling the PSG-1 rifle in his hands.

He knew he'd hit her. Not with the first shot, she had spun around at the last minute. But with the second, as she was trying to hit the deck. He just didn't know if he had done the job. He wanted to send a message to Lieutenant Lindsay Boxer and just wounding her friend wasn't good enough. Claire Washburn had to die.

He sat in the cover of the dark street, the barrel of the rifle protruding from the car window. He needed to make sure she was dead, but damn it, he didn't want to go into the house. She had a son and he might be in there. One of them might have called 911.

Suddenly, outside lights flashed from a house down the street. At another, someone stepped out onto the lawn.

'Goddamnit,' he seethed. 'Son of a bitch.' Part of him wanted to charge the shattered window and spray the room with a barrage. Washburn had to die. He didn't want to leave without finishing her.

From behind him came a noise. A car turned wildly onto the street, its horn blaring, bright lights flickering on and off. The car sped towards him like some meteor barreling right into his sight.

'What the hell . . .?'

Maybe she had called the cops. Maybe as soon as they heard the shots, the neighbors had. He couldn't risk it. She wasn't the one he would put himself on the line for. He wasn't going to get caught.

The honking, flashing car spun sharply into the driveway of the house. It screeched to a halt. The neighbors began to emerge from their homes.

He slammed the wheel with his hand and pulled in his gun. He put his car in gear and floored it.

It was the first time he had messed up. Ever. Jesus, he never made mistakes.

You're lucky, Doc. But you were target practice anyway.

It was the next one that mattered.

Chapter Seventy

I had taken off my makeup and curled up to watch the late news when Edmund's call came. My father was sitting next to me on the couch.

Claire's husband was frantic, stammering. The impossibility of what he was struggling to describe slammed into me with the force of a train. 'She'll be all right, Lindsay. She's at San Mateo County Hospital now.'

Insisting my father stayed behind, I yanked a fleece pullover over my head, tugged on some jeans and, throwing a top-hat on the roof of the car, raced down to Burlingame. I made the forty-minute drive in under twenty minutes.

I found Claire still in one of the treatment rooms, sitting upright, dressed in the same rust-colored suit I had left her in only three hours before. A doctor was applying a bandage to her neck.

'Jesus, Claire . . .' was all I could manage, my eyes hot and moist. I melted into Edmund, resting my head on his shoulder, and gave him my warmest, most grateful hug.

Then I threw my arms all over Claire.

'Go easy on the TLC, honey,' she winced, jerking her neck. Then she managed a smile. 'I always told you one day these fat cells would come in handy. It takes a helluva shot to reach anything vital in me.'

I was still squeezing her. 'Do you have any idea how lucky you are?'

'*Yeah*,' she exhaled. I could see it in her eyes. 'Believe me, I know.'

The bullet had only grazed her. The ER doctor had cleaned the wound, bandaged it, and was releasing her without even spending the night. Another inch and we wouldn't be talking now.

Claire reached out for Edmund's hand and smiled. 'My men did okay, didn't they? Both of them. Edmund's car scared the sniper away.'

Edmund grimaced. 'I should've chased that bastard myself. If I'd caught him . . .'

'Down, tiger,' Claire smiled. 'Let Lindsay be the heat. You stay a drummer. I always told you,' she said, squeezing his hand, 'Rachmaninov might be in his head, but when it comes to his heart, the man's all Dog E. Dog.'

Almost at once, the reality of what had almost happened seemed to overwhelm him. Edmund's bravado melted away. He sat down, just leaned against Claire for a while, and as he tried to speak, put a hand over his eyes. Claire squeezed his hand without speaking.

A little more than an hour later, after going through the

story with the Burlingame police, we walked the grounds outside her house.

'It was *him*, wasn't it, Claire? It was Chimera.' She shook her head, *yes*.

'He's a real cold sonovabitch, Lindsay. I heard him say, "Lean a little to the left, Doc." Then he started firing.'

Local cops and the San Mateo County Sheriff's office were still scrambling all over the house and yard. I had already called Clapper to come down and lend a hand.

Claire said, 'Why *me*, Lindsay?'

'I don't know, Claire. You're black. You work in law enforcement. I don't understand it myself. Why would he change his pattern?'

'We're talking calm and deliberate, Lindsay. It was like he was toying with me. He made it sound . . . *personal*.'

I thought I saw something I had never seen in her before. *Fear*. Who could blame her? 'Maybe you should take some time off, Claire,' I told her. 'Stay out of sight.'

'You think I'm gonna let him push me under a rock? That's not a possibility, Lindsay. No way I let him win.'

I gave her a gentle hug. 'You're okay?'

'I'm okay. He had his chance. Now I want mine.'

Chapter Seventy-One

I finally dragged myself back to my apartment sometime after two in the morning.

The events of the long, horrible day – Jill losing her child, Claire's terrifying ordeal – flipped by like some old-time nightmare film sequence. The man I was tracking had almost killed my best friend. *Why Claire? What could it mean?* Part of me felt responsible, dirtied by the crime.

My body groaned. I wanted to sleep. I needed to wash away the day. Suddenly, the door to the guest bedroom opened and my father shuffled out. In the madness of the day, I had almost forgotten he was here.

He was wearing a long white T-shirt and boxers with a seashell pattern. Somehow, with the deprivation of sleep, I found this funny.

'You're wearing boxers, Boxer,' I said. 'You're a witty old bastard.' Then I told him what had happened. As a former cop, he would understand. Surprisingly, my father was a good listener. Just what I needed right about then.

He came around to my side of the couch. 'You want

coffee? I'll go make it, Lindsay.'

'Brandy would do the trick better. But there's some Moonlight Sonata tea on the counter there if you're up to it.' It was nice to have someone here and he seemed eager to calm me.

I sank back in the couch, shut my eyes, and tried to figure out what I was going to do next. *Davidson, Mercer, and now Claire Washburn . . .* Why would Chimera come after Claire? What did it mean?

My father came back with a cup of tea and a snifter of Courvoisier two inches full. 'I figure, you're a big girl. So why not *both*.'

I took a sip of tea, then about half the brandy in a gulp. 'Oh, I needed that. Almost as much as I need a break on this case. He's leaving clues, but I still don't get it.'

'Take it easy on yourself, Lindsay,' my father said in the gentlest voice.

'What do you do,' I asked, 'when everyone in the world is watching and you have no idea what to do next? When you realize that whatever you're fighting isn't giving in, that you're fighting a monster?'

'That's about where we usually called in Homicide,' my father said with a smile.

'Don't try to make me laugh,' I begged. But my father had me smiling in spite of everything. Even more surprising to me, I was starting to think of him as my father.

His tone suddenly changed. 'I can tell you what I did when it really got tough. I took off. You won't do that, Lindsay. I can tell. You're so much better than me.'

He was looking squarely at me, no longer smiling.

What happened next I would never have believed. My father's arms just sort of parted, and almost without resistance I found myself burrowing into his shoulder. He wrapped his arms around me, a little tentatively at first, then, just like any father and any daughter, he squeezed me with tender care. I didn't resist. I could smell the same cologne I remembered as a child. It felt both strange and, at the same time, the most natural thing in the world.

Having my father hold me, unexpectedly, it felt like layers of pain were suddenly stripped away.

'You're going to catch him, Lindsay,' I heard him whisper, squeezing me and rocking. 'You will, Buttercup . . .'

It was just what I needed to hear.

'Oh, Daddy,' I said. Nothing more, though.

Chapter Seventy-Two

'Lieutenant Boxer,' Brenda buzzed me early the next morning, 'Warden Estes from Pelican Bay. Line two.' I picked up the phone, not expecting much.

'You asked if we had ever had a policeman imprisoned here,' Estes said.

I perked up immediately. 'And?'

'Mind you, I don't give a shit about some lunatic ravings from Weiscz. But I did go back through the old files. There *was* a case here that might have some relevance. Twelve years ago. I was the warden at Soledad when this scum arrived.'

I took the phone off speaker, pressing the receiver to my ear.

'We had him here for five years. Two of them in "iso." Then we shipped him back to Quentin. A special case. You may even remember the name.'

I picked up a pen and started racking my brain. A cop at Pelican? Quentin?

'Frank Coombs,' Estes said.

I did recognize the name. It was like a headline flashing back from my youth. *Coombs.* A street cop, he had killed a kid in the projects some twenty years before. Got run up on charges. Sent away. To any San Francisco cop, his name was like a warning bell for the use of excessive force.

'Coombs turned into more of a bastard in prison than he was on the outside,' Estes went on. 'He choked a cellmate blue down in Quentin, which is why they shipped him to us. After a stay in the SHUs, we were able to cure him of some of his anti-social tendencies.'

Coombs . . . I wrote down the name. I couldn't remember anything about the case except he had choked and killed this black kid.

'What makes you think this Coombs might fit?' I asked.

'As I said,' Estes cleared his throat, 'I don't much care about Weiscz's ravings. What made me call was that I asked some of our staff. When he was here, Coombs was a charter member of that little group of yours.'

'My group?'

'That's right, Lieutenant. *Chimera.*'

Chapter Seventy-Three

You know the saying – when one door slams in your face, another one opens.

Half an hour later, I rapped on my window for Jacobi. 'What do you know about Frank Coombs?' I asked when he came into my office.

Warren shrugged. 'Dirtbag street cop. Got some teenager in a stranglehold during a drug bust years ago. The kid died. Major departmental scandal when I was in uniform. Didn't he get a dime up in Quentin?'

'Uh-uh, *twenty*.' I slid Coombs's personnel file towards him. 'Now tell me something I can't find in here.'

Warren opened the file. 'As I remember, the guy was a tough cop, decorated, a solid arrest record, but at the same time I figure this file's got enough OCC reprimands for excessive force to rival the Rodney King case.'

I nodded, 'Keep going.'

'You read the file, Lindsay. He busted up a basketball game in one of the projects. Thought he recognized one of the players as some kid he put away for drugs, but was spat back out. The kid said something to him, then he took off. Coombs went after him.'

'We're talking about a black kid,' I interjected. 'They gave him fifteen to twenty, second degree manslaughter.'

Jacobi blinked. 'Where're we going with this, Lindsay?'

'*Weiscz*, Warren. At Pelican Bay. I thought he was just ranting, but something he said stuck. Weiscz said he'd given me something. He said it sounded like an inside job.'

'You dredged up this old file because Weiscz said it was an inside job?' Jacobi screwed his brow.

'Coombs was *Chimera*. He spent two years in the SHUs. Take a look . . . The guy had SWAT training. *He was qualified for marksman status.* He was an avowed racist. And he's *out*. Coombs was released from San Quentin a few months ago.'

Jacobi sat there, stone-faced. 'You're still short a motive, Lieutenant. I mean, granted, the guy was a major asshole. But he was a cop. What would he have against other cops?'

'He pleaded self-defense, that the kid was resisting. No one backed him, Warren. Not his partner, not the other officers on the scene, not the brass.

'You think I'm reaching?' I grabbed the file, skimmed through, and stopped where I had circled a single word in red marker. 'You said Coombs killed this kid in the projects?'

Jacobi nodded.

I pushed the page at him.

'*Bay View*, Warren. *LaSalle Heights*. That's where he

choked that kid. Those projects were torn down and rebuilt in 1990. They were renamed . . .'

'. . . Whitney Young,' Jacobi said.

Where Tasha Catchings had been killed.

Chapter Seventy-Four

My next move was to dial up Madeline Akers, Assistant Warden at San Quentin prison. Maddie was a friend. She told me what she knew about Coombs. 'Bad cop, bad guy, real bad inmate. A cold sonovabitch.' Maddie said she would ask around about him. Maybe Frank Coombs had told somebody what he planned to do once he got outside.

'Madeline, this absolutely can't leak out,' I insisted.

'Mercer was a friend, Lindsay. I'll do anything I can. Give me a couple of days.'

'Make it one, Maddie. This is vital. He's going to kill again.'

For a long time I sat at my desk, trying to piece together just what I had. I couldn't place Coombs at a crime scene. I had no weapon. I didn't even know where he was. But for the first time since Tasha Catchings was killed, I had the feeling I was onto something good.

My instinct was to ask Cindy to troll through the *Chronicle*'s morgue for old stories. These events had happened twenty years before. Only a few people in the department were still around from those days.

Then I remembered I had someone who'd been there staying under my own roof.

I found my father watching the evening news when I walked through the door. 'Hey,' he called. 'You're home at a decent hour. Solve your case?'

I changed my clothes, grabbed a beer from the fridge, then I pulled up a chair across from him.

'I need to talk to you about something.' I looked in his eyes. 'You remember a guy named Frank Coombs?'

My father nodded. 'There's a name I haven't heard in a long time. Sure, I remember him. Cop who choked the kid over in the projects. They brought him up on murder charges. Sent him away.'

'You were on the force, right?'

'Yes, and I knew him. Worst excuse for a cop I ever ran into. Some people were impressed with him. He made arrests, got things done. In his own way. It was different then. We didn't have review committees looking over our shoulder. Not everything we did got into the press.'

'This kid he choked, Dad, he was fourteen.'

'Why do you want to know about Coombs? He's in jail.'

'Not any longer. He's out.' I pulled my chair closer. 'I read that Coombs claimed he killed the kid in self-defense.'

'What cop wouldn't? He said the kid tried to cut him with a sharp object he took to be a knife.'

'You remember who he was partnered up with back then, Dad?'

'Jesus.' My father shrugged. 'Stan Dragula, as I recall. Yeah, he testified at the trial. But I think he died a few years back. No one wanted to work with Coombs. You were scared to walk through the neighborhoods with him.'

'Was Stan Dragula white or black?' I asked.

'Stan was white,' my father answered. 'I think Italian, or maybe Jewish.'

That wasn't the answer I had been expecting. No one had backed Coombs up. But why was he killing *blacks*?

'Dad, if it *is* Coombs doing these things . . . if he is out for some kind of revenge, why against blacks?'

'Coombs was an animal, but he was also a cop. Things were different then. That famous blue wall of silence . . . Every cop is taught at the Academy, keep your yap shut. It'll be there for you. Well, it didn't hold up for Frank Coombs; it came tumbling down on him. Everyone was glad to give him up. We're talking, what, twenty years ago? The affirmative action thing on the force was strong. Blacks and Latinos were just starting to get placed in key positions. There was this black lobby group, the OFJ—'

'Officers for Justice,' I said. 'They're still around.'

My father nodded. 'Tensions were strong. The OFJ threatened to strike. Eventually, there was pressure from the city, too. Whatever it was, Coombs felt he was handed over, hung out to dry.'

It started coming clear to me. Coombs felt he had been railroaded by the black lobby of the department. He had chewed on his hatred in prison. Now, twenty years later, he was back on the streets of San Francisco.

'Maybe, another time, this kind of thing might've been swept under the rug,' I said. 'But not then. The OFJ nailed him.'

Suddenly, a sickening realization wormed into my brain. 'Earl Mercer was involved, wasn't he?'

My father nodded his head. 'Mercer was Coombs's Lieutenant.'

Book Three

The Blue Wall of Silence

Chapter Seventy-Five

The next morning, the case against Frank Coombs, which only a day ago had seemed flimsy, was bursting at the seams. I was pumped.

First thing, Jacobi rapped at my door. 'One for your side, Lieutenant. Coombs is looking better and better.'

'How so? You make any progress with Coombs's PO?'

'You might say. He's gone, Lindsay. According to the PO, Coombs split from this transient hotel down on Eddy. No forwarding address, hasn't checked in, hasn't contacted his ex-wife.'

I was disappointed that Coombs was missing, but it was also a good sign. I told Jacobi to keep looking.

A few minutes later, Madeline Akers called from San Quentin.

'I think I've got what you want,' she announced. I couldn't believe she was responding so soon. 'Over the past year, Coombs was paired with four different cell-mates. Two of them have been paroled, but I spoke with the other two myself. One of them told me to stuff it, but the other, this guy Toracetti . . . I almost didn't even have to tell him what I was looking for. He said the minute he heard on the news about Davidson and Mercer, he knew it was Coombs. Coombs told him he was going to blow the whole thing wide open again.'

I thanked Maddie profusely. *Tasha, Mercer, Davidson . . .* It was starting to fit together.

But how did Estelle Chipman fit in?

A force took hold of me. I went outside and dug through the case files. It had been weeks since I'd looked at them.

I found it buried at the bottom. The personnel file I'd called up from Records: *Edward R. Chipman.*

In his thirty unremarkable years on the force, only one thing stood out.

He had been his district's representative to the OFJ . . . *The Officers for Justice.*

It was time to put this on the record. I buzzed Chief Tracchio. His secretary, Helen, who had been Mercer's secretary, said he was in a closed-door meeting. I told her I was coming up.

I grabbed the Coombs file and headed up the stairs to five. I had to share this. I barreled into the Chief's office.

Then I stopped, speechless.

To my shock, seated around the conference table were Tracchio, Special Agents Ruddy and Hull of the FBI, the press flack Carr, and Chief of Detectives Ryan.

I hadn't been invited to the latest task force meeting.

Chapter Seventy-Six

'This is bullshit,' I said. 'It's total crap. What is this, some kind of a men's club?'

Tracchio, Ruddy and Hull, Carr, Ryan. Five boys seated around the table – minus me, the woman.

The Acting Chief stood up. His face was red. 'Lindsay, we were about to call you up.'

I knew what this meant. What was going on. Tracchio was going to shift control on the case. *My* case. He and Ryan were going to hand it over to the FBI.

'We're at a critical moment in this case,' Tracchio said.

'You're damn right,' I cut him off. I swept my gaze over the group. '*I know who it is.*'

Suddenly, all eyes turned my way. The boys were silent. It was like the lights had been cranked up and my skin prickled as if it were cauterized.

I leveled my eyes back on Tracchio. 'You want me to lay it out for you? Or do you want me to leave?'

Seemingly dumbfounded, he pulled out a chair for me.

I didn't sit. I stood. Then I took them through everything,

and I enjoyed it. How I was skeptical at first, but then it began to fit. Chimera, Pelican Bay, his grudge against the police force. At the sound of Coombs's name, the departmental people's eyes grew wide. I linked the victims, Coombs's qualification as a marksman, how only a marksman could have made those shots.

When I finished, there was silence again. They just stared. I wanted to pump my arm in victory.

Agent Ruddy cleared his throat. 'So far, I haven't heard a thing that links Coombs directly to any of the crime scenes.'

'Give me another day or two and you will,' I said. 'Coombs is the killer.'

Hull, Ruddy's broad-shouldered partner, shrugged optimistically towards the Chief. 'You want us to follow this up?'

I couldn't believe it. This was *my* case. *My* breakthrough. *Homicide*'s. Our people had been murdered.

Tracchio seemed to mull it over. He pursed his thick lips, like he was sucking a last drop through a straw. Then he shook his head towards the FBI man.

'That won't be necessary, Special Agent. This has always been a city case. We'll see it through with city personnel.'

Chapter Seventy-Seven

Only one thing was standing in the way now. We had to find Frank Coombs.

Coombs's prison file mentioned a wife, Ingrid, who had divorced him while he was in prison and remarried. It was a long shot. The PO said he hadn't been in touch. But long shots were coming in right now.

'C'mon, Warren,' I nudged Jacobi, 'you're coming with me. It'll be like old times.'

'Awhh, ain't that sweet.'

Ingrid Bell lived on a pleasant, middle-class street off of Laguna, where Forest Hills wound down towards the flats of Outer Sunset.

We parked across the street, went up and rang the bell. No one answered. We didn't know if Coombs's ex-wife worked, and there was no car in the driveway.

Just as we were about to head back, an old-model Volvo station wagon pulled into the driveway.

Ingrid Bell looked about fifty, with stringy brown hair. She wore a plain, shapeless blue dress under a heavy gray sweater. She climbed out of the car and opened the rear hatch to unload groceries.

An old cop's wife, she ID'd us the minute we walked up. 'What do you people want with me?' she asked.

'A few minutes. We're trying to locate your ex-husband.'

'You got a nerve coming around here,' she scowled, hoisting two bags in her arms.

'We're just checking all the possibilities,' Jacobi said.

She snapped back, 'Like I told his parole officer, I haven't heard a word from him since he got out.'

'He hasn't been to see you?'

'Once, when he got out. He came by to pick up some personal stuff he thought I had held for him. I told him I threw it all out.'

'What kind of effects?' I asked.

'Useless letters, newspaper articles on the trial. Probably the old guns he kept around. Frank was always into guns. Stuff only a man with nothing to show for his life would find value in.'

Jacobi nodded. 'So what'd he do then?'

'What'd he do?' Ingrid Bell snorted. 'He left without a word about what life had been like for us for the past twenty years. Without a word about me or his son. You believe that?'

'And you have no idea where we could contact him?'

'None. That man was poison. I found someone who's treated me with respect. Adopted my boy. I don't want to see Frank Coombs again.'

I asked, 'You have any idea if he might be in touch with your son?'

'No way. I kept them apart since he went to prison. My son doesn't have any links to his father. And don't go buzzing around him. He's in college at Stanford.'

I stepped forward. 'Anyone who might know where he is, Ms Bell, it would be a help to us. This is a murder case.'

I saw the slightest sign of hesitation. 'I've lived a good life for seventeen years. We're a family now. I don't want anyone knowing this came from me.'

I nodded. I felt the blood rushing to my head.

'Frank kept up with Tom Keating. Even when he was locked away. Anyone knows where he is, it'd be him.'

Tom Keating. I knew the name.

He was a retired cop.

Chapter Seventy-Eight

Less than an hour later, Jacobi and I pulled up in front of condo 3A at the Blakesly Residential Community, down the coast in Half Moon Bay.

Keating's name had stuck in my mind from when I was a kid. He'd been a regular at the Alibi after the nine-to-four shift, where many afternoons I'd been hoisted up on a bar stool by my father. In my mind, Keating had a ruddy complexion and a shock of prematurely white hair. *God*, I thought, *that was almost thirty years ago.*

We knocked on the door of Keating's modest, slatted-wood condo. A trim, pleasant-looking woman with gray hair answered.

'Mrs Keating? I'm Lieutenant Lindsay Boxer of the San Francisco Homicide detail. This is Inspector Jacobi. Is your husband at home?'

'*Homicide?*' she said, surprised.

'Just an old case,' I said with a smile.

A voice called from inside, 'Helen, I can't find the damned clicker anywhere.'

'Just a minute, Tom. He's in the back,' she said, as she motioned us into the house.

We walked through the sparsely furnished house and into a sun room overlooking a small patio. There were several framed police photos on the wall. Keating was as I remembered him, just thirty years older. Gaunt, white hair thinning, but with that same ruddy complexion.

He sat watching an afternoon news show with the stock market tape streaming by. I realized he was sitting in a wheelchair.

Helen Keating introduced us, then, finding the clicker, turned the TV volume down. Keating seemed pleased to have visitors from the force.

'I don't get to many functions much since my legs went. Arthritis, they tell me. Brought on by a bullet to lumbar four. Can't play golf anymore,' he chuckled, 'but I can still watch the old pension grow.'

I saw him studying my face. 'You're Marty Boxer's little girl, aren't you?'

I smiled. 'The Alibi . . . A Coors and a 5-0-1, right, Tom?' A 5-0-1 was the call for back-up, and how they used to call for their favorite drink, an Irish whiskey with a beer chaser.

'I heard you were quite the big-shot these days,' Keating nodded with a toothy smile. 'So, what brings you two honchos down to talk to an old street cop?'

'Frank Coombs,' I said.

Keating's features suddenly turned hard. 'What about Frank?'

'We're trying to find him, Tom. I was told you might know where he is.'

'Why don't you call his parole officer? That wouldn't be me.'

'He's split, Tom. Four weeks now. Quit his job.'

'So they got Homicide following up on parole offenders now?'

I held Keating's eyes. 'What do you say, Tom?'

'What makes you think I'd have any idea?' He glanced towards his legs. 'Old times are old times.'

'I heard you guys kept in touch. It's important.'

'Well, you're wasting your time here, Lieutenant,' he said, suddenly turning formal.

I knew he was lying. 'When was the last time you spoke with Coombs?'

'Maybe just after he got out. Could be once or twice since then? He needed some help to get on his feet. I may have lent him a hand.'

'And where was he staying,' Jacobi cut in, 'while you were lending him this hand?'

Keating shook his head. 'Some hotel down on Eddy or O'Farrell. Wasn't the St Francis,' he said.

'And you haven't spoken with him since?' My eyes flicked towards Helen Keating.

'What do you want with the man anyway?' Keating snapped. 'He's done his time. Why don't you just leave him alone?'

'It would be easier this way, Tom,' I said. 'If you'd just talk to us.'

Keating pursed his dry lips, trying to size up where his loyalties fell.

'You put in thirty years, didn't you?' Jacobi said.

'Twenty-four.' He patted his leg. 'Got it cut short at the end.'

'Twenty-four good years. It'd be a shame to dishonor it in any way by not cooperating now . . .'

He shot back, 'You want to know who was a goddamn *expert* in lack of cooperation? Frank Coombs. Man was only doing his job, and all those bastards, supposedly his friends, looked the other way. Maybe that's the way you do things now, with your community action meetings and your sensitivity training. But then we had to get the bad guys off the streets. With the means that we had.'

'Tom,' his wife raised her voice, 'Frank Coombs killed a boy. These people, they're your friends. They want to speak with him. I don't know how far you have to take this duty and loyalty thing. Your duty's here.'

Keating glared at her harshly. 'Yeah, sure, my duty's here.' He picked up the TV clicker and turned back to me. 'Stay here all day if you like, I don't have the slightest idea where Frank Coombs is.'

He turned up the volume on his TV.

Chapter Seventy-Nine

'Fuck him,' Jacobi said as we left the house. 'Old school asshole.'

'We're halfway down the peninsula already,' I said to him. 'You want to drive down to Stanford? See Frankie's kid?'

'What the hell,' he shrugged, 'I can use the education.'

We hooked back onto 280 and made it to Palo Alto in under half an hour.

As we pulled onto the campus drive – the tall palms lining the road, the stately ochre buildings with their red roofs, the Hoover Tower rising majestically over the Main Quad – I felt the spell of being part of campus life. Every one of these kids was special and talented. I even felt some pride that Coombs's son, despite his rough beginnings, had made it here.

We checked in at the administrative office on the Main Quad. A dean's assistant told us Rusty Coombs was probably at football practice down at the field house. Said Rusty was a good student, and a great tight end. We drove there, and a student manager in a red Stanford cap took us upstairs and asked us to wait outside the weight room.

Moments later, a solidly built, orange-haired kid in a sweaty Cardinals' T-shirt wandered out. Rusty Coombs had a friendly face spotted with a few freckles. He had none of the dark, brooding belligerence I had seen in photos of his father.

'I guess I know why you guys are here,' he said, coming up to us. 'My mom called, told me.'

The heavy sound of weight irons and lifting machines clanged in the background. I smiled affably. 'We're looking for your father, Rusty. We were wondering if you have any idea where he might be?'

'He's not my father,' the boy said, and shook his head. 'My father's name is Theodore Bell. He's the one who brought me up with Mom. Teddy taught me how to catch a football. He's the one who told me I could make it to Stanford.'

'When was the last time you heard from Frank Coombs?'

'What's he done anyway? My mother said you guys are from Homicide. We know what's in the news. Everyone knows what's going on up there. Whatever he did before, he paid his time, didn't he? You can't believe just because he made some mistakes twenty years ago, he's responsible for these terrible crimes?'

'We wouldn't have driven all the way down unless it was important,' Jacobi said.

The football player shifted back and forth on the balls of

his feet. He seemed to be a likeable kid, cooperative. He rubbed his hands together. 'He came here once. When he first got out. I had written him a couple of times in jail. I met with him in town. I didn't want anybody to see him.'

'What did he say to you?' I asked.

'I think all he wanted was to clear his own conscience. And know what my mother thought of him. Never once did he say, "Hey, great job, Rusty. Look at you. You did good." Or, "Hey, I follow your games . . ." He was more interested in knowing if my mom had thrown out some of his old things.'

'What sort of things?' I asked. What would be so important that he would drive all the way here and confront his son?

'Police things,' Rusty Coombs said, and shook his head. 'Maybe his guns. That's what I remember about my father, Lieutenant. Him down in the basement, tinkering with his guns.'

I smiled sympathetically. I knew what it was like to look at your father with something less than admiration. 'He give you any idea where he might go?'

Rusty Coombs shook his head. He looked like he might tear up. 'I'm not Frank Coombs. I may have his name, I may even have to live with what he did, but I'm not him. Please leave our family alone. Please.'

Chapter Eighty

W ell, that sucked. Stirring up bad memories for
Rusty Coombs made me feel terrible. Even Jacobi
agreed.

We made it back to the office about four. We'd driven all
the way down to Palo Alto just to run into another dead
end. What fun.

There was a phone message waiting for me. I called
Cindy back immediately. 'There's a rumor floating around
that you've narrowed on a suspect,' she said. 'Truth or
dare?'

'We have a name, Cindy, but I can't tell you anything. We
just want to bring him in for questioning.'

'So there's no warrant?'

'Cindy . . . not just yet.'

'I'm not talking about a story, Lindsay. He went after our
friend. Remember? If I can help . . .'

'I got a hundred cops working on it, Cindy. Some of us
have even handled an investigation or two before. Please,
trust me.'

'But if you haven't brought him in, then you haven't *found* him, right?'

'Or maybe we haven't made the case yet. And Cindy, that's not for print.'

'This is *me* talking, Linds. Claire, too. And Jill. We're in this case, Lindsay. All of us.'

She was right. Unlike any other homicide case I had worked, this one seemed to be growing more and more personal. *Why was that?* I didn't have Coombs and I could use the help. The longer he stayed free, anything could happen.

'I do need your help. Go through your old files, Cindy. You just didn't go far back enough.'

She paused, then sucked in a breath. 'You were right, weren't you? The guy's a cop.'

'You can't go with that, sweetie. And if you did, you'd be wrong. But it's damned close.'

I felt her analyzing, and also biting her tongue. 'We're still going to meet, aren't we?'

I smiled. 'Yeah, we're going to meet. We're a team. More than ever.'

I was about to pack it in for the night when a call buzzed through to my line. I was sitting around thinking that Tom Keating had been lying. That he'd spoken to Coombs. But until we put out a warrant, Keating could hold back all he wanted.

To my utter surprise it was his wife on the phone. I almost dropped the receiver.

'My husband's a stubborn man, Lieutenant,' she started,

clearly nervous. 'But he wore the uniform with pride. I've never asked him to account for anything. And I won't start now. But I can't sit back. Frank Coombs killed that boy. And if he's done something else, I refuse to wake up every morning for the rest of my life knowing I abetted a murderer.'

'It would be better for everybody, Mrs Keating, if your husband told us what he knew.'

'I don't know what he knows,' she said, 'and I believe him when he says he hasn't spoken to Coombs in some time. But he wasn't telling the whole truth, Lieutenant.'

'Then why don't you start.'

She hesitated. 'Coombs *did* come by here. Once. Maybe two months ago.'

'Do you know where he is?' My blood started to rush.

'No,' she answered. 'But I did take a message from him. For Tom. I still have the number.'

I fumbled for a pen.

She read me the number: *434-9117*. 'I'm pretty sure it was some kind of boarding house or hotel.'

'Thank you, Helen.'

I was about to hang up when she said, 'There's one more thing. When my husband said he lent Coombs a hand, he wasn't telling the whole story. Tom did give him some money. He also let him rummage through some old things.'

'What sort of things?' I asked.

'His old department things. Maybe an old uniform, and a badge.'

That's what Coombs had been looking for in his ex-wife's house. His old police uniforms. My mind clicked. *Maybe he was going to use them to get close to his next victims . . .*

'That's all?' I asked.

'No,' Helen Keating said. 'Tom kept guns down there. Coombs took those, too.'

Chapter Eighty-One

Within minutes I traced the number Helen Keating had given me to a boarding house on Larkin and McAlister. The Hotel William Simon. My pulse was jumping.

I called Jacobi, catching him as he was about to sit down to dinner. 'Meet me at Larkin and McAlister. The Hotel William Simon.'

'You want me to meet you at a hotel? Cool. I'm on my way.'

'I think we found Coombs.'

We couldn't arrest Frank Coombs. We didn't have a single piece of evidence that could tie him directly to a crime. I might be able to get a search warrant and bust into his room, though. Right now, the most important thing was to make certain he was still there.

Twenty minutes later, I had driven down to the seedy area between the Civic Center and Union Square. The William Simon was a shabby, one-elevator dive under a large billboard with a slinky model wearing Calvin Klein underwear. As Jill would say, *yick*.

I didn't want to go up to the desk, flashing my badge and his photo, until we were ready to make a move. Finally, I thought, *what the hell*, and placed a call to the number Helen Keating had given me. After three rings, a male voice answered, 'William Simon . . .'

'Frank Coombs?' I inquired.

'*Coombs . . .*' I listened as the desk clerk leafed through a list of names. 'Nope.'

Shit. I asked him to double-check. He came back negative.

Just then, the passenger door of my Explorer opened, my nerves twanging like a bass guitar.

Jacobi climbed in. He was wearing a striped golf shirt and some sort of short, hideous Members Only jacket. His belly bulged at the waist. He grinned like a john. 'Hey, lady, what does an Andrew Jackson get me?'

'Dinner maybe, if you're treating.'

'We got an ID?' he asked.

I shook my head. I told him what I had found out.

'Maybe he's moved on,' Jacobi offered. 'How 'bout I go in and flash the badge. With Coombs's photo?'

I shook my head. 'How 'bout we sit here and wait.'

We waited for over two hours. Stakeouts are incredibly dull. They would drive the average person nuts. We kept our eyes peeled on the William Simon, going over every-thing from Helen Keating, to what Jacobi's wife was serving for dinner, to the 49ers, to who's sleeping with who at the Hall. Jacobi even sprung for a couple of sandwiches from a Subway.

At ten o'clock, Jacobi grumbled, 'This could go on forever. Why don't you let me go inside, Lindsay?'

He was probably right. We didn't even know if Helen Keating's number was current. She had taken it weeks ago.

I was about to give in when a man turned the corner on Larkin headed towards the hotel. I gripped Jacobi's arm. 'Look over there.'

It was Coombs. I recognized the bastard instantly. He was wearing an Army khaki coat, hands stuffed in his pockets, a floppy hat pulled over his eyes.

'Son of a fucking bitch,' Jacobi muttered.

Watching the bastard slink up to the hotel, it took everything I had not to jump out of the car and slam him up against the wall. I wished I could slap him in cuffs. But we had Chimera now. We knew where he was.

'I want someone stuck to him twenty-four hours,' I told Jacobi. 'If he makes the tail, I want him picked up. We'll figure out the charges later.'

Jacobi nodded.

'I hope you brought a toothbrush,' I winked. 'You've got first watch.'

Chapter Eighty-Two

A s they walked hand in hand down Twenty-fourth Street towards her Noe Valley apartment, Cindy admitted to herself that she was scared shitless.

This was the fifth time she and Aaron Winslow had been out together. They had seen Cyrus Chestnut and Freddie Hubbard at the Blue Door; been to 'Traviata' at the Opera; taken the ferry across the Bay to a tiny Jamaican café that Aaron knew. Tonight they had seen this dreamy film, *Chocolat*.

No matter where this went later, she enjoyed being with him. He was deeper than most men she'd dated, and he was definitely more sensitive. Not only did he read unexpected books like Dave Eggers' *A Heartbreaking Work of Staggering Genius* and *The Bonesetter's Daughter*, he lived the life that he preached. He worked twelve- to sixteen-hour days, was loved in his neighborhood, but he still managed to keep his ego in check. She'd heard it over and over again interviewing people for her story. Aaron Winslow was one of the good guys.

All the while, though, Cindy felt this moment looming in the distance. Hurtling closer and closer. Ticking. This was the natural step, she told herself. As Lindsay would say, their foxhole was about to explode.

'You seem a little quiet tonight,' Aaron said. 'You okay, Cindy?'

'No, I'm great,' she fibbed. She thought he was just about the sweetest man she had ever gone out with, but, *Jesus, Cindy, he's a pastor. Why didn't you think of this then? Is this a good idea? Think it through. Don't hurt him. Don't get hurt yourself.*

They stopped walking in front of the entrance to 2450 Noe and stood in the lighted arch. He sung a line from an old R&B tune, 'I've Passed This Way Before'. He even had a good singing voice.

There was no use postponing it any longer. 'Look, Aaron, someone has to say this. You want to come up? I'd like it if you did, *hate* it if you didn't.'

He exhaled, and smiled. 'I don't exactly know where to take this, Cindy. I'm a little out of my range. I, uh, I've never dated a blonde before. I wasn't expecting any of this.'

'I can relate to that,' she smiled. 'But it's only two floors up. We can talk about it there.'

His lip was quivering slightly, and when he touched her arm it sent a shiver down her spine. God, she did like him. And she trusted him.

'I feel like I'm about to cross this line,' he said. 'And it's not a line I can cross casually. So I have to know. Are we there together? In the same place?'

Cindy elevated herself on her toes and pressed her lips lightly against his mouth. Aaron seemed surprised, and at first stiffened, but slowly he placed his arms around her and gave himself over to the kiss.

It was just as she had hoped, that first real kiss. Tender and breathtaking. Through his jacket she could feel the rhythm of his heart pounding. She liked it that he was afraid, too. It made her feel even closer to him.

When they parted she looked in his eyes and said, 'We're there. We're in the same place.'

She took out her key and led him up the two floors to her place. Her heart was pounding too.

'It's great,' he said. 'I'm not just saying that.' A two-story wall of bookshelves and an informal open kitchen. 'It's you . . . Cindy, it seems silly that I haven't been up here before.'

'It wasn't for lack of trying,' Cindy grinned. God, she was so *nervous*.

He took hold of her again, this time giving her a longer kiss. He certainly knew how to kiss. Every cell in her body seemed alive. The small hairs on her arms, the warmth in her thighs; she pressed herself against him. She wanted, needed, to be close to him now. His body was slender, but he was definitely strong.

Cindy started to smile. 'So what were you waiting for?'

'I don't know. Maybe some kind of sign.'

She pressed herself into the grooves of his body, felt him come alive. '*There's* a sign,' she smiled, close to his face.

'I guess my secret's out now. Yes, I *do* like you, Cindy.'

Suddenly the phone rang, almost blasting in their ears.

'Oh, God,' she groaned. 'Go away, leave us alone.'

'I hope that's not another sign,' he laughed.

Each ring seemed more annoying than the last. Mercifully, the answering machine finally kicked on.

'Cindy, it's Lindsay,' the voice shot. 'I've got something important. *Please.* Pick. Up.'

'Go ahead,' Aaron said.

'Now that you're finally up here, don't use the time I'm on the phone to change your mind.'

She reached behind the couch, fumbled for the receiver, put it to her ear. 'I wouldn't do this for anyone but you . . .' she said.

'Funny, that's just what I was about to say. Listen to this.' Lindsay shared her news and Cindy felt a rush of triumph surge through her. This was what she had wanted. It had been her angle that put Lindsay onto him. Yes!

'Mañana,' she said, 'and thanks for the phone call.' She placed the receiver down, squeezed back with Aaron, and looked into his eyes.

'You wanted a sign. I think I've got the best one in the world.' A glimmer lit her face.

'*They found him, Aaron.*'

Chapter Eighty-Three

We kept watch all night at the William Simon. Unofficially. So far, Coombs hadn't come out again. I knew where he was. Now all I had to do was make the case.

That was the morning that Jill came back to work. I stopped at her office to bring her up to date. Coming off the elevator on the third floor, I ran into Claire, who must've had the same idea.

'Great minds and all that,' she said.

'I've got big news,' I told her, beaming with anticipation. 'C'mon . . .'

We knocked on her door and found Jill at her desk, looking a little peaked. Stacks of documents and legal files gave the impression she hadn't missed a single day. At the sight of us her blue eyes sprang alive, but as she stood, her arms outstretched for a hug, she seemed to be moving at half her usual speed.

'*Don't,*' I said. I went over and gave her a hug. 'You've got to take it easy.'

'I'm fine,' she answered, quickly. 'Abdomen's a little stiff, heart's a little broken. But I'm here. And this is the best thing for me.'

'You *sure* this is the smartest thing?' Claire asked her.

'It is for me,' Jill shot back. 'I promise, Doc, I'm *fine*. So please, don't start trying to convince me otherwise. You want to help me start to heal, just bring me up to date on what's going on.'

We looked at her, a little skeptically. But then I had to share the news. 'I think we found him.'

'Who?' Jill asked.

I beamed. '*Chimera.*'

Claire gave me a stare. She closed her eyes for a moment, as if in prayer, then opened them with a sigh.

Jill looked impressed. 'Jesus, you sonsabitches *have* been busy while I've been away.'

They asked all the right questions, and I laid it all out for them. When I told them the name, Jill muttered, '*Coombs* . . . I remember the case from law school.' A spark lit in her sharp blue eyes. 'Frank Coombs. He killed a teenage boy.'

'You're *sure* it's him?' Claire asked. She was still wearing a bandage on her neck.

'I hope so,' I said. Then, without any doubt, 'Yes, I'm sure it's him.'

'You arrest him yet?' Claire asked. 'Can I visit him in his cell? Hmmm? I've got this bullbat I've been meaning to try out.'

'Not yet. He's holed up at some dive in the Tenderloin.

We've got him under twenty-four-hour watch.'

I turned to Jill. 'What do you say, Counselor? I want to bring him in.'

She came over a little gingerly, and leaned on the corner of her desk. 'Okay, tell me exactly what you have.'

I went through each link: the loose connections to three of the victims; Coombs's history as a marksman; his documented grudge against blacks; how the OFJ had sealed his fate. But with each strand of evidence I saw her conviction dim.

'Jill, listen,' I held up my hand. 'He took a department-issued .38 from a retired cop and Mercer was killed with a .38. Three of the targets tie directly to his own history. I've got a guy in San Quentin who says he boasted he was out for revenge . . .'

'Thirty-eights are a dime a dozen, Lindsay. Do you have a match on the gun?'

'No, but Jill, Tasha Catchings' murder took place at the same spot where Coombs went down twenty years before.'

She cut me off. 'What about a witness who can place him at the scene? One witness, Lindsay?'

I shook my head.

'A print then, or a piece of clothing. Something that ties him to one of the murders?'

With an exasperated breath, I reacted, 'No.'

'Circumstantial evidence can convict, Jill,' Claire cut in. 'Coombs is a monster. We can't just let him stay out on the streets.'

Jill looked sharply at both of us. Jeez, she was almost the Jill of old. 'You don't think I want him as much as you? You don't think I look at you, Claire, and think just how close we came . . . But there's no weapon, barely a motive. You haven't even placed him within sight of a murder scene. If you bust in and don't find anything, you've lost him for good.'

'Coombs is Chimera, Jill,' I said. 'I know I don't have it buttoned up yet, but I've got a motive and links which tie him to three victims. As well as outside testimony that corroborates his intentions.'

'Jailhouse testimony,' said Jill. 'Juries laugh at it these days.'

She got up, came over and put a hand on both Claire's and mine. 'Look, I know how badly you want to close this. I'm your friend, but I'm still the law. Bring me anything, someone who saw him at a scene, a print he left on a door. Give me *anything*, Lindsay, and I'll be bashing down his door to get at him, same as you. Turn him upside down, rattle him until his spare change falls out.'

I stood there, teeming with frustration and anger, but knowing that Jill was right. I shook my head and made my way towards the door.

'What are you going to do?' asked Claire.

'*Rattle* the fucker. Turn his life upside down.'

Chapter Eighty-Four

Fifteen minutes later, Jacobi and I picked up Cappy outside the William Simon and headed into the run-down lobby of the hotel. Behind the front desk a sleepy-eyed Sikh was leafing through a newspaper in his native tongue. Jacobi thrust Coombs's photo and his badge in front of the man's startled eyes.

'What room?'

It took about three seconds for the turbaned clerk to squint at the photo, flip through a bound black register, and in a tight accent stammer, 'T-ree-oh-sevon. He is registered with the name *Burns* . . .' He pointed. 'Ele-vator to the right.'

Moments later, we stood in the dingy, paint-chipped hallway on the third floor, across from Coombs's room, flicking our automatics off safety.

'Remember, we're only talking,' I cautioned. 'Keep your eyes open for anything we can use.'

Jacobi and Cappy nodded, then each took a position straddling the door. Cappy knocked.

No one answered.

He knocked again. 'Mr Frank Burns?'

Finally, a heavy, grumbling voice. 'Go the fuck away. Get lost, huh? I'm paid up through Friday.'

Jacobi shouted, 'San Francisco Police, Mr Burns. We got you your morning coffee.'

There was a long pause. I heard some commotion, the sound of a chair being dragged and a drawer closed. Finally, the sound of footsteps coming closer and a voice barking, 'What the fuck do you want?'

'Just to ask a few questions. You mind opening the door?'

It took about a minute of waiting with our fingers tensed on the triggers for the door to finally unlatch.

It swung open, revealing Coombs's angry face.

Chimera.

His face was round and heavy, with eyes that sagged into deep-set craters. Short, graying hair, a large, flat nose, mottled skin. He had on a white, short-sleeve undershirt pulled over rumpled gray trousers. And his eyes *burned* with hatred and disdain.

'*Here,*' exclaimed Jacobi, swatting him in the chest with a rolled-up *Chronicle*, 'your morning paper. Mind if we come in?'

'Yeah, I mind,' Coombs scowled.

Cappy smiled. 'Anyone ever tell you you're a dead ringer for this cat who used to be on the force? What the hell was the cat's name? Oh yeah, Coombs. *Frank Coombs*. You ever hear that from anybody before?'

Coombs blinked, impassively, then his mouth curled into a half-smile. 'Wouldn't you know, I get boarded on planes for him all the time.'

If he recognized Jacobi or Cappy from years ago on the force, he didn't register it, but he squinted a look of familiarity as his gaze fell on me. 'Don't tell me, after all this time, you bozos are the department's welcome home committee?'

'How 'bout you let us in?' Jacobi asked.

'You come with a warrant?' Coombs leered.

'I told you nicely, we're just delivering your morning paper.'

'Then make a fucking scene. C'mon,' Coombs said between gritted teeth. His eyes were something else; they burned a hole right into the back of your skull.

Cappy pressed the door firmly in his face, then he and Jacobi pushed their way into the room. 'As long as we're here, we might as well run a couple of questions by you.'

Coombs rubbed his unshaven face, glaring vicious darts at us. He finally pulled out a wooden chair from a small table and took a seat with his arms wrapped around its back. 'Fuckers,' he muttered. 'Useless shitbirds.'

The tiny hotel room was littered with newspapers, Budweiser bottles lined up on the sill, cigarette butts in Coke cans. I had the sense that if I could only poke around, *something was there*.

'This is Lieutenant Boxer of the Homicide detail,' Jacobi started in. 'We're Inspectors Jacobi and Thomas.'

'Congratulations,' Coombs grinned. 'I feel safer already.

What do you Three Stooges want?'

'Like I said,' Jacobi cut in, 'you should read the papers. Keep abreast of what's going on. You follow what's in the news much?'

'You got something to say, say it,' Coombs said.

'Why don't you start by telling us where you were three nights ago,' I started. 'Tuesday? Around eleven o'clock.'

'Why don't you kiss my ass,' Coombs sneered. 'You want to play games, let's play. I was either at the ballet, or the opening of that new art exhibition. I can't recall. My schedule's too full these days.'

'Simplify it for us,' Cappy glared.

'Sure. Yeah. Actually, I was with friends.'

'These friends,' Jacobi cut in, 'they have names, phone numbers? I'm sure they'd be happy to vouch for you.'

'Why?' Coombs's mouth puckered into a slight grin. 'You got someone who says I was somewhere else?'

'I guess what I was thinking,' I met his eyes, 'was when was the last time you made it out to Bay View? Your old stomping grounds? Maybe I should say – your choking grounds.'

Coombs's glare stiffened. I could tell he wanted to wrap his hands around my neck.

'So he *does* read the papers,' Cappy chortled.

The ex-con glared. 'What the fuck, Inspector, you think I'm some rookie whose knees start to shake when you wag your dick at him? Sure, I read the papers. You assholes can't solve your case, so you come up here and shake my bush for old times. You've got zip on me, otherwise you wouldn't be lap dancing in my face and we'd be having this talk down at the Hall. You think I killed all those dingo bastards, then lock me up. Otherwise – Oh, look at the time, my town car's waiting. Are we done?'

I wanted to take him by the throat and smack his smug face against the wall. But Coombs was right. We *couldn't* take him in. Not with what we had. 'There are a few questions you're going to have to answer, Mr Coombs. You'll have to answer why three people are dead who had a connection to your manslaughter charge twenty years ago. You'll have to answer what you were doing on the nights that they were killed.'

The veins on Coombs's forehead started to bulge. Then he calmed, and his mouth curled into a smile. 'You must be up here, Lieutenant, 'cause you've got some eyewitnesses that can place me at one of the murder scenes.'

I glared in his face without answering.

'Or my prints all over some weapon? Or fibers from this rug, right, or my clothing? You just came up here to let me turn myself in with dignity?'

I stood there inches from Chimera, watching his arrogant grin. 'You think just because you Affirmative Action flunkees come up here and look tough at me, I'm gonna shove up my ass and say, "Hey, stick it here . . ."? It gives me a real kick seeing those assholes drop one by one. You took my life away. You want to make me sweat, Lieutenant, then *pretend* you're real cops. Find something that will stick.'

I stood there, glaring into those cold, haughty eyes. I

wanted to take him down so bad. I was tempted. 'Consider yourself a murder suspect, Mr Coombs. You know the routine. Don't leave town. We'll be back to see you soon.'

I nodded at Cappy and Jacobi. We got up and moved towards the door.

'One more thing,' I turned back with a grin of my own. 'Just so you know. From Claire Washburn . . . *Lean a little to the left, huh, asshole.*'

Chapter Eighty-Five

I was totally wired after work. There was just no way I could go home and unwind.

I headed down Brannan towards Potrero, my mind replaying the gut-stabbing interview with Coombs. He was taunting us, laughing in our faces, knowing we couldn't bring him in.

I knew who Chimera was . . . but I couldn't touch him.

I stopped at a light, not wanting to go home, but not knowing where else to go. Cindy had a date; Jill and Claire were home with their husbands; I probably could have a date, if I made myself the least bit available.

I thought about calling Claire, but my cell phone was down – I needed to recharge the damn battery. I wanted to do something; the urgency was ripping through me.

If I could only get into Coombs's hotel room . . . I felt torn between heading home, or possibly making the biggest mistake of my career. My rational voice said, *Lindsay, go home, get him tomorrow. He's going to mess up soon.*

The pounding in my heart said, *Uh-uh, baby . . . stay on him.*

Rattle the fucker.

I swung my Explorer onto Seventh and headed for the Tenderloin district. It was almost nine o'clock.

My car seemed to drive itself to the William Simon. My chest felt tight and pressurized. Pete Worth and Ted Morelli had night watch, and as I pulled up, I spotted them in a blue Acura. They had orders, if Coombs left, to follow and radio in. Earlier that day Coombs had sauntered out, strolled conspicuously around the block, and finally settled in a coffee shop to read the paper. *He knew he was being watched.*

I climbed out of my Explorer and went over to Worth and Morelli. 'Any sign?'

Morelli leaned out of the driver's side window. 'Nada, Lieutenant. He's probably up there watching the Kings game. The scumbag. He knows that we're stuck down here. Why don't you go home? We've got him covered for the night.'

Much as I hated to admit it, he was probably right. There was nothing much I could do here.

I started the engine again and flashed a wave to the boys as I passed by. But at the corner, on Eddy, some controlling impulse restrained me from leaving. It was like something was saying, *what you want is here.*

He knows he's being watched. And? . . . He wants to show up the SFPD.

I drove up Polk, behind the William Simon. I passed

pawn shops, an all-night liquor store, a storefront Chinese take-out. A parked patrol car stood at the end of the block.

I drove past the rear of the hotel. Several garbage cans outside. Not much else. The street was deserted. I turned off my lights and sat there. I don't know what I was expecting to happen, but I was driving myself crazy.

I finally climbed out of the Explorer and went inside the back door of the hotel. *Rattle the fucker.* I was thinking about going back upstairs to talk to Coombs again. Yeah, maybe we could watch the Kings game together.

There was a narrow, dingy bar just off the lobby. I took a peek inside, saw a couple of real skulls, but not Frank Coombs. Goddamnit, a murderer was here in this hotel, a cop murderer, and we couldn't do a thing about it.

A movement near the back stairs caught my eye. I ducked back inside the shadowy bar. A real oldie was playing on the juke, Sam and Dave's 'Soul Man'. I watched a person coming down the stairs, casting glances around like the Fugitive.

What the hell was this?

I recognized the camouflage jacket, the floppy hat pulled over his face. I stared hard to be sure.

It was Frank Coombs.

Chimera was on the move.

Chapter Eighty-Six

Coombs ducked into the kitchen of a greasy spoon attached to the hotel. I waited a few seconds, then I followed him outside.

Now I was the one keeping my head down, casting furtive looks. I saw Coombs, but he'd changed. He'd put on a white kitchen jacket and a greasy chef's hat. I remembered my cell phone – and then that it was dead. I wasn't on duty; I hadn't really needed it.

Coombs walked right out the back door of the hotel. Before I had a chance to signal the patrol car, *discreetly*, he ducked into an alleyway.

I looked down the alley and saw it angled towards the street where I was parked. I ran for my car.

Thank God, I could still see him. Coombs hurried across the street, not twenty feet in front of my car. I still hoped I'd have a chance to signal the patrol car, but I didn't.

Coombs ducked into an empty lot, heading towards Van Ness. I was angry at our people – they had let him out. They'd blown it.

I waited until he disappeared into the lot, then I spun the Explorer around and headed towards the intersection at Eddy. At the light I made a right, throwing on the car lights. At Van Ness I cut the corner sharply. The busy street was crowded. A Kinko's, a Circuit City, people passing by.

I watched where I thought the lot might empty out.

I sat there, scanning up and down the block. *Could he have beaten me out here? Could he have slipped into the crowd? Shit!*

Suddenly, up ahead, I spotted the camouflage jacket, slinking out of an alley between the Kinko's and a Favor shoe store.

He'd dumped the kitchen jacket and hat.

I was pretty sure he hadn't seen me. He looked around in both directions, then, hands in pockets, started south towards Market. I wanted to run him down with my car.

At the next intersection I spun the Explorer around and headed back on the other side of the street, about twenty yards behind.

He was pretty good at this. He moved well. He was obviously in shape. Finally, he seemed satisfied he'd made a clean escape. *Nearly.*

At Market Street Coombs jogged into the middle of the street at a BART station. He hopped an electric bus, heading south.

I followed as the bus continued south on Mission. Each time it stopped I slowed on the brakes, cranking to see if

Coombs had jumped off. He never did. He was taking it out of the City Center.

Out near Bernal Heights, at the Glen Park Station, the bus hung at the stop for a few seconds. Just as it was starting up again, Coombs hopped off.

It was too late for me to stop. I had no choice but to pass right by. I hunched low, every nerve in my body on edge. I'd been on lots of stakeouts, tailed dozens of cars, but never with so much at risk.

Coombs hung on the platform, scanning in both directions. I had to continue on. Out of the rearview mirror I watched him. He seemed to be following my car as it faded out of sight.

Damn! All I could do was drive. I was incredibly angry, so pissed. When I was sure I was out of sight, I accelerated, climbing a residential hill, cutting a three-point U-turn out of a driveway, and prayed Coombs would still be there.

I sped across the street and spun around to the Glen Park Station from the other side.

The sonovabitch was gone! I scanned frantically in every direction, but there was no sign of him. I pounded the wheel in anger. 'Fucker!' I yelled.

Then, about thirty yards ahead, I spotted a mustard-colored Pontiac Bonneville pulling out of a side street, then stopping on the side of the road. The only reason I fixed on it was that it was the only thing moving.

Suddenly, there was Coombs. He ducked out of a store-front and jumped into the Bonneville's passenger's side door.

Back at'ya, I said to myself.
Then the Bonneville sped away.
So did I.

Chapter Eighty-Seven

I followed, ten car lengths or so behind. The Bonneville spun onto the entrance ramp for 280 and headed south. I hung at a distance, my pulse racing. I was pretty much running on adrenaline now. I had no choice except to follow Coombs as best I could.

After a few miles, the Bonneville signaled and veered onto the exit for South San Francisco. It wound through the working-class part of town, then up a steep street that I knew to be South Hill. The streets grew dark and I turned off my lights.

The Bonneville turned down a dark, isolated street. Middle-class row houses badly in need of repair. At the end of the street it pulled into the driveway of a white clapboard house perched on a hill overlooking the valley. The location was pretty enough, but the house was a shambles.

Coombs and his partner got out of their car, talking. They went into the house. I turned into a dark driveway three houses down. I'd never had such a chilling feeling of being alone. It was just that I couldn't let Coombs go, couldn't let him run on us.

I pulled the Glock out of my glove compartment and checked the clip. Full load. *Jesus Christ, Lindsay. No vest, no back-up, no cell phone that works.*

I crept along the shadowy sidewalk towards the white house, the automatic at my side. I was good with the gun, but *this* good?

Several beat-up cars and pick-ups were parked in a random pattern at the front of the driveway. The downstairs lights were on. I could hear voices. *Well, I'd come this far.*

I made my way up a narrow driveway towards the garage. It was a two-car stand-alone, separated from the main house by a blacktop walkway. The voices grew louder. I tried to listen but they were too far away. I took a breath and moved closer. Hugging the house, I looked inside a window. If Coombs looked like he was going to stay for a while, then I could get back-up here.

Six outlaw types, beer bottles, smokes, huddled around a table. Coombs was one of them. On the arm of one man I spotted a tattoo that made it all so clear.

The head of a lion, head of a goat, tail of a reptile.

This was a meeting of Chimera.

I inched closer, trying to hear. Suddenly came the rumble of another car climbing South Hill. I froze. I clung to the house, hugging the space between the main house and the garage. I heard the car door slam, then voices and footsteps coming my way.

Chapter Eighty-Eight

I saw two men coming, one with a blond beard and long ponytail, the other in a sleeveless denim vest, with massive tattooed arms. I had absolutely nowhere to go.

They fixed on me. 'Who the hell are you?'

Two possibilities: back away with my gun aimed at them; or make a stand and take Coombs in right now. The latter seemed the best idea to me.

'*Police*,' I shouted, freezing the two new arrivals. My automatic was extended with both hands. 'San Francisco Homicide. Get your hands up.'

The two men had measured, unpanicked reactions. They glanced at each other, calculatingly, then back at me. I was sure they were armed, and so were the others inside. A terrifying thought flashed through me . . . *I could die here.*

Noise erupted from all over. Two other men arrived from the street. I spun around, jerking my gun at them.

Suddenly, the lights inside the house went out. The driveway got dark, too. *Where was Coombs? What was he doing now?*

I jerked into a shooting crouch. This wasn't about Coombs anymore.

I heard a noise behind me. Someone coming fast. I spun in that direction – and then I was blindsided by somebody else. I was grabbed hard, taken down. I hit the ground under a couple of hundred pounds.

Then I was looking at a face I didn't want to see. A face I hated.

'Look what the tide rolled in,' Frank Coombs grinned. He wagged a .38 at my eyes. 'Marty Boxer's little girl.'

Chapter Eighty-Nine

C oombs crouched down close and leered at me with that haughty, smirking grin I'd come to hate already. Chimera was right here. 'Seems *you're* the one who's leaning to the left a little now,' he said.

I had just enough clear-headedness to realize what incredible trouble I was in. Everything that could have possibly gone wrong, had.

'This is a murder investigation,' I said to the men around me. 'Frank Coombs is wanted in connection with four killings, including two cops. You don't want a piece of that.'

Coombs continued to grin. 'You're wasting your breath, if you think that bullshit carries any weight here. I heard you talked to Weiscz. Neat guy, huh. Friend of mine.'

I forced myself into a sitting position. How the hell did he know I'd been to Pelican Bay? 'People know I'm here.'

Suddenly, Coombs's fist flashed out. He caught me flush on the jaw. I felt a warm ooze fill my mouth, my own blood. My mind flickered for some way to escape.

Coombs continued to smile down at me. 'I'm gonna do

what you bastards did to me. Take something precious from you. Take something you can never have back. You don't understand anything yet.'

'I understand enough. You killed four innocent people.'

Coombs laughed again. His coarse hand stroked my cheek. The venom in his stare, the coldness of his touch nearly made me retch.

I heard the gunshot, loud and close by, only it was Coombs who howled and grabbed his shoulder.

The others scattered. There was chaos in the darkness and I was as confused as anyone. Another bullet whined through the air.

A skinny thug with tattoos yelped and grabbed his thigh. Two more shots thudded into the garage wall.

'What the fuck is going on?' Coombs yelled. 'Who's shooting?'

More shots rang out. They were coming from the shadows at the end of the driveway. I got up and ran in a crouch away from the house. No one stopped me.

'Here,' I heard someone shout up ahead. I churned my legs towards the sound. The shooter was crouched up ahead, behind the mustard-colored Bonneville.

'Let's go,' he hollered.

Then, all at once, I saw, but I couldn't believe my eyes.

I reached out and fell into the arms of my father.

Chapter Ninety

We sped away from the house, getting most of the way to South San Francisco before we could even speak. Finally, my father pulled his car into the busy parking lot of a 7-11. I faced him, still breathing hard, my heart pounding.

'Are you okay?' he asked in the softest voice I could imagine.

I nodded, not quite sure, taking an inventory of where it hurt. *My jaw . . . the back of my head . . . my pride.*

Slowly, the wail of questions that needed to be answered crept through the daze.

'What were you doing there?' I stammered.

'I've been worried about you. Especially after somebody came after your friend Claire.'

The next thought hit me hard. 'You've been following me?'

He dabbed the corner of my mouth with his thumb to wipe away a trickle of blood. 'I was a cop for twenty years. I followed you after you left work tonight. Okay.'

My head rung in disbelief, but somehow it didn't matter. Then, staring at my father, something else flashed in my mind. Something that wasn't adding up. I remembered Coombs leering over me. 'He knew who I was.'

'Of course he knew. You met him face to face. You're in charge of his case.'

'I don't mean from the case,' I said. 'He knew about *you*.'

My father's eyes looked confused. 'What do you mean?'

'That I was your daughter. He knew. He called me, "Marty Boxer's little girl".'

A light was blinking from a beer sign in the 7-11 window. It illuminated my father's face.

'I already told you,' he said. 'Coombs and I were familiar. Everybody knew me back then.'

'That wasn't what he meant.' I shook my head. 'He called me, "Marty Boxer's little girl". It was about *you* . . .'

I had a flash of my face-to-face with Coombs this morning at the hotel. I'd had the same fleeting sensation then. That he knew me. That there was something *between him and me*.

I pulled away, my voice straining. 'Why were you following me? I need to hear everything.'

'To protect you. I swear. To do the right thing for once.'

'I'm a cop, Dad, not your little Buttercup. You're holding something back. You're involved in this somehow. You want to do the right thing for once, this is the time to start.'

My father leaned back his head, eyes fixed straight ahead. He sucked in a sharp breath. 'Coombs called me when he got out of jail. He managed to trace me down south.'

'Coombs called *you*?' I said, wide-eyed, completely in shock. 'Why would he call you?'

'He asked how I'd enjoyed the last twenty years of my life, while he was away. If I'd made something of myself. He said it was time to pay me back.'

'Pay you back? Pay you back for what?' As soon as I asked the question, the answer shot through me. I stared hard into my father's lying eyes.

'You were there that night, weren't you? You were in this twenty years ago.'

Chapter Ninety-One

My father averted his eyes. I'd seen the shamed and guilty look before – too many times – when I was just a little girl.

He started to explain. *Here we go again, huh, Daddy?*

'Six of us got to the crime scene, Lindsay. I was only there by chance. I was subbing for this guy, Ed Dooley. We were last on the scene. I didn't see shit. We got there after everything had been played out. But he's been badgering us, all of us, ever since.

'I never knew he was Chimera, Lindsay,' my father said. 'That you have to believe. I never heard of this cop, Chipman, until you told me the other day. I thought he was just threatening me.'

'Threatening you, Dad?' I blinked in disbelief. My heart was breaking a little. 'Threatening you with what? Please make me understand. I *really* want to understand.'

'He said he was going to make me feel the way *he* did all these years. Watching himself lose everything. He said he was going after you.'

'That's why you came back,' I sighed, 'wasn't it? All that stuff about wanting to set things right. Make amends with me. That wasn't it at all.'

'No,' he shook his head. 'I'd already pissed away so much. I couldn't let him take the rest, the part that was good. That's why I'm here, Lindsay. I swear it. I'm not lying this time.'

My head was ringing. I had a murder suspect loose. Shots had been fired. I didn't know what to make of this. What to do about my father. How much he really knew. How to deal with Coombs now. *With Chimera* . . .

'You're telling me the truth? For once? This is my case, my big, important case. I have to know the truth. Please don't lie to me, Dad.'

'I swear,' he said, his eyes hooded with shame. 'What're you going to do?'

I glared at him. 'About what? About Coombs, or *us* . . .?'

'About this whole mess. What happened tonight.'

'I don't know,' I swallowed. 'But I do know one thing . . . If I can, I'm bringing Coombs in.'

Chapter Ninety-Two

By ten the next morning I had a search warrant in my hands. It granted access to Coombs's room at the William Simon. Half a dozen of us rushed over there in two cars.

Coombs was out in the open. There were things we could nail him for: the attempted murder of a police officer, and resisting arrest. I had put out an APB on him and sent in a team to go over the meet house where everyone had scattered the night before.

I asked Jill to meet Jacobi and me at the William Simon. I was hoping against hope that we'd find something in Coombs's room that would tie him to one of the murders. If we did, I wanted a warrant in motion immediately.

The same Indian desk clerk let us into the room. It was unkempt, a row of crushed beer bottles and soda cans lining the window sill. The only furniture was a metal-frame bed with a thin mattress, and a chest of drawers with his toiletries on top.

'Whatd'ya expect,' Jacobi smirked, 'a Holiday Inn?'

Several newspapers were littered about, *Chronicle*s and *Examiner*s. Nothing out of the ordinary. On a ledge to the side of the bed, my eyes fell on a small marksmanship trophy – a prone sharpshooter aiming a rifle and the inscription: *Regional 50 Meter Straight Target Champion*, inscribed to Frank Coombs.

It made my stomach turn.

I went over to the desk. Stuck under the phone were crumpled receipts and a few numbers I didn't recognize. I found a map of San Francisco and the surrounding areas. I yanked out the drawers of the desk. An old Yellow Pages, some take-out menus to local restaurants, an out-of-date city guide.

Nothing . . .

Jill looked at me. She shook her head, grimaced.

I kept searching the room. Something had to be here. *Coombs was Chimera . . .*

I kicked a desk drawer in, sending a lamp toppling to the floor. In the same frustrated fit I grabbed hold of the mattress and angrily ripped it off the bed.

'It's here, Jill. Something has to be.'

To my surprise, a manila envelope that had been between the mattress and the box springs fell to the floor. I picked it up and spilled the contents onto Coombs's bed.

It wasn't a gun, or something taken from the victims, but it was a virtual history of the Chimera case. Newspaper articles, some of them going back twenty years to the trial, one from *Time* magazine, detailing the history of the case. One, headlined *Police Lobby Demands Coombs Arrest*, had a picture of an Officers for Justice rally at City Hall Square. Scanning through it, my eye was drawn by a slashing red circle Coombs had made, highlighting a quote ascribed to a group spokesman: *Patrol Sergeant Edward Chipman*.

'*Bing-o*,' Jacobi whistled.

Continuing on, we came upon articles on the trial and copies of letters from Coombs to the POA demanding a new trial. A faded copy of the original Police Commission's report on the incident in Bay View. There were lots of angry comments penned in the margins by Coombs. '*Liar*', boldly underlined, and '*Fucking coward*'. A red bracket highlighted the testimony of Field Lieutenant Earl Mercer.

Then a series of current articles, tracing the most recent murders: Tasha Catchings, Davidson, Mercer . . . A blurb in the *Oakland Times* about Chipman, with a scrawled-in comment: 'A man without honor dishonors everything.'

I looked at Jill. It wasn't perfect; it wasn't something we could tie directly to a murder case. But it was enough to remove all doubt that we had found our man. 'It's all here,' I said. 'At least we can make this stick for Chipman and Mercer.'

She thought a while, then finally bunched her lips together and gave me a satisfied nod.

As I rebundled the file, perfunctorily leafing through the last few items, something hit my eye. My jaw stiffened.

It was a newspaper clipping, from the first press conference after the Tasha Catchings murder. The photo showed Chief Mercer standing behind several microphones.

Jill noticed my changed expression. She took the

clipping out of my hand. *'Oh God, Lindsay . . .'*

In the photo's background, behind Mercer, were several people connected to the investigation. The mayor, Chief of Detectives Ryan, Gabe Carr.

Coombs had drawn a bold, red circle around one face. *My face.*

Chapter Ninety-Three

By the end of the day, Frank Coombs's description was in the hands of every cop in the city. This was personal. We all wanted to bring him down.

Coombs had no belongings, no real money, no network that we knew of. By all reckoning, we should have him soon.

I asked the girls to get together, down in Jill's office, after everyone else had left. When I arrived they were cheerful and smiling, probably thinking about congratulating me. The newspapers had Coombs's picture on the front page. He *looked* like a killer.

I sank down on the leather couch next to Claire.

'Something's wrong,' she said. 'I don't think we want to hear this.'

I nodded. 'I need to talk about something.'

As they listened, I described my experience the night before. The *real* version. How tailing Coombs had been risky and impulsive, though I didn't have any real choice. How I had gotten trapped. How, when I was sure there was no hope, my father had rescued me.

'Jesus, Lindsay.' Jill's jaw hung incredulously. 'Will you *please* try to be more careful?'

'I know,' I said.

Claire shook her head. 'You said to me the other day, *I don't know what I would do without you*, and you go off taking a risk like that. Don't you think it works the same for us? You're like a sister. Please stop trying to be a hero.'

'A cowboy,' Jill said.

'Cowgirl,' Cindy chimed.

'A couple of seconds either way,' I smiled, 'you guys would be out on a membership drive about now.'

They sat staring at me, somber and serious. Then a ripple of laughter snaked its way around the room. The thought of losing my girls, or them losing me, made what I had done seem all the more insane. Now, it was funny.

'Thank God for Marty,' Jill exclaimed.

'Yeah, good old Marty,' I sighed. 'My dad.'

Sensing my ambivalence, Jill leaned forward. 'He didn't hit anyone, did he?'

I took a breath. 'Coombs. Maybe someone else.'

'Was there blood at the scene?' asked Claire.

'We've been over the house. It was rented to this small-time punk who's disappeared. There was evidence of blood in the driveway.'

They stared back in silence. Then Jill said, 'So how'd you leave it, Lindsay? With the department?'

I shook my head. 'I *didn't*. I kept my father out of it.'

'Jesus, Lindsay,' Jill shot back, 'your dad may have shot

someone. He stuck his nose into a police situation and fired his gun.'

I looked at her. 'Jill, he saved my life. I can't just turn him in.'

'But you're taking a huge risk. For what? His gun is properly licensed. He was your father, and he was following you. He saved you. There's no crime in that.'

'Truth is,' I swallowed, 'I'm not sure he was following me.'

Jill shot me a hard look. She wheeled her chair closer. 'You want to run that by me again?'

'I'm not sure he was following *me*,' I said.

'Then why the hell was he there?' Cindy shook her head.

All their eyes fell on me.

Piece by piece, I laid out the exchange with my father in the car after the raid. How, after I confronted him, my father had admitted to being a material witness twenty years ago in Bay View. 'He was there with Coombs.'

'Oh, shit,' Jill said with blank eyes. 'Oh, Jesus, Lindsay.'

'That's why he came back,' I said. 'All those uplifting conversations about reconnecting with his little girl. His little Buttercup. Coombs was threatening him. He came back to face him down.'

'That may be,' said Claire, reaching out for my hand, 'but he was threatening him with you. He came back to protect you, too.'

Jill leaned forward, her eyes narrowed. 'Lindsay, this may not be about protecting your dad from getting involved. He may have known Coombs was killing people, and not come forward.'

I met her eyes. 'These past few weeks, having him back in my life, it was like, all of a sudden I could put aside the things he had done, the hurt he caused, and he was just a person, who made some mistakes, but who was funny, and needing, and who seemed happy to be with me. When I was little, I dreamed of something like this happening, my dad coming back.'

'Don't give up on him yet,' Claire said.

Cindy asked, 'So, if you don't think your father came back for *you*, Lindsay, what *is* he protecting?'

'I don't know.' I looked around the room, my eyes stopping at every face. 'That's the big question.'

Jill got up, went over to the credenza behind her desk, and hoisted up a large cardboard box-file. On the front was marked: Case File 237654A. *State of California vs. Frank C. Coombs.*

'I don't know either,' she said, patting it. 'But I'll bet the answer's somewhere in here.'

Chapter Ninety-Four

As soon as she got to work the next morning, Jill opened the case file and waded in. She told her secretary to hold all calls and cancelled what only yesterday had seemed an urgent meeting on a murder case she'd been working on.

With a mug of coffee on her desk and her DKNY suit jacket slung over her chair, she lifted out the first heavy file. The massive trial record – pages and pages of testimony, motions and judicial rulings. In the end, it would be better that she didn't find anything. That Marty Boxer ended up being a father who had come back to protect his kid. But the prosecutor in her wasn't convinced.

She groaned and started the file.

The trial had taken nine days. It took the rest of the morning for her to go through it. She sifted through the pre-trial hearings, jury selection, the opening statements. Coombs's previous record was brought out. Numerous citations for mishandling situations on the street where blacks were involved. Coombs was known for off-color jokes and pejorative remarks. Then came a painstaking re-creation of the night in question. Coombs and his partner, Stan Dragula, on patrol in Bay View. They encounter a schoolyard basketball game. Coombs spots Gerald Sikes. Sikes is basically a good kid, the prosecution conveys. Stays in school, is in the band; one blemish when he had been rounded up two months before in a sweep of the projects looking for pushers.

Jill read on.

As Coombs busts up the game, he starts taunting Sikes. The scene gets ugly. Two more patrol cars arrive. Sikes shouts something at Coombs, then he takes off. Coombs follows. Jill studied several hand-drawn diagrams illustrating the scene. After the crowd is subdued, two other cops give chase. Patrol Officer Tom Fallone is the first to arrive. *Gerald Sikes is already dead.*

The trial and notes run over three hundred pages . . . thirty-seven witnesses. A real mess. It made Jill wish she'd been the prosecuting attorney. But nowhere was there anything implicating Marty Boxer.

If he was there that night, he was never called.

By noon, Jill had made her way through the depositions of witnesses. The murder of Sikes had taken place in a service alley in between Buildings A and B in the Whitney Young projects. Residents claimed to have heard the scuffle and the boy's cries for help. Just reading the depositions turned Jill's stomach. Coombs was Chimera; he had to be.

She was tired and discouraged. She'd spent half a day plowing through the file. She had almost gotten to the end when she found something odd.

A man who claimed he'd witnessed the murder from a fourth-story window. *Kenneth Charles.*

Charles was a teenager himself. He had a juvie record. Reckless mischief, possession. He had every reason, the police said, to create trouble.

And no one else backed up what Charles said he saw.

As she read through the deposition, a throbbing built in Jill's head until it was sharp, stabbing. She buzzed her secretary. 'April, I need you to get me a police personnel file. An old one. From twenty years ago.'

'Give me the name. I'm on it.'

'Marty Boxer,' Jill replied.

Chapter Ninety-Five

A chilly Bay breeze sliced through the night as Jill huddled on the wharf outside the BART terminal station.

It was after six. Men in blue uniforms, still wearing their short-billed caps, came out of the yard, their shift over. Jill searched the exiting faces. He may have been a juvie with a police record twenty years before, but he had straightened his life out. He'd been decorated in the service, married, and for the past twelve years worked as a motorman with BART. It had taken April only a few hours to track him down.

A short, stocky black man in a black leather cap and a 49ers windbreaker waved good-bye to a few coworkers and made his way over to her. He eyed her warily. 'Office manager said you were waiting for me? Why's that?'

'Kenneth Charles?' Jill asked.

The man nodded.

Jill introduced herself and handed him her card. Charles's eyes widened. 'I don't mind saying, it's been a long time since anyone at the Hall of so-called Justice took an interest in me.'

'Not you, Mr Charles,' Jill answered, trying to set him at ease. 'This is about something you might have witnessed a long time ago. You mind if we talk?'

Charles shrugged. 'You mind walking? My car's over here.' He motioned her through a chain link gate to a parking lot on the wharf.

'We've been digging through some old cases,' Jill explained. 'I came across a deposition you had given. The case against Frank Coombs.'

At the sound of the name, Charles came to a stop.

'I read your deposition,' Jill went on. 'What you said you saw, I'd like to hear about it.'

Kenneth Charles shook his head in dismay. 'No one believed anything I said back then. They wouldn't let me come to trial. Called me a punk. Why you interested now?'

'You were a kid with a rap sheet who'd been in the system twice,' Jill answered honestly.

'All that's true,' Kenneth Charles said, 'but I saw what I saw. Anyway, there's a lot of water under the bridge since then. I'm twelve years towards my pension. If I read right, a man served twenty years for what he did that night.'

Jill met his eyes. 'I guess I want to make sure the right man did spend twenty years for that night. Look, this case hasn't been reopened. I'm not making any arrests. But I'd like the truth. Please, Mr Charles.'

Charles took her through it. How he was watching TV and smoking weed, how he'd heard scuffling outside his window, shouting, then a few muffled cries. How, when he looked out, there was this kid being choked.

Then, as Jill listened, everything changed. She took in a sharp breath.

'There were *two* men in uniform. *Two* cops holding Gerald Sikes down,' Charles told her.

'Why didn't you do something?' Jill asked.

'You have to see it like it was back then. Then, you wore blue, you were God. I was just this punk, right?'

Jill looked deeply into his eyes. 'You remember this second cop?'

'I thought you said you weren't making any arrests?'

'I'm not. This is something personal. If I showed you a picture, you think you could pick him out?'

They had arrived at a shiny new Toyota. Jill opened her briefcase, took out the picture. She showed it to him. 'Is the policeman you saw one of these men, Mr Charles?'

He stared at the photo for a long moment. Then he pointed to one face and said, 'That's the man I saw.'

Chapter Ninety-Six

I spent that whole day at the Hall, on the phone with the field or at a grid map of the city, overseeing the manhunt for Frank Coombs.

We placed a watch on several of his known acquaintances and places where we thought he might run, including Tom Keating's. I did a trace on the yellow Bonneville that had picked Coombs up, and ran the phone numbers found on his desk. No help there. By four, the guy who had rented the house in South San Francisco had turned himself in, insisting it was the first time he had met with Coombs.

Coombs had no money, no belongings. No known manner of transport. Every cop in the city had his likeness. *So where the hell was he?*

Where was Chimera? And what would he do next?

I was still at my desk at seven-thirty when Jill walked in. She was only a few days out of the hospital. She had on a brown wrap raincoat, with a Coach briefcase slung over her shoulder. 'What're you still doing here?' I shook my head. 'Go home and rest.'

'You got a minute?' she asked.

'Sure, pull up a chair. Afraid I don't have a beer to offer.'

'Don't worry,' she smiled, opening her bag and removing two Sam Adams's. 'I brought my own.' She tilted one towards me.

'What the hell,' I sighed. We had no trace on Coombs, and it was clear in Jill's face something was bothering her. I figured it was Rich, already humping some new deal, leaving her alone again.

But as soon as she unzipped her case, I saw the blue personnel folder. And then a name, *Boxer, Martin C.*

'I must've told you,' Jill said, cracking her beer and setting herself down across from me, 'my father was a defense lawyer back in Highland Park.'

'Only a hundred times.' I flashed her a smile.

'Actually, he was the best lawyer I ever saw. Totally prepared, unswayed by race or what a client could pay. My dad, the totally upright man. Once, I watched him work a case at night at home for six months to overturn a conviction of an itinerant lettuce farmer who was falsely convicted on a rape charge. A lot of people back then were pushing my dad to run for Congress. I loved my dad. Still do.'

I sat there silently, watching her eyes grow moist. She took a swig of beer. 'Took me until I was a senior in college to realize the bastard had cheated on my mother for twenty years. The big upstanding man, my hero.'

I broke into a faint smile. 'Marty's been lying to me all along, hasn't he?'

Jill nodded, pushing my father's dog-eared personnel file along with a deposition across my desk. The deposition had been folded open to a page highlighted in yellow. 'You might as well read it, Lindsay.'

I braced myself, and as dispassionately as I could, I read through Kenneth Charles's testimony. Then I read it over again. All the while, a sinking feeling of disappointment. And then fear. My first reaction was not to believe it; anger filled me. But at the same time, I knew it had to be true. My father had lied and covered up his whole life. He had conned and bullshitted and disappointed anyone who ever loved him.

My eyes welled up. I felt so betrayed. A tear burned its way down my cheek.

'I'm so sorry, Lindsay. Believe me, I hated to show you this.' Jill reached out a hand and I took it, squeezed hard.

For the first time since becoming a cop, I had no idea what to do. I felt a chasm widening; it couldn't be filled with anything that resembled duty, or responsibility, or right.

I shrugged, draining the last of my beer. I smiled at Jill. 'So, whatever happened to your father? Is he still with your mom?'

'*Fuck*, no,' she said. 'She was so tough sometimes, so cool. I just loved her. She threw him out when I was in law school. He's been living in a two-bedroom condo in Las Colinas ever since.'

I started to laugh, a painful laugh that mixed with the disappointment and the tears. When I stopped, I was left with this crushed feeling in my heart, and all these questions that wouldn't go away. How much had my father known? What had he kept silent about? And finally, what was his connection to Chimera?

'Thanks,' I said. I squeezed Jill's hand. 'I owe you, sweetie . . .'

'What are you going to do, Lindsay?'

I folded my jacket over my arm. 'What I should've done eleven years ago. I'm going to find out the truth.'

Chapter Ninety-Seven

My father was in the middle of a game of solitaire when I got home.

I shook my head, slightly averting my eyes. I trudged into the kitchen, pulling a Black and Tan out of the fridge. I came over and sank into the chair across from him.

My father looked up, maybe feeling the heat of my eyes. 'Hey, Lindsay.'

'I was thinking, Dad, about when you left . . .'

He continued flipping through the deck of cards. 'Why do you want to go through that now?'

I kept my gaze on him. 'You took me down to the wharf for some ices. Remember? I do. We watched the ferries coming in from Sausalito. You said something like, "I'm gonna get on one of those in the next few days, Buttercup, and I won't be back for a while." You said it was something between you and Mom. And for a while I waited. But for years, I always wondered, *Why did you have to leave*?'

My father's lips moved as if he was trying to frame a response, then he stopped.

'You were dirty, weren't you? It was never about you and Mom. Or the gambling, or the booze. You helped Coombs murder that boy. That's what it was all along. Why you left. Why you came back. None of it had anything to do with *us*. It was all about you.'

My father blinked, trying to spit out a reply. 'No . . .'

'Did Mom even know? If she did, she always gave us the party line, that it was your gambling, and the alcohol.'

He put down the deck of cards. His hands were trembling. 'You may not believe it, Lindsay, but I always loved your mother.'

I shook my head, and I wanted to get up and hit my father. 'You couldn't have. No one could hurt someone they love that much.'

'Yes, they can.' He wet his lips. 'I've hurt *you*.'

We sat there, frozen in silence for a few moments. The washed-over anger of so many years was hurtling back at me.

'How did you find out?' he asked.

'What does it matter? I was going to find out eventually.'

He looked stunned, like a fighter hit with a solid uppercut. 'That trust, Lindsay . . . it's been the best thing to happen to me in twenty years.'

'Then why did you have to use me, Dad? You used me to get to Coombs. You and Coombs killed that boy.'

'I didn't kill him,' my father said, and shook his head back and forth, back and forth. 'I just didn't do anything to stop him.'

A breath came out of him that seemed like it had been

held inside for twenty years. He told me how he had run after Coombs and found him in the alley. Coombs's strong hands were wrapped around Gerald Sikes's throat. 'I told you things were different then. Coombs wanted to teach him a little respect for the uniform. But he kept squeezing. "He's got something," he sneered at me. I shouted at him, "Let go." When I realized it had gone too far, I went for him. Coombs laughed at me. "This is my territory, Marty-boy. If you're scared, get the fuck out of here." I didn't know the kid was going to die . . . When Fallone came on the scene, Coombs let the kid drop and said, "Little bastard was trying to pull a knife on me." Tom was a Vet; he sized it up fast. Told me to get lost. Coombs laughed, "Go . . ." No one ever disclosed my name.'

My eyes stung with tears. My heart felt like it had a rip in it. 'Oh, how could you? At least Coombs stood up. But *you* . . . you ran.'

'I know I ran,' he said. 'But I didn't run the other night. I was there for you.'

I closed my eyes, then opened them again. 'It's truth time. You weren't there for *me*. You were following *him*. That's why you came back here. Not to protect me . . . to protect yourself. You came back to kill Frank Coombs.'

My father's face turned ashen. He ran his hand through his white hair. 'Maybe at first,' he swallowed. 'But not *now* . . . It changed, Lindsay.'

I shook my head. Tears were running down my cheeks and I angrily wiped them away.

'I know you think that everything that comes out of my

mouth is a lie. But it's not. The other night, helping you escape was the proudest moment of my life. You're my daughter. I love you. I always have.'

My eyes were still wet and words came out I wished I could grab back. 'I want you to go. I want you to pack up and go back to wherever you were for the past twenty years. I'm a cop, Dad, not your little Buttercup. Four people have been killed so far. You're involved somehow. And I have no idea how much you know or what you're hiding.'

My father's face went slack. I could see in the evaporating glow of his eyes how much this hurt.

'I want you out,' I said again. 'Right now.'

I sat there, my arms folded around Martha, while he went into the guest room. A few moments later, he came out with his things packed. He looked small suddenly, and alone.

Martha's ears stood up. She sensed that something was wrong. She moseyed over to him and he gently patted her head.

'Lindsay, I know how much reason I've given you to hate me, but don't do this now. You've got to watch out for Coombs. He's going to come after you. Please, let me help . . .'

My heart was breaking. I knew that the minute he walked out that door, I would never see him again.

'I don't need your help,' I said. Then I whispered, 'Goodbye, Daddy.'

Chapter Ninety-Eight

Frank Coombs leaned stiffly against a payphone on the corner of Ninth and Bryant. His eyes were riveted on the Hall of Justice. It had all been leading here.

The pain in his shoulder cut through his body, as if someone with a scalpel was probing at the edges of the wound. For two days he had kept undercover, slipping down to San Bruno, hiding out. But his picture was on the cover of every paper. He had no money. He couldn't even go back and get his things.

It was almost two o'clock. The afternoon sun pierced his dark glasses. There was a crowd on the front steps of the Hall. Lawyers huddling in discussions.

Coombs took in a calming breath. *Hell, what do I have to be afraid of?* He continued to stare towards the Hall of Justice. *They should be afraid.*

The service revolver was holstered to his waist, thanks to old faithful Tom Keating. The clip was filled with hollow points. He extended his shooting arm. Okay. He could do this.

Coombs turned towards the payphone. He placed a quarter in the slot and dialed. *No more second chances. No more waiting. This was his time. Finally, after twenty years in hell.*

On the second ring, a voice answered, 'Homicide Detail.'

'Put me through to Lieutenant Boxer.'

Chapter Ninety-Nine

We had a line on one of Coombs's prison cronies who had fled to Redwood City. I was waiting for a call back.

All morning I had pushed the murder case forward, while in the back of my mind I replayed the devastating scene with my father. Was I right to judge him for things that had happened twenty years before? More important, *what was my father's involvement with Chimera?*

I was finishing a sandwich at my desk when Brenda stuck her head in. 'Call on line one, Lieutenant.'

'Redwood City?' I asked as I reached for the phone.

Brenda shook her head. 'This person said you would know him. Said he was an old friend of your father's.'

My body stiffened. 'Put it on four,' I said. Four was the common line shared by the office. 'Start a trace, Brenda. *Now . . .'*

I jumped out of my chair, urgently signaling to Jacobi in the outer room. I held up four fingers, pointing to the phone.

In seconds, the office exploded into a state of alert. Everybody knew this had to be Chimera.

We needed ninety seconds to get a solid read on the trace. Sixty to narrow it down to a sector of town. *If* he was even calling from town. Lorraine, Morelli, Chi, all ran in, their faces tight with anticipation.

I picked up the phone. In the squad room, Jacobi picked up as well. 'Boxer,' I said.

'Sorry we missed out on all the real fun the other night, Lieutenant,' Coombs laughed. 'I wanted to do you. In my own special way.'

'Why are you calling?' I asked. 'What do you want, Coombs?'

'I have important things to tell you. Might help you make sense of the last twenty years.'

'I'm fine with them, Coombs. You were put away for killing a kid.'

He chuckled, grimly. 'Not *my* twenty years. *Yours.*'

My heart jumped. I was talking to a man who had raised a pistol to my head. I had to engage him. Anger him. Anything to keep him on the goddamn line.

I looked at my watch, thirty-five seconds had gone by. 'Where are you, Coombs?'

'Always the departmental small talk, huh, Lieutenant? I'm starting to lose some respect for you. You're supposed to be a smart chick. Make your Marty-boy proud. So tell me, how come all these people are dead, and you still don't have it figured right?'

I could feel him sneering at me. God, I hated this man.

'What is it, Coombs? What haven't I figured out?'

'I heard your daddy ran out on you about the time I went to jail,' he said.

I knew what he was building up to tell me. Still, I had to keep him on the line. In the outer room, Jacobi was listening, but he was also watching me.

Coombs snickered, 'You probably thought that the old man was jacking off some barmaid. Or that he left some bad markers out on the street.' Coombs put on a voice of mock sympathy. 'God, it must've been tough when he took off and your mom died.'

'I'm going to enjoy nailing you, Coombs. I'll be there when they start the drip at San Quentin.'

'Too bad you won't have the chance, sweetheart. But I wanted to tell you something important – *listen* – your old man *did* leave markers. *To me.* I own them . . . I took the fall. For him. For the whole police department. I own them all. I did the time. But guess what, little Lindsay . . . I wasn't alone.'

Every fiber in my body tightened. My chest nearly exploded with rage. I glanced at Jacobi. He nodded to me as if to say, *a few more beats . . . keep him on*.

'You want me, Coombs? I saw the photo in your room. I know what you want. I'll meet you, anywhere.'

'You want the killer so bad it's almost touching. But sorry, I have to pass on your offer. I've got one more date.'

'*Coombs,*' I said, glancing at the clock, 'you want me, let's go at it. Can you beat a woman, Frank? I don't think you can.'

'Sorry, Lieutenant. Thanks for the fun talk. But it seems like, everything that happens, you're just a tad too late. I still don't think broads belong in the department. Just an opinion.'

I heard a click.

I ran out into the squad room. Cappy had a line going with Dispatch. I was desperately hoping Coombs hadn't used a cell phone. Cells were the hardest to trace. *One more date* . . . I didn't know what the hell Coombs was threatening. What was next? What?

'He's still in the city,' Cappy shouted to me. He reached for a pen. 'He's in a phone booth. They're trying to narrow it down.'

The detective started to write, then he looked up, wide-eyed. His face was screwed in disbelief. 'He's in a booth . . . at the corner of Tenth and Bryant.'

All of our eyes met, and then everybody in the room was moving.

Coombs was calling from two blocks away.

Chapter One Hundred

I strapped on my Glock and yelled a call for Closest Available Unit. Then I charged out of the office. Cappy and Jacobi trailed on my heels.

Just two blocks away . . . What was Coombs going to do?

I didn't wait for the elevator. I bounded down the back stairs as fast as my legs would carry me. In the lobby, I pushed through staffers and civilians standing around and burst through the glass doors leading to Bryant Street.

There was the usual mass of people milling around on the front steps at lunchtime: lawyers, bondsmen, detectives. I turned my gaze south towards Tenth, craning my head to spot anyone who looked like Coombs.

Nothing.

Cappy and Jacobi caught up to me. 'I'll go ahead,' Cappy said.

Then it hit me. *One more date . . . Coombs was still here, wasn't he?* He was at the Hall of Justice.

'Police!' I screamed, alerting the unsuspecting crowd. 'Everybody stand alert!'

I scanned through the startled crowd for his face. My Glock was at the ready. Bystanders looked at me in wide-eyed surprise. Several crouched down or started to move away.

This is what I remember about what happened next:

A uniformed cop came up the stairs, walking towards me. I hardly noticed; I was scanning for Coombs's face.

The uniform came out of the crowd, the face obscured behind sunglasses and the visor of his hat. He was holding out his hand.

I focused right past him, scanning down the street, searching for Coombs. Then I heard someone shout my name. 'Hey! *Boxer!*'

Everything exploded on the steps of the Hall. Jacobi, Cappy, yelling. *'Gun!'*

My eyes flashed towards the cop. In that instant, the strangest thing came clear to me. *His blues* ... He was wearing a patrolman's uniform that I hadn't seen in a while. I fixed on the face, and to my shock it was Coombs ... It was Chimera. I was the date he was planning to keep.

Someone spun me from behind as I raised my Glock. 'Hey!' I yelled.

I saw Coombs's gun spurt orange. Twice. Nothing I could do to stop it.

Then everything got incredibly crazy and confused. Chaos. Terror.

I know that I got off a shot before my body went numb with pain.

I saw Coombs lurch forward, his glasses flying off, his gun pointed my way. He staggered, but he was still coming for me. His dark eyes glared with hate.

Then a scary shooting gallery erupted in front of the Hall. A cacophony of loud, echoing pops . . . *five, six, seven* in rapid succession, coming from all directions. People were screaming, running for cover.

Coombs's blue uniform erupted in bursts of bright red. Cappy and Jacobi were firing at him. His body hurtled backwards, jerking with the hits. His face showed terrible pain. The air was laced with a burning cordite smell. The echo of each shot crashed in my ears.

Then it was eerily quiet. The silence was startling to me.

'*Oh, Jesus,*' I remembered saying, finding myself down on the concrete steps. I didn't know for sure if I'd been shot.

Jacobi was leaning over me. 'Lindsay, stay right there. Be still.' His hands were on my shoulders and his voice echoed through my brain.

I nodded, inventorying my body for a wound. Shouts and wails echoed all around, people rushing everywhere.

I reached for Warren's arm and slowly pulled myself up. 'Lindsay, stay down. I'm telling you now.' He tried to give me an order.

Coombs was on his back, ruptures of crimson oozing out of his blue shirt.

I pushed by Jacobi. I had to see Coombs, had to stare into his eyes. I hoped he was still alive, because when the monster took his last breath, I wanted him staring up at me.

A few uniforms had formed a protective ring around the body, ordering everyone to stay clear.

Coombs was still alive, labored sounds escaping from his heaving chest. An EMS team came running, two techs lugging equipment. One, a woman, began ripping at Coombs's bloody shirt. The other was taking his pressure and setting up an IV.

Our eyes met. Coombs's gaze was waxy, but then his mouth twitched into an ugly smile. He tried to say something to me.

The EMS woman was backing people off, shouting out his vitals.

'I have to hear what he's saying,' I told the tech. 'Give me a minute here.'

'He can't talk,' she said. 'Give him room to breathe, Lieutenant. He's dying on us!'

'I have to hear,' I said again, then I knelt down close. Coombs's uniform shirt had been cut open, a mosaic of ugly wounds exposed.

His mouth quivered. He was still trying to talk. *What did he want to tell me?*

I leaned closer, the blood on Coombs smearing my blouse. I didn't care. I put my ear close.

'One last . . .' he whispered. Every breath was a fight for him now. Was this how it ended? Coombs taking his secrets straight to hell?

One last . . .? Target? Victim? I stared into his eyes, saw the hatred still there.

'One last *what*, Coombs?' I asked.

Blood bubbled out of his mouth. He took in a hard breath, husbanding the last of his strength, straining against the power of his own death.

'One last *surprise.*' He smiled.

Chapter One Hundred and One

C himera was dead. It was over, thank God.

I had no idea what Coombs had meant, but I wanted to spit his words back in his face. *One last surprise . . .* Whatever it was, Chimera was gone. He couldn't hurt us anymore.

I hoped it didn't mean he had left one last victim before he died.

'C'mon, Lieutenant,' Jacobi muttered. He pulled me up gently.

Suddenly, my legs buckled. I felt like I had no control over the lower part of my body. I saw the look of alarm on Warren's face. 'You're hit,' he uttered, wide-eyed.

I looked down at my side. Jacobi peeled back my jacket and a wet red gash appeared on my right abdomen. All of a sudden my head began to spin. A current of nausea rose.

'*We need help here,*' Jacobi shouted to the EMS tech. He and Cappy eased me back to the ground.

I found myself staring over at Coombs, as the female tech who had peeled away the dead man's shirt rushed over to me. *God, this was so unreal.* They took off my jacket, slapped a blood pressure monitor on my arm. It was as if it was happening to somebody else.

My gaze stayed fixed on the killer, the goddamn Chimera. Something a little strange, something not tracking. What was it?

I pulled myself out of Jacobi's grip. 'I have to see something . . .'

He held me back. 'You have to stay right here, Lindsay. There's an ambulance on the way.'

I pulled away from Jacobi and Cappy. I got up and went over to the body again. Coombs's police uniform had been peeled back off his chest and arms. Raw wounds spotted his chest. But something was missing; something was all wrong. What was it?

'Oh my God, Warren,' I whispered. 'Look.'

'*Look at what?*' Jacobi frowned. 'What the hell is wrong with you?'

'Warren . . . there's no tattoo.'

My mind flashed back. Claire had discovered pigments from the killer's tattoo under Estelle Chipman's fingernails.

I put my hands underneath Coombs's shoulders and rolled him slightly. *There was nothing on his back. No tattoos anywhere.*

My mind was whirling. This was unthinkable – but Coombs couldn't be Chimera.

Then I passed out.

Chapter One Hundred and Two

I opened my eyes in a hospital room, the constraining pull of an IV line stuck in my arm.

Claire was standing over me.

'You are a lucky girl,' she said. 'I talked to the doctors. Bullet grazed your right abdomen but didn't lodge. What you've basically got is one of the nastiest floor burns you'll ever see.'

'I heard floor burns go well with powder blue, don't they?' I said softly, my lips parting in a weak smile.

Claire nodded, tapping the taped bandage on her neck. 'So I'm told. Anyway, congratulations. You've earned yourself a cozy desk job for the next couple of weeks.'

'I already have a desk job, Claire,' I said. I blinked a confused look around the hospital room, then I pulled myself up into a sitting position. My side ached like it was on fire.

'You did good, girl,' Claire squeezed my arm. 'Coombs is dead, and now safely ensconced in hell. There's a mob of people outside who want to talk with you. You're gonna have to get used to the accolades.'

I closed my eyes, thinking of the misplaced attention about to come my way. Then, through the haze, it hit me. What I had discovered before I blacked out.

My fingers gripped Claire's arm. 'Frank Coombs didn't have a tattoo.'

She shook her head and blinked back. 'So?'

It hurt to talk, so the words came out in a whisper. 'The first murder, Claire . . . Estelle Chipman . . . She was killed by a man with a tattoo. You said it.'

'I could've been wrong.' Claire shook her head.

'You're never wrong.' I flashed my eyes.

She eased back on her stool, her brow creased. 'I'm doing the autopsy on Frankieboy tomorrow morning. There could be a highly pigmented section of skin, or a discoloration somewhere.'

I managed a smile. 'Autopsy? My professional opinion is that he was shot.'

'Thanks,' Claire grinned, 'but someone's got to take the bullets out of him and match them up. There'll be an inquiry.'

'Yeah.' I blew out a gust of air, and dropped my head on the pillow. The whole incident, seeing the cop coming up to me, realizing it was Coombs, the flash of his gun, all came back to me as broken fragments.

Claire stood up, brushed her suit skirt. 'You ought to get some rest. Doctor said they might release you by tomorrow. I'll check back in the AM.' She leaned down and gave me a kiss. Then she made her way to the door.

'Hey, Claire . . .'

She turned back. I wanted to say how much I loved her, how grateful I was to have such a friend. But I just smiled and said, 'Keep your eyes peeled for that tattoo.'

Chapter One Hundred and Three

I spent the rest of the day trying to rest. Unfortunately, a steady stream of brass and press paraded through my room. It was credit by association, soundbite time. Everyone wanted to have their picture taken with the wounded hero cop.

The mayor stopped by, accompanied by his press liaison and Chief Tracchio. They held an impromptu press conference at the hospital, praising me, citing the great work done by the city's Homicide detail, the same unit that they had almost pulled off the case.

After the commotion finally died down, Cindy and Jill dropped in. Jill brought a single rose in a glass vase and placed it on my bedside table. 'You won't be in here long enough to warrant more,' she grinned.

Cindy handed me a wrapped videotape. I opened it. *Zena, the Warrior Princess.* She winked, 'I hear she does her own stunts too.'

I pulled myself up and lifted my stiff arms around them in a hug. '*Don't* squeeze back,' I winced with a smile.

'They giving you any good pills?' Jill grinned.

'Yeah. Percocets. You should try this sometime. Definitely worth the risk.'

For a moment, we all just sat there without talking.

'You did it, Lindsay,' Cindy said. 'You may be fucking crazy, but no one can say you're not a helluva cop.'

'Thanks.'

'Don't think this getting shot thing lets you out of my exclusive. I'll give you some time to recover. How's six?'

'Right,' I chuckled. 'Bring me back a chicken enchilada from Susie's.'

'Doctor said we could only come in for a minute,' said Jill. 'We'll call you later.' They both smiled and backed towards the door.

'You know where to find me, ladies.'

Around five, Jacobi and Cappy stuck their heads in.

'We were wondering where you were?' Jacobi muttered, deadpan. 'You didn't show up for the afternoon meeting.'

I grinned, climbed out of bed a little stiffly. 'You guys are the heroes. All I did was dive out of the way to save my butt.'

'Shit,' Cappy shrugged, 'we just wanted to say that despite the fact the mayor's recommending you for the Medal of Honor, we still love you.'

I smiled, tugged at my green hospital gown and slowly lowered myself into a chair. 'You guys got a bead on what happened?'

'Chimera came at you is what happened,' Jacobi said. 'He shot, we took him out. End of story.'

I tried to remember the sequence of events. 'Who got off the shots?'

'I got four,' Jacobi said. 'Tom Perez, from Robbery, was next to me. He got off two.'

I looked at Cappy.

'Two,' he added. 'But shots were coming from all around. IAB's taking statements.'

'Thanks,' I smiled, gratefully. Then my expression changed. I looked at the two of them. 'How do you figure this? The same guy who takes out Tasha Catchings and Davidson like it's a lay-up from a hundred yards, only *grazes* me from point blank range?'

Jacobi looked at me a little confused. 'Is there something you're trying to tell us, Lindsay?'

I sighed. 'All along we were looking for a guy with a tattoo, right? The same man who killed Estelle Chipman. Linchpin of the case.'

They nodded, blankly.

'There was none on Coombs. Not a mark.'

Jacobi shot a glance at Cappy, then back at me. 'What're you trying to say? That Coombs isn't our man? That we tied him into each of the murders, found those clippings in his room. That he tried to pop you. Not once, but twice. But that it wasn't him?'

My mind wasn't working clearly. The events of the day, the medication. It was chicken shit compared to everything that pointed clearly at him. 'I guess what I mean is, you ever know Claire Washburn to be wrong?'

'No,' Jacobi shook his head, 'but I don't know you to be

wrong too often, either. Jeez, I can't believe I said that.'

They told me to get a good night's sleep.

'My gut feeling,' Jacobi said, turning back, 'is that when the medication wears off and you have a chance to look at everything in the light of day, you'll see you made a pretty good bust.'

I smiled at them. 'We all did.'

That night I couldn't sleep. I lay on my back, my side throbbing, but I was also feeling the blurry warmth of a couple of Percocets. I looked around the dark room, strange, unnatural, and the truth sunk in about how lucky I was to be alive.

Jacobi was right, it *was* a good bust. Coombs was a murderer. All the facts played out. He was trying to kill me at the end.

I shut my eyes and tried to drift off, but the tiniest voice tolled in my head. One voice, sneaking through all that was certain, all that seemed plausible.

I tried to force myself to sleep but the voice got louder.

How could he have missed?

Chapter One Hundred and Four

I was released the following morning.

Jill came and got me, pulling her gold Range Rover up to the curb outside San Francisco General as they wheeled me out in a chair. The press was there. I waved to all my new pals, but I refused to talk to them. The first stop was home, a quick hug for Martha, a shower, a change of clothes.

By the time I walked into room 450 at the Hall with a slightly stiff gait, it was as if it was business as usual: the entire detail gave me a round of applause.

'Game ball belongs to you, Lieutenant,' Jacobi said, handing me the brush.

'C'mon,' I waved them off, 'let's wait for the inquiry.'

'The inquiry? What's that gonna prove?' he said. 'Do the honors.'

'LT,' said Cappy, his eyes clear and proud, 'we've been saving it. For you.'

'Do it, LT.'

Maybe for the first time since Mercer promoted me, I felt

like the head of Homicide, and that all the doubts of worth and rank I'd carried with me my whole career were markers on an old journey, miles behind.

I went over to the board where our active cases were listed and I brushed Tasha Catchings' name off the board. Art Davidson's, too.

I was filled with a quiet but exultant joy. I felt relief and satisfaction.

You can't bring the dead back. You can't even make sense of why things happen. All you can do is the best you can to let the living believe their souls are at peace.

The detectives circled around me and watched.

I wiped Earl Mercer's name off the slate.

Chapter One Hundred and Five

I fielded phone calls for the next couple of hours. But mostly I just sat at my desk, giving some thought to my deposition. There was an inquiry pending on the Coombs shooting, standard practice whenever a policeman fires a gun.

The whole incident was still a blur to me. The doctors told me it might be like that for a while. A kind of repressed shock.

I had a flash of that out-of-date uniform, and Coombs's eyes, burning into me. His arm extended, the orange spurt of his gun. I was sure that someone shouted my name, probably Cappy or Jacobi, then someone else said, '*Gun!*'

And my own Glock, flopping up in slow motion, knowing I was a beat too late, seeing the spurt of his gun. Then the gunfire, from all directions, *pop, pop, pop, pop, pop* . . . Finally, I put it out of my mind and went back to work.

About an hour later I was leafing through the file on one of our new outstanding cases when Claire appeared at my door.

'Hey!'

'Hey, back at you, Lindsay.'

I know Claire. I know her look when she's found what she expected and has put doubt to rest. And I know the look when it's not so kosher.

This time she was definitely wearing that not-kosher look.

'You didn't find any tattoo, did you?' I said.

She shook her head. Her expression couldn't have been more troubled if she had found something culpable about Edmund, or one of her own sons.

I motioned her in and shut the door. 'Okay, so what *did* you find?'

She shrugged, somberly. 'I guess, I found out why Coombs missed.'

Chapter One Hundred and Six

Claire sat down and started to explain. 'I was doing a routine histology, in the substantia nigra—'

'In English, Claire,' I cut in. '*S'il vous plait? Por favor?*'

She smiled. 'I scooped some cells, mid-brain. Coombs was hit nine times. Six were nine millimeter. Two .20s. One .40 from the rear. That one smacked into his cervical spine. It's the only reason I would have been in there in the first place. I was looking for a specific cause of death.'

'So what *did* you find?'

Her gaze bore right through me. 'A marked absence of neurons . . . live nerve cells.'

I sat upright. My heart was in my throat. 'Meaning what, Claire?'

'Meaning, Coombs had Parkinson's, Lindsay. And not an unadvanced case.'

Parkinson's. My first thought was, *that's why he missed.* That I had been so damn lucky . . .

Then, watching the look of blank-eyed nullity grow into alarm on Claire's face, I knew it wasn't so simple.

'Lindsay, someone with Coombs's stage of Parkinson's could *never* have pulled off those shots.'

My mind went back to the scene at the LaSalle Heights Church. Tasha Catchings, felled by that incredible shot. And Art Davidson, the top of his head blown off . . . the bullet had come through the window from an adjoining roof at least a hundred yards away.

I fixed on Claire's eyes. 'You're sure about this?'

She nodded, slowly, 'I'm not a neurologist . . .' But then with unwavering clarity, 'Yes, I'm sure. I'm absolutely positive. His state of Parkinson's could never have allowed the necessary interaction between hand and brain for such a shot. His case was too progressed.'

With an almost nauseating chill, I flashed through all the things we knew about our killer. We had been certain that Chimera had a tattoo. But Coombs didn't have one. Then he barely grazed me on the steps of the Hall from point blank range. And now this, *Parkinson's*. Whoever Chimera was, he was certifiable as a marksman. That much was irrefutable.

We looked at each other and I uttered the unutterable. 'Jesus, Claire, Coombs isn't our man.'

'Right,' she said. 'So who is, Lieutenant?'

Chapter One Hundred and Seven

For a long time we just sat there, letting the stunning realization, and panic, sink in.

The newspapers, the TV, every sane person in the entire city was celebrating Chimera's death. Just an hour ago, I had wiped the murder case off the board.

'Coombs was trying to tell me something,' I said to Claire, recalling his dying moments. ' "*One last . . .*" he whispered, and when I asked him, "*One last what?*", he seemed to smile. "*One last surprise.*" He *knew* Chimera was still out there, Claire. He knew we would find out. The bastard was laughing at me as he drew his last breath. It has to be somebody else in his group. There's another madman.'

Claire pressed her lips. 'Lindsay, if I could've come back with any other conclusion . . .'

I didn't know exactly what to do with this new information. The pattern had fit so seamlessly. Bay View . . . Chimera. The file in Coombs's room. And how he had come at me. I couldn't believe that somehow I had been wrong. And then the question again: *If not Coombs, who?*

The last thing I wanted to do was go upstairs and shatter the celebration of all the bureaucrats and brass. But at the same moment Claire and I were gaping at each other in disbelief, the real killer was out there, possibly scoping another hit. *Jesus, this just didn't make sense.*

'Come with me,' I said, sucking in the sharp pain in my side. I ambled down the hall to Charlie Clapper's office.

'The returning hero.' The rotund CSU man stood up and smiled. 'A little bent over at the waist, but otherwise you look okay.'

'Charlie,' I said, 'how long until we have a match on the gun?'

'Gun?' He screwed his brow.

'Coombs's gun. How long until we can match it up against the piece that killed Mercer.'

'It's a little late, gorgeous, if you're trying to narrow down your suspects. I'd start with the dude on Claire's slab.'

'When, Charlie?' I shot back. 'How long till you get a match?'

'Maybe Monday,' he shrugged. 'We've got to scan the inside of the gun, get a reading on the—'

'*Tomorrow*, Charlie,' I said. 'I *need* it by tomorrow.'

'Lindsay,' he said, looking a little confused, 'what the hell is going on?'

I turned to Claire, a swallow of bile making an unpleasant retreat into my chest. 'We have to bring this upstairs.'

We grabbed an elevator up to the sixth floor. I was so

dumbfounded and racked with emotions, I hardly felt the pain shooting through my side. We barged into Acting Chief Tracchio's office. He was scribbling at his desk.

'What are you doing here?' he exclaimed. 'You should be home. Good God, Lieutenant, if anyone has a well-earned leave coming to them—'

I stopped him in mid-sentence. Then I told him what Claire had found. Suddenly, Tracchio looked as if he had swallowed a mouthful of bad oysters.

'I don't buy this, Lieutenant,' he said. 'You solved the case. It's over.'

'You may not buy it,' Claire said, firmly, 'but I've never been so sure of anything in my professional life. There is *no way* Coombs could've pulled off those shots.'

'But this is all speculation,' Tracchio objected. 'The links to the Sikes killing . . . Coombs's Chimera background . . . his qualifications with weapons. These are all facts. *Your* facts, Lieutenant.' He wagged his finger at me, stabbing me point by point with my own analysis. 'No one else could possibly have fit that profile. I can't argue with your conclusions, Dr Washburn, but eliminating Coombs . . .'

'We can match up his DNA against the sample of skin we found under Estelle Chipman's nails,' Claire replied, 'which is what I'm going to do. But I'll bet my reputation against yours, they *don't*.'

'In the meantime, we have to reopen the case,' I said.

'Reopen the case?' Tracchio gasped. 'I'm not going to give any such order.'

'If Chimera's still out there,' I pressed, 'he could be

planning another hit right now. I suspect that he is.'

'Only yesterday morning,' Tracchio blurted, 'you were one hundred per cent sure Coombs was Chimera.'

'That was yesterday,' I said. 'We told you why it's changed. Right now I'm about one hundred per cent sure Coombs *isn't* Chimera.'

'What you've told me is medical speculation. I want solid proof. Get me the DNA check.'

'That could take days,' Claire said. 'A week . . .'

'Then match the ballistics,' Tracchio ordered. 'Chief Mercer was killed with a .38. I'll guarantee you Clapper will show it was the same gun.'

'I'm on it. But in the meantime—'

'There is no *meantime*, Lieutenant. As far as I'm concerned, you did one hell of a job. Put your own life on the line. What you should be on now is medical leave, not trying to start another investigation.'

Claire and I looked at each other.

Then Tracchio picked up a few papers, the way figures of authority learn to communicate that a meeting is over. *Fuck him.*

Back in the hallway, I looked at Claire. 'I'm about to bring the whole city down on us. You better be damn sure.'

''Course I'm sure,' she replied. 'What are you going to do?'

'I'm going to wait for ballistics, Claire. And pray that nothing happens in between. I'm also putting everybody back on the investigation.'

Chapter One Hundred and Eight

'**C**indy Thomas, is that you?'

Aaron Winslow almost couldn't believe what his eyes were telling him. When Cindy opened the door to her apartment, she was wearing a tailored black pantsuit, slingback heels, a solitaire diamond necklace. Directly behind her, he could see her dining room – lit candles, china, silver flatware and crystal.

Cindy stepped forward and gave Aaron a kiss. Then she pulled away. God, she did look stunning. She was absolutely radiant tonight.

'All right, I have a confession to make,' she said. 'The Armani suit belongs to my friend Jill, the lawyer. So do the Ferragamo shoes. If I spill anything on the Armani, or as much as scuff the shoes, she'll never talk to me again.'

Cindy smiled and took Aaron's hand.

'Come in, don't be too afraid. Even though I am. Tonight we celebrate the end of a horrible siege, and a terrible man.'

Aaron had started to laugh. 'You certainly look beautiful for the celebration.'

Cindy continued to beam. 'Yes, and I prepared almond-crusted chicken, a romaine salad, orzo pasta with peas and mint. Unfortunately, the chicken happens to be one of only three dinners I know how to make.'

'Your honesty is refreshing,' Aaron said. 'Who belongs to the china and crystal?'

Cindy laughed out loud as she led him into the dining room. Jeez, she felt a little like Bridget Jones.

'Believe it or not, the china and crystal is all mine. My mother has been giving me pre-wedding gifts since I was eighteen. I thought Wedgwood and Waterford would be perfect for our special night. The grub is ready. Let's do it.'

'May I help you serve the feast?' Aaron asked.

'That would be just perfect. Like everything else tonight.'

Everything was, actually, and a few minutes later they were seated at the dining table with the delicious-looking food in front of them.

Cindy tapped her wine glass. 'I want to make a toast,' she said.

Just then, Aaron saw a reflection moving in the mirror over the sideboard behind Cindy. His heart fell. Not again; not here.

'Cindy, no!' he screamed. Suddenly, he was out of his chair and diving head first across the dining table. He only hoped he was in time.

He took Cindy and most of her china and crystal down.

Everything hit the floor with a crash, just as the first shot shattered the dining-room window. Several more shots followed in quick succession. Trailer fire. Chimera was here. He was coming for them now.

Cindy had the presence of mind to grab the cord and pull the phone off the console in the hallway. She pressed the number four on her quick dial, then SPEAKER, and she heard Lindsay's voice.

'He's here at my apartment. He's shooting at Aaron and me!' she screamed over the phone. 'Chimera is here and he's still shooting!'

Chapter One Hundred and Nine

T his couldn't be happening, but it was.

I called for all available units, then I rushed to Cindy's apartment. I got there as fast as humanly possible. Maybe a little faster. I saw Cindy and Aaron standing on the front porch. Half a dozen patrol cars were parked all around the house. But they were still targets, weren't they?

My hands were clutched tightly as I ran to her. I hugged Cindy and she was still trembling badly. I'd never seen her look so vulnerable, so afraid and lost.

'Thank God a patrol car was here in minutes, Lindsay. It either scared him off, or he was gone already.'

'Are you all right?' I turned my attention to Aaron. He and Cindy both had stains all over their clothes. It looked like they'd had a food fight. What the hell had happened here?

'Aaron saved me,' Cindy said in a whisper. He just shook his head and held Cindy's hand. There was a tenderness between them that touched me a great deal.

'He's losing it,' I muttered, more to myself than to either

of them. Whoever Chimera was, he was in a rage. Obviously he wanted to hurt me, or anyone I was close to. Or maybe he was offended by the idea of Aaron Winslow and Cindy. That could be part of it. He wasn't planning his hits so carefully now; he was reckless and rattled, but still very dangerous.

And he was out there somewhere. Maybe even watching us right now.

'C'mon, let's go back inside,' I said.

'Why, Lindsay?' asked Cindy. 'That's where he shot at us the first time. Who the hell is this guy? What does he want?'

'I don't know, Cindy. Please go inside, sweetie.'

Inspectors were already checking where the shots had come from. CSU was after the caliber of the weapon. But I knew. And I knew that it was him, *Chimera*.

I'm still here, he was telling us. Telling me.

Warren Jacobi's blue Ford pulled up, and I watched him hurry out and come to a stunned stop at the grisly scene. He walked up to me slowly. 'The two of them okay?'

'Yeah. They're inside now. Jesus, Warren. This has something to do with me. It has to.'

I rested my head on his shoulder for a second. Tears welled in my eyes, and I felt them come. They ran down my cheeks, hot and stinging.

'I'm gonna kill this guy,' I whispered.

Jacobi held me even tighter. Good old Warren.

We were back at zero. I had no idea who it was. I didn't know where we would start to look for him.

A black Lincoln town car wound its way along the barricaded street and swooshed up to the curb. The door opened and a grim-faced Chief Tracchio stepped out, surveying the shooting scene.

He caught my eye with a guilty swallow, the flashing red lights of the crime scene reflected in his glasses.

I glared at him. *Proof enough?*

Chapter One Hundred and Ten

That next morning, half of Homicide banged our heads together in the conference room, re-examining every piece of evidence, every assumption we had made. As the meeting was ending, I took Jacobi aside. 'One other thing, Warren. I want you to look at something for me. Make certain that Tom Keating really is in a wheelchair.'

By one o'clock I had to take a break. I needed thinking time outside the box. We weren't seeing something.

I had to talk to the girls, so I called them together for a quick lunch at the Rialto across the street from the Hall. Even Cindy said she was coming. She insisted on it.

When she arrived everybody hugged her and tears came into our eyes. None of us could believe Chimera had come after Cindy and Aaron – but he certainly had.

'This is crazy,' I said, as we huddled around a table, nibbling at salads and calzones. 'Everything matched. Coombs's past, Chimera, the incident in Bay View. Everything pointed there. We *can't* be wrong.'

'What you need to do first,' Claire cautioned, 'is take the

pressure off yourself. It's horrible, what's happened. But we can't get too emotional.'

'I know that,' I exhaled. 'It's probably what the killer wants. Jesus.'

Jill shuffled in her seat. 'Listen, Coombs has to be at the center of this. Too many things check out. He may not have pulled the trigger, but what if he got someone else to? What about those asshole buddies of his in South San Francisco?'

'Two are still missing,' I said, 'but my gut tells me, no. Oh hell, I don't know anymore. Everybody in Homicide is stumped. Coombs was one madman. Who the hell is the other one?'

'You checked everything you found in his hotel room?' Cindy asked. She had been unusually quiet until then.

'Checked, double-checked,' I replied.

For what seemed like the tenth time, my mind went to the tiny, disheveled hotel room – the suitcase full of Coombs's prison things, the clippings stashed under his bed, the numbers on the desk, his letters . . .

Except this time something hit . . .

Cindy was asking if we ever considered the possibility someone was trying to set Coombs up, but I didn't respond. My mind was elsewhere . . . rooted back in that dingy hotel room. The line of beer cans and cigarette butts on the sill above the bed. *Something else there.* I had never given it a second thought. I squinted into space, trying to visualize the sight. Then I saw what I was looking for – and what I might have missed.

'Lindsay,' Claire cocked her head, 'everything all right?'

'Earth to Lindsay,' Jill taunted.

Cindy put her hand on my wrist. 'Lindsay, what's going on?'

I grabbed my bag and stood up. 'We've got to get back to the Hall. I think I just figured something out.'

Chapter One Hundred and Eleven

E vidence taken into custody is kept under lock and key in a large storage room in the basement of the Hall.

Fred Karl, the day duty officer, looked a little annoyed at the four of us. 'This isn't a social room,' he scowled, pushing a clipboard in my direction and pressing a button that opened the chain-link gate. 'You and Ms Bernhardt can sign and go in. These other two, they'll have to wait out here.'

'Arrest us, Fred,' I said, waving everyone through.

The contents of Coombs's hotel room had been placed in a large storage bin near the back. I led the girls to the spot, and hung my jacket on a ledge as I pulled a couple of large bins down from the shelf coded with Coombs's case number. I started rummaging through the contents.

'Would you mind telling me just what the hell we're looking for?' Jill asked, and seemed annoyed. 'What the hell didn't I see?'

'You saw it perfectly,' I said as I pawed through Frank

Coombs's effects. 'So did I. But neither of us put it together at the time. Look at this.'

Like a silver chalice, I picked up the polished brass trophy of a prone sharpshooter aiming a rifle. *Regional 50 Meter Straight Target Champion*, the inscription plate read. That was what I remembered from the first time I saw the trophy.

But the name above it changed everything.

Frank L. Coombs . . . *Not Frank C.* Francis Laurence, not Francis Charles.

Rusty Coombs . . . The trophy had been awarded to Coombs's son.

All of a sudden, every assumption and insight changed for me. Maybe because of all the paperwork I had looked at recently, Coombs Sr's full name had sunk into my consciousness.

Frank C. was the father; Frank L. the son.

'I'm not my father,' I remembered Rusty Coombs saying. I could see his face now; the convincing act he'd put on for Jacobi and me.

Jill sat back on the floor, stunned. 'You're telling me, Lindsay, that these horrifying murders were committed by Coombs's son? The boy at Stanford?'

Cindy blurted, 'I thought he hated his father. I thought they hadn't been in touch.'

'So did I,' I said. 'He fooled everyone, didn't he.'

We stood there, seeking each other's eyes in the dark basement room. Did the new theory work? Did it stand up to scrutiny? My mind flashed again – the white van, the getaway car from Tasha Catchings' murder . . . It had been stolen from Mountain View. Palo Alto and Mountain View were only a few minutes apart.

'The owner of the white van,' I said, 'taught Anthropology at a community college down there. He said he took on students from other schools. Sometimes, some of the jocks . . .'

All of a sudden, things were fitting into place. 'Maybe one of them was Rusty Coombs?'

Chapter One Hundred and Twelve

I hurried back upstairs. The first thing I did was place a call to Professor Stasic at Mountain View Junior College. I was only able to get his voice mail. I left an urgent message for him to call me.

I punched the name Frank Coombs Jr into the CCI databank computer. The father's old conviction came up, but nothing on the son. No criminal record.

I felt that if the kid was cold enough to commit these terrible crimes, he had to be in the system somewhere. I typed his name in the juvie databank. These records were sealed, unable to be used in a court, but we had access. After a few seconds, a file shot back. *A long one.* I blinked at the screen.

Rusty Coombs had had run-ins with the law at least seven times from the time he was thirteen.

In 1989, he'd been brought before a juvie court for shooting a neighbor's dog with a pellet gun.

A year later, he'd been indicted for criminal mischief for killing a goose in a corporate park.

At fifteen, he and a friend had been charged with desecrating a public place for spray painting a synagogue with anti-Semitic slogans.

He had been charged, but not convicted, with throwing beer bottles through a neighbor's window. The complainant was black.

He was alleged to be part of a high school gang. The Kott Street Boys, known for race-based attacks on blacks, Latinos and Orientals.

One after another, I read on, stunned. Finally, I called Jacobi into my office. I laid the whole thing out for him. Rusty Coombs's violent past. His name on the marksmanship trophy. The stolen van in Mountain View, not that far from Palo Alto.

'Obviously, they've seriously relaxed the admission requirements at Stanford since I applied,' Jacobi snorted.

'No jokes, Warren. Please. So what do you think? I'm losing it, right? Am I crazy?'

'Not so crazy we shouldn't pay the kid another visit,' he said.

There were other things we could do to be sure. We could wait and see if his DNA matched what was found under Estelle Chipman's nails. But that took time. The more I thought about it, the more Rusty Coombs made sense.

My brain was buzzing now. A tremor of recognition reverberated through me. 'Oh my God, Warren. *The white chalk . . .'*

Jacobi leaned forward and narrowed his eyes. 'What about it?'

'The white powder Clapper found at two of the scenes.'
I recalled an image of Rusty Coombs, his freckled face and
wide lineman's shoulders in a sweaty Stanford T-shirt. The
epitome of a superior kid who'd turned his life around,
right?

'Remember when we met him?'

'Sure, the gym at Stanford.'

'He was lifting weights. What do weightlifters use,
Warren, to hold onto the bar so it doesn't slip?' I stood up.
My mind settled on the vivid image of Rusty Coombs
rubbing his thick, white hands.

'They use chalk,' Jacobi muttered.

Chapter One Hundred and Thirteen

Jogging back from afternoon practice, Rusty Coombs took the four-mile loop from the Field House around South Campus. He decided to make the last two hundred meters an all-out sprint.

A police car wailed past him. Then another speeding cruiser.

At first, the sight of the cruisers jolted him. But as he watched the cars trail away, he relaxed. His muscular legs churned on.

Everything was fine, just fine. He was safe here at Stanford. One of the privileged few, right?

He went back to what he'd been thinking about before the cops rudely interrupted. If he could get his body fat down to 7.8, and slice his time in the 40 another tenth or two, he could maybe move up to the third round of the NFL draft. Third round meant guaranteed bonus. Stick to the plan, he told himself. Fantasies had a way of becoming real; *at least his did*.

Rusty chugged onto Santa Cruz, a block away from the

frat house where he and several of the football players lived. As he turned down the street, his body slammed to a halt.

What the fuck . . . they're here for me!

The street was ablaze with flashing lights. Police cars, three of them, and two maroon Campus Security vehicles in front of *his* house. A crowd milling in the street. Town cops weren't allowed on campus for anything trivial. No, this was bigger, *wide-screen* . . .

He knew in a sickening flash that everything was over. He wouldn't even have the chance to cut the lights out on the little bitch who had killed his father. His legs still moved, jogging in place.

What shot through his mind was, *how the fuck could they have known? Who figured it out? Not Lindsay Boxer!*

A geeky student in baggy red shorts with a red knapsack thrown over his shoulder came up the street towards him. Rusty continued to jog in place. 'Hey, what the hell's going on?'

'Police looking for someone,' the guy said. 'At DU. Must be something big, 'cause everyone's saying cops from San Francisco are on the way.'

'No shit,' Rusty muttered. 'All the way from San Francisco, huh?'

Too bad, he thought. He was pissed. He was also sorry it had to end. But he'd always fantasized about how this might play out.

He reversed himself and started jogging back in the direction of the Main Quad. His stride picked up speed, swiftly and powerfully.

Rusty Coombs turned his head as another police car, siren wailing, shot by. No point hiding out any longer. The cops were here in numbers.

Fortunately, he had the perfect ending.

Chapter One Hundred and Fourteen

Jacobi and I sped down 280 towards Palo Alto at a steady ninety. Signs for Burlingame, San Mateo, and Menlo Park shot past. We were pumped to take this creep down within the hour.

I was hoping we could take Rusty Coombs by surprise. Maybe as he came out of a class. There were thousands of students on the Stanford campus. He was armed, and very dangerous, so I wanted to avoid a confrontation if I could.

I had arranged to meet Lieutenant Joe Kimes of the Palo Alto Violent Crimes Detail at the Dean of Students' Office in the Main Quad. As we closed in on Palo Alto, Kimes called back. He reported that Coombs couldn't be found. He had no scheduled classes that afternoon. He wasn't at his residence, or the stadium where the Stanford football team had finished practice about an hour ago.

'Does he know there's an APB out on him?' I asked. 'What's happening down there, Joe?'

'It's hard to keep a low profile here,' Kimes said. 'He could've seen our cars.'

I was starting to worry. I'd hoped we could get to Coombs before he knew we were coming. He liked attention – he wanted to be a star.

'What do you want us to do?' Kimes asked.

'I want you to put the local SWAT team on alert. Meanwhile, try to find the big creep, Joe. Don't let him out of our trap. And Joe, this guy is extremely dangerous. You have no idea.'

Chapter One Hundred and Fifteen

The elevator ascended rapidly, and when it opened, Chimera looked out on the observation deck of the Hoover Tower, more than two hundred and fifty feet over Stanford's Main Quad.

There was no one up there on the deck. No one to bother him, no one to kill right away. Just the flat, blue sky, the concrete WPA-style dome, the giant Carillon bells that tolled thunder across the campus.

Rusty Coombs flicked off the elevator power switch, freezing the doors open. Then he slung the black nylon duffel bag he was carrying onto the floor and leaned against the concrete wall, his back to one of the eight barred windows. He opened the bag, removing his disassembled PSG-1, the sniper's scope, two additional pistols along with clips of ammunition.

This was something else – breathtaking, actually. The bomb, right? He could see mountains to the south and west, the outline of San Francisco to the north. It was a clear blue day. Everything was calm, perfect. The Stanford campus stretched out before him. Students crept like little ants down below. The best and the brightest.

He began to hook together the rifle, clicking the barrel seamlessly into the stock, fitting in the customized shoulder rest, until the assembled piece rested in his arms like a prized instrument.

A seagull perched on the Carillon bells. He aimed and squeezed the trigger in a dry run. *Click.*

Then he screwed the sniper's sight onto the stock. He snapped in a twenty-four-round clip.

He crouched behind the cement restraining wall. The wind rattled by, sounding like a gust snapping a canvas sail. The sky was a gorgeous turquoise blue. *I'm going to die, and you know what, I really don't care.*

Students were casually traversing crosswalks, lounging and reading on the green. Who knew . . .? Who suspected any danger? He could have his pick. *He could immortalize any of them.*

Rusty Coombs swung the barrel of his rifle through the metal bars in the dome's six-foot-high windows. He squinted through the sight and searched out the first target. Students popped into view: a pretty Japanese girl with auburn hair and dark glasses nuzzling her Caucasian boyfriend on the green. A geek in a bright yellow sweatshirt riding a yellow bicycle. He shifted the sight. A black student with long corn braids walking towards the students' bookstore. Coombs smiled. Sometimes it even amazed him how much hatred he had inside. He was smart enough to know that he didn't just despise them, he despised himself. Despised his buffed-up body, the imperfections only he knew about, but most of all, he hated his thoughts, his obsessions, the way his goddamn mind worked. He'd felt so alone for so goddamn long. Like right now.

In the distance he caught sight of a blue Explorer with flashing lights. It pulled up in front of the Administration Building. The tight-assed bitch from San Francisco jumped out of the passenger door. His heart pounded.

She was here. He'd have his chance at her after all.

His father had been taken away when he was a little kid, his hands cuffed, legs shackled. His mother had held him back, her glare contemptuous. Didn't they see? Didn't they see how much it hurt him? *I love you, Dad* . . . Didn't they see he was going to lose his father forever? Then that look, that cold smirk he would remember for the rest of his life. His father pushing him away. *Be a man*, he snorted.

'Am I being a man?' Rusty Coombs whispered now.

He placed the sight on the pretty Oriental girl smooching her boyfriend on the lawn. Christ, he hated both of them. Disgraces to their races.

Then, as a second thought, he swung the rifle over to the jig girl with the cornstalks, a gold, heart-shaped pendant bobbing on her neck, a glint in her brown eyes.

It's just my nature, he smirked, coiling his finger around the cold, metal trigger.

Chimera was back in business.

Chapter One Hundred and Sixteen

As the Explorer screeched to a stop outside of the Administrative Building, Jacobi and I got out and cut through the arched Spanish loggia overlooking the Main Quad.

We ran right into Kimes, barking orders into a hand-held radio. He was with a grim-faced Dean of Students, Felix Stern. 'We still haven't found Rusty Coombs,' Kimes told me. 'He was seen on the Quad twenty minutes ago. Now he's disappeared again.'

'How are we doing with that SWAT team?' I asked him.

'They're on their way now. You think we'll need them?'

I shook my head. 'I hope not. We won't need them if Coombs got spooked and split.'

Just then, we heard shots. I knew that none of the police would fire first. Besides, it sounded like rifle-fire.

'I think he's still here,' Warren Jacobi dead-panned.

Screams of panicked students echoed down the loggia. Then they started to run towards us, fleeing the green.

Someone shouted, 'He's in the Hoover Tower. The

fucker, the fucking madman!'

Jacobi, Kimes and I ran right into the stampeding students. Joe Kimes was on the radio. 'Shots fired! All personnel and EMS to the Hoover Tower. Use extreme caution!'

We got to the green in the next few seconds. Students were hiding behind trees, pillars, large flower pots, anything that afforded some cover.

Two students were down on the green. One of them was a black woman, a bloody circle widening on her chest. Goddamn him. Goddamn *Chimera*.

'Stay down! Stay where you are!' I yelled across the Quad. 'Please keep your heads down!'

A shot rang out from the tower. Then a second and a third. A male student dropped from behind a shuttered bench.

'Please stay down!' I screamed again. 'Stay the hell down!'

I fixed my eyes on the belfry of the tower, searching for a shape, a gun, anything to set Rusty Coombs's position.

Suddenly, two more shots echoed from the tower. Coombs was definitely up there. There was no way we could protect this many people. He had us where he wanted us. Chimera was still winning.

I grabbed Kimes. 'How would I get up there?'

'No one's going up there,' Joe Kimes snapped back, 'without a SWAT escort.' His eyes were wide and frozen. He shouted into the radio. 'All SWAT and medical teams to the Main Quad! Sniper is shooting from the Hoover Tower. At least three down.'

I looked him in the eye. 'How do I get up there, Joe?' I demanded. 'I'm going, so tell me the best way.'

'There's an elevator on the ground floor,' Dean Stern cut in.

I pulled my Glock out of my side holster and checked the smaller Beretta I had fastened to my ankle. Chimera was up in that dome, raining bullets down.

My eyes fixed on a wooden kiosk that would provide some cover. Jacobi reached for my arm. But he knew he wasn't going to stop me.

'You wouldn't give me a minute to grab us both a vest, would you, LT?'

'I'll see you up there, Warren.' I winked. Then I broke for the tower in a tight crouch.

And somewhere in the back of my mind, I wondered – *why am I doing this?*

Chapter One Hundred and Seventeen

Jesus, he felt good.

Chimera pulled back the rifle and sat with his back against the hard concrete wall. In a moment, hell on earth was going to bust loose in the Quad. SWAT teams, snipers, maybe even helicopters. He knew he had the advantage – he didn't care if he died.

He fixed on the big Carillon bells. He'd always liked the stupid, damn bells. When they played, you could hear them all over campus. He wondered, when this was over, when he was no longer around, if he could have bells played at his funeral. Yeah, right.

Then he realized he was alone in the Hoover Tower, and had just killed five people. What a fucking day this had been – what a life he'd had. He was going down in history, no doubt about that anymore.

He lifted himself up and peered over the side. Suddenly, everything was pretty quiet down there. The Quad had been cleared. Soon there'd be a high-tech SWAT team on the scene, then he'd just have to take out as many as he could get. They were going to have to earn their overtime pay.

But for now, up here, man, everything was beautiful . . .

Then he spotted Lindsay Boxer. He squinted through the rifle sight to be sure. The 'hero cop' who had killed his father. She had run from the cover of the Administrative Building, zigzagging in a crouch towards the towers. He was glad she was here. Suddenly, everything had changed. *He could still bring this bus in on time . . .*

He followed the darting shape, and gently closed his left eye. He let his breathing slow to an almost meditative beat.

He was thinking that his father had taken nine shots.

So should she.

He drew in a breath, and fixed the crosshairs on her white blouse.

You're a dead woman.

Chapter One Hundred and Eighteen

I t was quiet now in the Quadrangle. Rusty Coombs was either taking a breather or reloading. I figured I had about fifty yards to the base of the tower. Long ways.

Let's do it. Me and you, pal.

I headed for the little wooden kiosk. I felt a kind of controlled hysteria. Not good. I knew I was a target, and that Coombs could shoot.

Suddenly, I heard a gun burst *behind* me. I glanced and saw Jacobi firing at the tower.

Before Coombs could train on me, I darted under the cover of thick poplar branches; then the cover of another small building only a few yards from the base of the tower.

I looked around and saw Jacobi with Kimes. He shook his head. I knew it meant, *please, Lindsay, stay put. I can't do back-up once you're in the tower.* I winked at him almost apologetically.

I ran along the walls of the tower until I found an entrance on the north side. I headed up the stairs and found myself in a marbled, WPA-style lobby.

Elevators straight ahead.

I pressed for the elevator, over and over, my gun trained on the doors. They didn't open. I slammed my fist against the polished chrome doors. I screamed, *'Police!'* The shouts echoed down the halls. I needed someone, anybody. I had no idea how to get up to the tower from here.

An older man in a maintenance uniform emerged from a corridor. He recoiled at the sight of my gun.

'Police,' I yelled. 'How do I get up there?'

'Man's blocked the elevator,' he said. 'Only way up is the auxiliary stairs.'

'Show me. Please. It's a matter of life or death.'

The caretaker led me through a door and up to the third floor, then down a corridor to a narrow set of stairs. 'You got yourself thirteen flights. Fire door at the top. Opens from both sides.'

'Wait in the lobby and tell anyone who comes that I'm up here,' I said as I headed into the narrow stairwell. 'That's a matter of life or death, too.'

'Yes, ma'am. Understood.'

I started up. Thirteen flights. And I didn't know what to expect at the top. My heart was racing and my blouse clung to my back with cold sweat.

Lucky thirteen. With each story, my breaths grew tighter and sharper. My legs began to ache, top to bottom, and I run four times a week. I didn't know if I was crazy, going in there without back-up. No, hell, I *knew* I was crazy.

Finally, I pushed past twelve and reached the top. A sealed window gave me a view, the Main Quad spread out below. *Jesus.* Only a solid metal fire door separated me from Chimera. My heart was exploding.

Through the door I heard more shooting. *K-pow, k-pow, k-pow.* He was at it again. I was scared that someone else might be killed. I was angry, pissed, I wanted him so bad. I checked my Glock and sucked in a breath. *Oh God, Lindsay, whatever you do, do it fast.*

The fire door had one of those heavy emergency levers that had to be pushed down to release.

I pressed it down and burst onto the tower roof.

Chapter One Hundred and Nineteen

I was struck by a blast of blinding sunlight. Then the chilling sounds: *k-ping, k-ping, k-ping* . . . the ejecting shells from the rifle jangling to the floor.

Rushing onto the deck, I spotted Coombs. He was kneeling over an opening with his rifle extended through the bars.

Suddenly, he pivoted towards me.

His gun exploded in my direction. A deafening burst, orange flashes clanging off iron and stone, ricocheting all around the roof. Loud, metallic dings.

I dove away from the door, peeling off a burst of four shots. I didn't know if I'd hit him. I sucked in a breath, waiting for a stab of pain to see if he'd hit me. He hadn't.

'It's a lot harder when somebody's shooting back at you,' I yelled.

I was crouched behind a tall metal grating. I saw it housed a collection of seven massive bells. Each looked like it could shatter my eardrums with a single ring. The rest of the tower roof was no more than an eight-foot-wide path.

It circled the bells, with viewing openings every six feet or so in the wall.

Coombs was on the other side, the bells acting as a cover for both of us.

His voice called out, an easy, arrogant twang. 'Welcome to Camelot, Lieutenant. All those big-shot brains down there . . . and now you coming all the way up here just to talk to *me*.'

'I brought along friends. They won't be talking, Rusty. They'll be looking for any shot to take you down. Why die like this?'

'I don't know, seems like a good plan to me. You want to die up here with me, be my guest,' Rusty Coombs called back.

I squinted through the grating, trying to get a fix on where Coombs was. Across the belfry, I heard him shove in a fresh clip.

'I'm glad it's you. I mean, it's fitting, don't you think? You nail my dad, now I get to do the same to you.'

His voice seemed to shift, *as if he was circling*.

I started to circle as well, my Glock aimed towards the corner of the bell housing.

'I don't want you to die up here, Rusty.'

'A little slow on the uptake, aren't you, Lieutenant? Just like always. I gave you everything I could think of. The van, the 911 . . . What did I have to do, send you a fucking e-mail and say, "*Hey, fellas, I'm over here . . .*"? Took you long enough to figure it out. Cost a few lives along the way.'

Suddenly, a burst of gunfire rattled the iron grating,

bullets clanging loudly off the bells.

I ducked down, holding my head between my hands.

'Your father's gone,' I shouted. 'This doesn't bring him back.'

Where was he now? I peered through a gap in the grating. *Brain freeze.*

There was Rusty Coombs. He was smiling at me, his father's smug, hateful grin.

I saw the rifle extended through the bell housing.

In that instant, I saw a sudden flash, felt a recoil of brute force. Then the powerful impact of the shot hurled me backwards.

I landed hard on my back, scurried for cover as Coombs rushed around for a clear shot. My fingers groped for my Glock. *Jesus, my gun wasn't there.*

Coombs had shot it out of my hand!

He walked forward until he stood over me. His rifle was pointed at my chest. 'You have to admit, I sure can shoot, huh?'

Every lingering hope was gone. His eyes were green and held such a cold, impassive burn. I hated this bastard so much.

'Don't add any more deaths,' I said, my mouth completely dry. 'SWAT teams are coming. Kill me, five minutes later it'll be you.'

He shrugged. 'At this point, it's gonna be a bitch to square myself with the coach. People like you,' he stared blankly, 'you don't have the slightest idea what it's like. You bastards took my father.'

I watched his finger move to the trigger and realized I was going to die. I said a silent prayer, and I thought, *I don't want to die.*

Then the deepest ear-splitting sound reverberated. It had the force of a building crashing down. One resounding gong was followed by another, then another. I had to grab my ears to keep from going deaf.

It was the bells. They were going off, and it was the loudest noise I'd ever heard – by a lot. The entire tower shook with the thunderous sound.

Coombs's face twisted into a contortion of shock and pain. He staggered, reflexively crunching into a ball to protect himself.

When I saw him coil up, I reached inside my pant leg. I pulled out the Beretta strapped to my ankle.

Everything happened so quickly, like a film with the action running but the sound a high-pitched distortion.

Coombs, seeing me, swung his rifle into firing position.

I fired three times, spurts jerking back my hand. *The bells continued to gong . . . over and over.*

Three crimson bursts spattered across Coombs's broad chest. The force sent him tumbling backward.

Then the bells again. Each ear-splitting clang felt like a sledge-hammer slamming into my skull.

Coombs came to rest in a sitting position. He gazed down, saw his torn flesh. He blinked with a glazed, mystified look. He raised his rifle towards me. 'You die too, bitch!'

I squeezed the trigger of the Beretta. The bells gonged as

a final blast thudded into his throat. He grunted loudly and his eyeballs rolled back into his head.

I realized that my hands were cupping my ears again. My head ached. I crawled to Coombs and kicked his rifle away. The bells continued to gong, a melody that was unidentifiable to me, maybe an answer to my prayer.

My eye fixed on something as I knelt beside Coombs. 'There it is,' I whispered.

A curled reptilian tail in red and blue, leading into the body of a goat with the fierce and proud heads of a lion and a goat. *Chimera . . .* One of my shots had pierced the wicked beast's torso. It looked dead, too.

I heard shouts coming from behind, but I continued to kneel over Coombs. I felt I had to answer what he'd said at the end. *You don't know what it's like . . . to lose your father.*

'Oh yes I do,' I told his still eyes.

Chapter One Hundred and Twenty

This time the newspapers had it right. *Chimera was dead.* The multiple homicide case was closed.

There was no great joy in the final outcome, at least not for me. Homicide didn't get together and wipe the board clean. There were no toasts with the girls. Too many people had died. I was lucky not to have been among them. So were Claire and Cindy.

I took a few days off, to give my side and hand some time to heal, and the IAB teams a chance to piece together what had happened at the shooting scenes. I hung out with Martha, took some long walks along the Marina Green and Fort Mason Park as the weather turned damp and cold.

Mostly, I replayed the events of the horrible case. It was the second time I'd had to fight a killer one on one. Why was that? What did it mean? What did it say about my life and what it had come to?

For a moment, I'd had an important piece of my own past given back, a father I never knew. Then that gift was taken away. My father had disappeared into the dark hole from which he had crept. I knew I would never see him again.

In those days, if I could have come up with one meaningful thing I wanted to do with my life, I might have said, *let's give it a ride*. If I could paint, or had some secret urge to open a boutique, or the stick-to-it-ive-ness to write a book . . . It was so hard to find even the thinnest slice of affirmation.

But by the end of the week, I just came back to work.

Late that first day I got a buzz from Tracchio to come up to his office. As I walked in, the Chief stood up and shook my hand. He told me how proud he was, and I almost believed him.

'Thanks,' I nodded, and even smiled. 'That what you wanted to say?'

Tracchio took off his glasses. He shot me a contrite smile. 'No. Sit down, please, Lieutenant.'

From the edge of his large walnut desk, he picked up a red folder. 'Preliminary Findings on the Coombs Shooting. Coombs, *Senior*.'

I regarded it tentatively. I didn't know if some IAB bureaucrat had found something suspicious.

'There's nothing to worry about,' Tracchio assured me. 'Everything checks out. A perfectly clean shooting.'

I nodded back. So what was this all about?

'There is one thing outstanding, though.' The Chief stood and leaned against his palms on the front of his desk. 'The ME lifted nine rounds out of Coombs's body.

Three belonged to Jacobi's nine millimeter. Two came from Cappy's. Two .20s from Tom Perez out of Robbery. One from your Glock. That's *eight*.'

He stared down at me. 'The ninth bullet didn't match up.'

'Didn't match?' I raised my eyes. It didn't make sense. The commission had every gun from every cop who was involved, including mine.

Tracchio reached into a desk drawer. He came back with a plastic baggie containing a flattened, slate-gray round, about the same color as his eyes. He handed it to me. 'Take a look . . . Forty caliber.'

A jolt of electricity surged through me. *Forty caliber . . .*

'Funny thing is,' his eyes bore in, 'it *did* match up to these . . .' He produced a second baggie containing four more rounds, nicked, flattened.

'We took these out of the garage and trees outside that house in South San Francisco where you followed Coombs.' Tracchio kept his eyes fixed on me. 'That make any sense to you?'

My jaw hung like a dead weight. It didn't make sense, except . . . I flashed back to the scene on the steps of the Hall.

Coombs rushing towards me, his arm extended; that frozen moment before I fixed on his face. From behind him, the thing I always remembered but couldn't put away: *a voice, someone shouting my name.*

In the mêlée there was a *pop*, then Coombs lurched.

The bullets didn't match up. Coombs had been shot with a

.40 caliber handgun. My father's gun . . .

I thought of Marty, his promise as he stood in my doorway that last time. *Lindsay, I'm not running anymore.* My father had shot Frank Coombs on those steps. He had been there for me.

'You didn't answer, Lieutenant. That make any sense to you?' Tracchio asked again.

My heart was bouncing side to side in my chest. I didn't know what Tracchio knew, but I was his hero cop. Catching Chimera would erase the *'Acting'* in front of his title. And like he said, it was a clean shooting.

'No, Chief,' I answered. 'It doesn't make any sense.'

Tracchio fixed on me, weighing the file in his hand, then nodded, placing it at the bottom of a heavy pile of other reports.

'You did a good job, Lieutenant. Nobody could have done better.'

Epilogue

I'll Fly Away

Chapter One Hundred and Twenty-One

Four months later . . .

It was a sparkling, clear March afternoon when we all came back to the LaSalle Heights Church.

Five months after that first bloody attack, every chink in its exterior walls had been sanded and painted over with fresh white paint. The arched opening where the church's beautiful stained-glass window had shone was draped with a white curtain erected for today's event.

Inside, VIPs from the city government sat shoulder-to-shoulder with proud parishioners and families gathered for the occasion. News cameras rolled from the side aisles, recording the proceedings for the evening news.

The choir, dressed in white gowns, belted out 'I'll Fly Away', and the chapel seemed to swell and resonate with the triumphant power of the raised voices.

Some people clapped with the music, others tearfully wiped their eyes.

I stood in the back with Claire and Jill and Cindy. My body tingled with awe.

As the choir concluded, Aaron Winslow stepped up to the pulpit, proud and handsome as ever in a black suit and dress shirt. He and Cindy were still together, and we all liked him, really liked *them*. The crowd quieted down. He looked around the packed house, smiling peacefully, and in a composed voice, began, 'Only a few months ago, the play of our children was rocked by a madman's nightmare. I watched as bullets desecrated this neighborhood. This choir that sings for you today was gripped with terror. We all wondered, "Why?" How was it possible that only the youngest and the most innocent of us was struck?'

Cries of 'Amen' echoed down from the rafters. Cindy whispered against my ear, 'He's good, isn't he? Best of all, he means it.'

'And the answer is,' Winslow declared to the hushed room, 'the only answer can be, so that she could pave the way for the rest of us to follow.' His eyes scanned the room. 'We are all linked. Everyone here, the families who have suffered loss, and those who have simply come to remember. Black or white, we are all diminished by hate. Yet somehow, we heal. We carry on. We *do* carry on.'

At that moment, he nodded towards young children dressed in their Sunday suits, flanking the large white curtain. A girl in braids, no more than ten, tugged on a cord, and the canvas fell to the floor with a loud *whap*.

The church became awash in brilliant light. Heads turned, followed by a collective gasp. Where once shards of fallen glass had left a jagged hole, a stunning stained window shone intact. Cries of acclamation rang out, then everyone began to clap. The choir started up softly in a hymn. It was so damn beautiful.

As I listened to the moving voices, something stirred inside me. I glanced at Cindy, Claire and Jill, thinking, reliving just how much had happened since I'd last stood in this place, since Tasha Catchings had been killed.

Tears welled in my eyes and I felt Claire's fingers at my side. She probed for my hand, squeezing me by the fingertips. Then Cindy cradled her arm through mine.

From behind, I felt Jill bracing my shoulder. 'I was wrong,' she whispered in my ear. 'What I said when they were wheeling me into the OR. The bastards don't win. We do. We just have to wait to the end of the game.'

The four of us stared at the beautiful stained-glass window. A sweet and gentle robed Jesus was motioning to disciples, a yellow nimbus around his head. Four or five followers were trailing behind. One of them, a woman, turned to wait for someone else, her arm extended . . .

She was reaching towards the outstretched hand of a young, black girl.

The girl looked like Tasha Catchings.

Two weeks later, a Friday night, I'd invited the girls over for dinner. Jill said she had big news that she wanted to share.

I was coming back from the market, grocery bags in hand. In the vestibule of my walk-up, I fumbled for the mail. The usual catalogs and bills. About to move on, I noticed a thin white envelope, the standard Air Mail variety with red and blue arrows, the kind they give you at the post office.

My heart jumped as I recognized the script.

It was postmarked *Cabo San Lucas, Mexico*.

I rested the grocery bags against the wall, then I sat on the steps and split the envelope open. I lifted out a folded piece of lined paper. Inside, a small Polaroid photo.

'My beautiful daughter,' the letter began in an edgy scrawl, 'by now you must know everything. I've come a long way down here, but I have stopped running.

'You no doubt have some idea of what happened that day at the Hall. You modern cops have it all over old slugs like me. What I wanted you to know was that I wasn't afraid to have it come out. I hung around for a few days to see if the story broke. I even called you at the hospital once. *That was me* . . . I knew you didn't want to hear from me, but I wanted to hear that you were all right. And of course – you are just fine.

'These words are not enough to let you know how sorry I am for having disappointed you again. I was wrong about a lot of things, and now I know you can't leave everything behind. I knew that the moment I saw you again. Why has it taken me my whole life to let such a simple lesson sink in?

'But I was right about one thing. And it's more important than anything else. No one is ever so big not to need help every once in a while . . . even from their father.'

The letter was signed, 'Your stupid Dad,' then below it, 'who truly loves you.'

I sat reading the note a second time, holding back a rush of tears. So Marty had finally found a place where nothing would follow him. Where no one would know him. I choked with the sad realization that I might never see him again.

I flipped around the grainy photograph.

There was Marty ... in a ridiculous Hawaiian shirt, posing in front of some dilapidated fishing boat raised on a scaffold, maybe twelve feet long. There was a little note on the bottom: *'New start, new life. I bought this boat. Painted it myself. One day, I'll catch you a dream . . .'*

At first, I laughed. What a jerk, I thought to myself, shaking my head. What the hell did he know about boats? Or fishing? The closest my father ever got to the ocean was when he was assigned to crowd control on Fisherman's Wharf.

Then something grabbed my eye.

In the background of the photo, past the proud countenance of my father, against the masts and hulls of the blue marina and the beautiful sky . . .

I squinted hard, trying to make out the lettering on the freshly painted hull of his new yawl.

The single word scrawled there, in plain white letters, in his own simple hand.

The name of the boat: *Buttercup.*

Turn the page for a preview of the next compelling thriller in the Women's Murder Club Series.

3rd DEGREE

JAMES PATTERSON

AND ANDREW GROSS

CHAPTER ONE

I t was a clear, calm, lazy April morning, the day the worst week of my life began.

I was jogging down by the Bay with my Border collie, Martha. It's my thing Sunday mornings – get up early and cram my meaningful other into the front seat of the Explorer. I try to huff out three miles, from Fort Mason down to the bridge and back. Just enough to convince myself I'm bordering on something called *in shape* at thirty-six.

That morning, my buddy Jill came along. To give her baby Lab, Snake Eyes, a run, or so she claimed. More likely, to warm herself up for a bike sprint up Mount Tamalpais or whatever Jill would do for *real* exercise later in the day.

It was hard to believe that it had been only five months since Jill lost her baby. Now here she was, her body toned and lean again.

'So, how did it go last night?' she asked, shuffling

---

407 ———

sideways beside me. 'Word on the street is, Lindsay had a date.'

'You could call it a date ...' I said, focusing on the heights of Fort Mason, which weren't getting closer fast enough for me. 'You could call Baghdad a vacation spot, too.'

She winced. 'Sorry I brought it up.'

All run long, my head had been filled with the annoying recollection of Franklin Fratelli, 'asset remarketing' mogul (which was a fancy way of saying he sent goons after the dot-com busts who could no longer make the payments on their Beemers and Franck Mullers). For two months Fratelli had stuck his face in my office every time he was in the Hall, until he wore me down enough to ask him up for a meal on Saturday night (the short ribs braised in port wine I had to pack back into the fridge after he bailed on me at the last minute).

'I got stood up,' I said, mid-stride. 'Don't ask, I won't tell the details.'

We pulled up at the end of Marina Green, a lung-clearing bray from me while Mary Decker over there bobbed on her toes as if she could go another loop.

'I don't know how you do it,' I said, hands on hips, trying to catch my breath.

'My grandmother,' she said, shrugging and stretching out a hamstring. 'She started walking five miles a day when she was sixty. She's ninety now. We have no idea where she is.'

We both started to laugh. It was good to see the old Jill trying to peek through. It was good to hear the laughter back in her voice.

'You up for a mochachino?' I asked. 'Martha's buying.'

'Can't. Rick's flying in from Chicago. He wants to bike up to see the Dean Friedlich exhibit at the Legion of Honor as soon as he can get in and change. You know what the puppy's like when he doesn't get his exercise.'

I frowned. 'Somehow it's hard for me to think of Rick as a puppy.'

Jill nodded and pulled off her sweatshirt, lifting her arms.

'Jill,' I gasped, 'what the hell is *that*?'

Peeking out through the strap of her exercise bra were a couple of small, dark bruises, like fingermarks.

She tossed her sweatshirt over her shoulder, seemingly caught off-guard. 'Mashed myself getting out of the shower,' she said. 'You should get a load of how *it* looks.' She winked.

I nodded, but something about the bruise didn't sit well with me. 'You sure you don't want that coffee?' I asked.

'Sorry ... You know El Exigente, if I'm five minutes late, he starts to see it as a pattern.' She whistled for Snake Eyes and started to jog back to her car. She waved. 'See you at work.'

'So how about you?' I knelt down to Martha. 'You

409

look like a mochachino would do the trick.' I snapped on her leash and started to trot off toward the Starbucks on Chestnut.

The Marina has always been one of my favorite neighborhoods. Curling streets of colorful, restored townhouses. Families, the sound of gulls, the sea air off the Bay.

I crossed Alhambra, my eye drifting to a beautiful two-story townhouse I always passed and admired. Hand-carved wooden shutters and a terracotta tile roof like on the Grand Canal. I held Martha as a car passed by.

That's what I remembered about the moment. The neighborhood just waking up. A redheaded kid in an FUBU sweatshirt practicing tricks on his Razor. A young woman in overalls hurrying around the corner, carrying a bundle of clothes.

'C'mon, Martha.' I tugged on her leash. 'I can taste that mochachino.'

Then the townhouse with the terracotta roof exploded into flames. I mean, it was as if San Francisco were suddenly Beirut.

CHAPTER TWO

'Oh, my god!' I gasped as a flash of heat and debris nearly knocked me to the ground.

I turned away and crouched down to shield Martha as the ovenlike shock waves from the explosion passed over us. A few seconds later, I turned to pull myself up. Mother of God ... I couldn't believe my eyes. The townhouse I had just admired was now a shell. Fire ripped through the upper floor.

In that instant I realized that people could still be inside.

I tied Martha to a lamppost. Flames gusted just fifty feet away. I ran across the street to the blazing home. The first floor was gone. Anyone up there didn't have a chance.

I fumbled through my fanny pack for the cell phone. Frantically, I punched in 911. 'This is Lieutenant Lindsay Boxer, San Francisco Police Department, Shield two-seven-two-one. There's been an explosion at the corner of Alhambra and Pierce. A residence. Casualties likely. Need full medical and fire support. Get them moving!'

I cut off the dispatcher. Procedure told me to wait, but if anyone was in there, there was no time. I ripped off my sweatshirt and wrapped it loosely around my face. 'Oh, Jesus Christ, Lindsay,' I said, and held my breath.

Then I pushed my way into the burning house.

'Is anyone there?' I shouted, choking immediately on the gray, raspy smoke. The intense heat bit at my eyes and face, and it hurt just to peek out from the protective cloth. A wall of burning Sheetrock and plaster hung above me.

'Police!' I shouted again. 'Is anyone there?'

The smoke felt like sharp razors slicing into my lungs. It was impossible to hear above the roar of the flames. I suddenly understood how people trapped in fires on high floors would leap to their death rather than bear the intolerable heat.

I shielded my eyes, pushing my way through the billowing smoke. I hollered a last time, 'Is anyone alive in here?'

I couldn't go any farther. My eyebrows were singed. I realized I could die in there.

I turned and headed for the light and cool that I knew were behind me. Suddenly, I spotted two shapes, the bodies of a woman and a man. Clearly dead, their clothes on fire.

I stopped, feeling my stomach turn. But there was nothing I could do for them.

Then I heard a muffled noise. I didn't know if it was real. I stopped, tried to listen above the rumble of the fire. I could hardly bear the pain of the blistering heat on my face.

There it was again. It was real, all right.

Someone was crying.

CHAPTER THREE

I gulped air and headed deeper into the collapsing house. 'Where are you?' I called. I stumbled over flaming rubble. I was scared now, not only for whoever had cried but for myself.

I heard it again. A low whimpering from somewhere in the back of the house. I headed for it. 'I'm coming!' I shouted. To my left, a wooden beam crashed. The farther I went, the more trouble I was in. I spotted a hallway where I thought the sounds came from, the ceiling teetering where the second story used to be.

'Police!' I yelled. 'Where are you?'

Nothing.

Then I heard the crying again. Closer this time. I stumbled down the hallway, blanketing my face. *C'mon, Lindsay ... Just a few more feet.*

I pushed through a smoking doorway. *Jesus, it's a kid's bedroom.* What was left of it.

A bed was overturned on its side up against a wall. It was smothered in thick dust. I shouted, then heard the noise again. A muffled, coughing sound.

The frame of the bed was hot to the touch, but I managed to budge it a little bit from the wall. *Oh, my God ...* I saw the shadowy outline of a child's face.

It was a small boy. Maybe ten years old.

The child was coughing and crying. He could barely speak. His room was buried under an avalanche of debris. I couldn't wait. Any more time, the fumes alone would kill him – and me.

'I'm gonna get you out of here,' I promised. Then I wedged myself between the wall and the bed and, with all my strength, heaved it away from the wall. I took the boy by the shoulders, praying I wasn't doing him harm.

I stumbled through the flames, carrying the boy. Smoke was everywhere, searing and noxious. I saw a light where I thought I had come in, but I didn't know for sure.

I was coughing, the boy clinging to me with his petrified grip. 'Mommy, Mommy,' he was crying. I squeezed him back, to let him know I wasn't going to let him die.

I screamed ahead, praying that someone would answer. 'Please, is anyone there?'

'Here,' I heard a voice through the blackness.

I stumbled over debris, avoiding new hot spots flaming up. Now I saw the entrance. Sirens, voices.

The shape of a man. A fireman. He gently took the boy out of my arms. Another fireman wrapped his arms around me. We headed outside.

Then I was out, dropping to my knees, sucking in mouthfuls of precious air. An EMT put a blanket round me. Everyone was being so good, so professional. I collapsed against a fire truck up on the sidewalk. I almost threw up, then I did.

Someone put an oxygen mask over my mouth and I took several deep gulps. A fireman bent over me. 'Were you inside when it happened?'

'No.' I shook my head. 'I went in to help.' I could barely talk, or think. I opened my fanny pack and showed him my badge. 'Lieutenant Boxer,' I said, choking. 'Homicide.'

CHAPTER FOUR

'I'm all right,' I said, forcing myself out of the EMT's grasp. I made my way over to the boy, who was already strapped onto a gurney. He was being wheeled into a van. The only motion in his face was a slight flickering in his eyes. But he was alive. My God, I had saved his life.

Out on the street, onlookers were being ringed back by the police. I saw the redheaded kid who'd been riding his Razor. Other horrified faces crowded around.

All of a sudden I became aware of barking. Jesus, it was Martha, still tied to the post. I ran over to her and hugged her tightly as she licked my face.

A fireman made his way to me, a division captain's crest on his helmet. 'I'm Captain Ed Noroski. You okay?'

'I think so,' I said, not sure.

'You guys in the Hall can't be heroes enough on your own shift, Lieutenant?' Captain Noroski said.

'I was jogging by. I saw it blow. Looked like a gas explosion. I just did what I thought was right.'

'Well, you did good, Lieutenant.' The fire captain looked at the wreckage. 'But this was no gas explosion.'

'I saw two bodies inside.'

'Yeah,' Noroski said, nodding. 'Man and a woman. Another adult in a back room on the ground floor. That kid's lucky you got him out.'

'Yeah,' I said. My chest was filling with dread. If this was no gas explosion …

Then I spotted Warren Jacobi, my number one inspector, coming out of the crowd, badging his way over to me.

Warren had the 'front nine,' what we call the Sunday-morning shift when the weather gets warm.

Jacobi had a paunchy ham hock of a face that never seemed to smile even when he told a joke, and deep, hooded eyes impossible to light up with surprise. But when he fixed on the hole where 210 Alhambra used to be and saw *me*, sooty, smeared, sitting down, trying to catch my breath – Jacobi did a double take.

'Lieutenant? You okay?'

'I think so.' I tried to pull myself up.

He looked at the house, then at me again. 'Seems a bit run-down, even for your normal fixer-upper, Lieutenant. I'm sure you'll do wonders with it.' He held in his grin. 'We have a Palestinian delegation in town I know nothing about?'

I told him what I had seen. No smoke or fire, the upper floor suddenly blowing out.

'My twenty-seven years on the job gives me the premonition we're not talking busted boiler here,' said Jacobi.

'You know anyone lives in a place like this with a boiler on the upstairs?'

'No one I know lives in a place like this. You sure you don't want to go to the hospital?' Jacobi bent down over me. Ever since I'd taken a shot in the Coombs case, Jacobi'd become like a protective uncle with me. He had even cut down on his stupid sexist jokes.

'No, Warren, I'm all right.'

I don't even know what made me notice it. It was just sitting there on the sidewalk, leaning up against a parked car, and I thought, *Shit, Lindsay, that shouldn't be there.* Not with everything that had just gone on. A red school knapsack. A million students carry them. Just sitting there.

I started to panic again. I'd heard of secondary explosions in the Middle East. If it was a bomb that had gone off in the house, who the hell knew? My eyes went wide. My gaze was fixed on the red bag.

I grabbed Jacobi. 'Warren, I want everyone moved back away from here, *now*. Move everybody back, now!'

CHAPTER FIVE

From the back of a basement closet, Claire Washburn pulled out an old, familiar case she hadn't seen in years. 'Oh, my God ...'

She had woken up early that morning, and after a cup of coffee on the deck, hearing the jays back for the first time that season, she threw on a denim shirt and jeans and set about the dreaded task of cleaning out the basement closet.

First to go were the stacks of old board games they hadn't played in years. Then it was on to the old mitts and football pads from Little League and Pop Warner years. A quilt folded up that was now just a dust convention.

Then she came upon the old aluminum case buried under a musty blanket. *My God.*

Her old cello. Claire smiled at the memory. Good Lord, it had been ten years since she'd held it in her hands.

She yanked it from the bottom of the closet. Just seeing it brought back a swell of memories: hours and hours of learning the scales, practicing. 'A house without music', her mother used to say, 'is a house without life.' Her husband Edmund's fortieth birthday was the last time she had played.

Claire unsnapped the clips and stared at the wood grain on the cello. It was still beautiful, a scholarship gift from the music department at Hampton. Before she realized she would never be a Yo-Yo Ma and headed to med school, it had been her most cherished possession.

A melody popped into her head. That same, difficult passage that had always eluded her: the first movement of Haydn's Cello Concerto in D Major. Claire looked around, as if embarrassed. What the hell, Edmund was still sleeping. No one would hear.

Claire lifted her cello out of the felt mold. She took out the bow, held it in her hands. *Wow ...*

A long minute of tuning, the old strings stretching back into their accustomed notes. A single pass, just running the bow along the strings, brought back a zillion sensations. Goose bumps. She played the first bars of the concerto. Sounded a little off, but the feel came back to her. 'Ha, the old girl's still got it,' she said with a laugh. She closed her eyes and played a little more.

Then she noticed Edmund, still in his pajamas, watching her, standing at the bottom of the stairs. 'I know I'm out of bed' – he scratched his head – 'I remember putting on my glasses, even brushing my teeth. But it can't be, 'cause I must be dreaming.'

Edmund hummed the opening bars that Claire had just played. 'So, you think you can finish off the next passage? That's the tricky part.'

'Is that a dare, Maestro Washburn?'

He smiled mischievously.

It was then that the phone rang. Edmund picked up a cordless on the handset. 'Saved by the bell,' he groaned. 'It's the office. On Sunday, Claire. Can't they *ever* give you a break?'

Claire took the phone. It was Freddie Rodriguez, a staffer at the ME's office. Claire listened, then she set down the phone.

'My God, Edmund … there's been an explosion downtown! Lindsay's been hurt.'

4th of July

James Patterson and Maxine Paetro

Detective Lindsay Boxer and the Women's Murder Club make a courageous return for their most thrilling case ever – one that could easily be their last.

In a late-night showdown, Lindsay has to make an instant-aneous decision: in self-defence she fires her weapon – and sets off a chain of events that leaves a police force disgraced, a city divided and a family destroyed. Now everything she's worked for her entire life hinges on the decision of twelve jurors.

To escape the media circus, Lindsay retreats to the picturesque town of Half Moon Bay. Soon after, a string of grisly murders punches through the community. There are no witnesses; there is no pattern. But a key detail reminds Lindsay of an unsolved murder she worked on years ago. As summer comes into full swing, Lindsay and her friends in the Women's Murder Club battle for her life on two fronts: in court, and against a ruthless killer.

Working with MAXINE PAETRO, JAMES PATTERSON fine-tunes the tension like never before in this breathtaking addition to the bestselling detective series.

Praise for JAMES PATTERSON'S No. 1 bestselling novels:

'The sort of street-sharp dialogue you can slice your page-turning finger to the bone on . . . This is murder mystery at its best' *Mirror*

'Brilliantly terrifying . . . so terrifying I had to stay up all night to finish it' *Daily Mail*

'Unputdownable. It will sell millions' *The Times*

978 0 7553 4929 6

headline